"I arrived (

She stared a̶̶ ̶t̶h̶e̶ ̶d̶i̶r̶t̶y̶ ̶c̶l̶o̶t̶h̶e̶s̶.̶ "In the livestock car?"

The woman was oblivious to her role in his dishevelment, but he was a diplomat. He changed his tone to astonishment. "Can you believe someone nearly ran me over in the middle of the street? A reckless driver behind a black gelding with three white stockings." His hand brushed the dust from his clothes, allowing her time to comprehend his implication.

She looked at her horse, a perfect match for his description. "I didn't see anyone in the street."

"I was the fellow hugging the ground." Logan put his hat on. "Now if you'll excuse me, I have business to take care of before someone else makes an attempt on my life."

Praise for Laura Freeman's
IMPENDING LOVE AND WAR

"With a realistic sequence on a canal boat, great humor as Cory explains courtship to the dunderhead Douglas, and Tyler's ingenious argument in the ending courtroom scene, this spicy story hits every note."

~*Akron Beacon Journal*

Impending Love and Death

by

Laura Freeman

Impending Love Series

This is a work of fiction. Names, characters, places, and incidents are either the product of the author's imagination or are used fictitiously, and any resemblance to actual persons living or dead, business establishments, events, or locales, is entirely coincidental.

Impending Love and Death

Cover Art by *Debbie Taylor*

The Wild Rose Press, Inc.
PO Box 708
Adams Basin, NY 14410-0708
Visit us at www.thewildrosepress.com

Publishing History
First American Rose Edition, 2015
Print ISBN 978-1-5092-0386-4
Digital ISBN 978-1-5092-0387-1

Impending Love Series
Published in the United States of America

Dedication

To my husband, Terry,
for his support in my writing career.

Chapter One

Logan Pierce clutched the brown leather satchel of government contracts as he disembarked from the train at the Darrow Falls depot. He had worked too hard obtaining signatures and promises of support to lose his work to a thief or gust of wind. President Abraham Lincoln may have declared war against the secessionists, but the U.S. Department of the Treasury had to find a way to pay for it. One more stop and he could return to Washington City, his assignment completed.

Built on a rise of land, the train station overlooked the town. Stone and wooden buildings surrounded a town square bordered by trees. The bell tower of a church rose above the treetops on the northern end of the square. The tranquility of Darrow Falls on a warm summer day provided a pleasant contrast to the noisy chaos of Washington.

Logan had left Washington City crowded with soldiers anticipating the first major battle of the war. He'd almost missed his train eight days ago, entertained by the patriotic music of the bands and colorful parades of soldiers as they marched out of the city on the morning of July 16, 1861. He had been in Cleveland when news of the victory and then defeat at Bull Run on July 21 was announced. Accounts of the battle were in yesterday's *Cleveland Morning Leader*, two days after the battle. The newspaper announced the victory in one column and next to it, told the story of how the battle had been lost. Once type was set, it was too expensive to remove, so both accounts were printed side by side in the same paper. Correspondents covering the battle called the men cowards. What had gone wrong?

Logan claimed his traveling chest on the wooden platform of the depot. "Do you know a reputable place to spend the night?"

"Take River Road to the Darrow Falls Inn." The porter pointed to an inn painted red, which stood out in comparison to the other plainer buildings surrounding the square. "Mrs. Stone is one of the best cooks around."

"Can you arrange for someone to deliver my trunk to the inn?"

"The Wheeler boy can do that. Matt takes the mail and any deliveries into town." The porter looked around. "Ought to be here by now."

Logan opened his satchel and withdrew a letter. "Do you know where Glen Knolls is?"

The porter shook his head no. "Could ask Marcus Wheeler. That's Matt's father. His store is next to the Town Hall on River Road. He's the postmaster and knows everyone in town."

Logan tipped the man for his trouble and walked along the dusty road toward town. The Darrow Falls Inn was on the southwest corner of Darrow Falls and River Roads. The two-story building had an open breezeway with rooms on each side and a large wrap-around porch facing town. Several men were seated at small tables, sipping coffee or smoking cigars. Across the street were the livery stable and a corral with half a dozen horses. He might need a horse to ride to Glen Knolls if the farm was more than a couple of miles out of town.

Logan paused at Darrow Falls Road. A long row of businesses stretched along the west side of the street and faced an open town square where sheep grazed. More shops lined the far side of the square. A few buggies and horses were tethered along the square under shade trees. Wheeler's dry goods store was across the street on the opposite corner.

Logan strolled toward the store. He didn't hear the buggy bearing down on him until the horse snorted a last minute warning. He leaped to the side, dust billowing from the impact when he hit the ground. He coughed to clear his lungs and stood, brushing the dirt from his black wool suit. The frock coat reached mid-thigh on his tall frame. He tugged on the black silk vest and made sure his watch wasn't broken. Then he gathered his top hat, satchel, and searched for his attacker.

The driver had stopped at a hitching post opposite Wheeler's store.

Logan headed for the buggy. The reckless ruffian needed to be more careful. The driver stood, and her pale yellow skirt billowed out of the rectangular box that formed the structure of the buggy frame. She retrieved something from the padded bench seat and bumped her wide flat straw hat on the canopy designed to protect occupants from the sun or foul weather.

The woman shouldn't be allowed behind the reins of a horse. The backside of her crinoline skirt wiggled, and the long ties dangling from a large blue satin bow tied around her waist echoed the motion as she searched for the metal step on the side of the buggy. She stumbled and screamed.

Logan dropped his satchel and caught her around the waist. His hands nearly encircled the tightly drawn corset beneath the sheer cotton dress. Small blue flowers were scattered on the field of yellow fabric. He eased her to the ground.

Her oversized bonnet tied with a matching blue satin ribbon had fallen forward and covered her face, but her exposed hair was a subtle blending of bronze and copper in the sunlight. The colorful strands reminded Logan of fire, both beautiful and dangerous. Her hair was worn in an intricate knot of braids with yellow and blue ribbons woven among them, matching the colors in her dress.

Logan's hands remained on her small waist. She trembled beneath his touch. Her crinoline was caught on the step she had missed before her tumble, and her skirt was hiked in the air. She struggled to free the bottom wire that formed a bell-shaped support for her skirt.

"Allow me." Logan extended his arm around her. He glanced at the shapely legs in white stockings before plucking the hoop from the step.

She raised her bonnet and stared. "I don't know you." She had cool blue eyes with long dark lashes. A sharp contrast for a fiery redhead. Her pale skin blushed beneath his gaze.

"Logan Pierce. Rescuer of damsels in distress." He removed his stove top hat and bowed before retrieving the satchel he had dropped in order to catch her.

She smoothed her skirt. "I meant you're not from

Darrow Falls. I know nearly everyone in town, and you're a stranger."

"I arrived on the train," Logan said.

She stared at his dirty clothes. "In the livestock car?"

The woman was oblivious to her role in his dishevelment, but he was a diplomat. He changed his tone to astonishment. "Can you believe someone nearly ran me over in the middle of the street? A reckless driver behind a black gelding with three white stockings." His hand brushed the dust from his clothes, allowing her time to comprehend his implication.

She looked at her horse, a perfect match for his description. "I didn't see anyone in the street."

"I was the fellow hugging the ground." Logan put his hat on. "Now if you'll excuse me, I have business to take care of before someone else makes an attempt on my life."

She followed him across the street. "I'm surprised you're still alive with such a disagreeable nature."

"People love me," Logan defended. "You are the first person to try to kill me."

"I've never harmed anyone. I simply didn't see you in the street."

He waved his hand in front of her eyes. "Are you blind?"

****

Jem Collins refused to reply. The man's rudeness was unforgiveable. Logan may have been dressed like a gentleman in a long coat and matching trousers, but he lacked any manners. He smoothed blonde bangs away from an angelic face, the fine lines of his nose and jaw etched by a skilled artist. He must be wearing a

5

disguise.

Why had he created the story about her nearly running him over with her buggy? She hadn't seen anyone in the street. But she'd been in a hurry, and the sun had been in her eyes. Had the shadow in her path been Logan? Did she owe him an apology? Hardly. His antagonistic behavior negated any guilt on her part. "Are you prone to hallucinations?"

He opened the door to the store. "If I am, then you don't exist." He proceeded inside ahead of her.

Jem removed her gloves and chose a smashed tomato in a tin bucket by the door.

"Miss Jenny, that tomato is rotten," Marcus Wheeler announced.

Logan swirled around, his cinnamon eyes wide, and maneuvered his hat in front to block any throw.

She tossed the tomato into the slop bucket. Logan's expression of horror had been reward enough. She entered the cool, dark interior of the store. "Did you imagine something?"

Logan refused to turn his back. "Does the sheriff know you've escaped?"

"Sheriff Lane Carter is next door at the Town Hall," Marcus said. "Do you need him?"

"Not unless Helen of Troy wants to start a war."

Was the comparison a compliment or insult? "Helen of Troy didn't start a war. Her husband did and used her as an excuse."

Logan's jaw was clenched, and his lips narrowed in a snarl. "Men died needlessly because of her, including her lover."

"She didn't want anyone to die for her or go to war," Jem defended. "Her husband claimed he was recovering stolen property."

"And you believe she was more than a pretty ornament?" Sarcasm dripped from every word he spoke.

"Yes. Her lover recognized her value even if her husband did not."

His voice was low, a whisper in her ear. "I'm sure he left her value in coin beside the bed."

Jem gasped, turning her back to him. She surveyed the merchandise, her eyes adjusting to the shadows and bands of light streaming through the sectioned window. A sewing machine was on display along with a set of hand-painted dishes and lace trimmed tablecloths. Less expensive pots and pans hung from the rafter beams. Yard goods were stored on shelves along with scissors, thread, and needles. Barrels of salt and wheat flour crowded the floor. A sign advertising granulated sugar for eight cents a pound and rice for seven cents a pound was placed near the scale.

The proprietor stood behind a counter waiting on a customer. His long bushy sideburns compensated for his bald head. He wore a wide apron with pockets for holding his sales book, pencils, and other items. The sleeves of his linen shirt were rolled to his elbows. His jacket hung on a peg behind him. Marcus smiled. "You'll have to wait, Miss Jenny. Matt hasn't returned from the train with the mail bag."

Paula Stone, the owner of the Darrow Falls Inn, turned. Paula was a stout woman with a face full of freckles and a large permanent bump on her forehead that hinted of a wild childhood. Now, in her forties, she hadn't slowed her pace. She was purchasing guest room linens. "Hello, Miss Beecher."

Jem removed her bonnet and tossed her soft leather gloves inside. "It's Mrs. Collins."

Paula frowned. "But you're one of the Beecher girls, aren't you?"

"Yes, Mrs. Stone. I'm Jennifer, but I married Ben Collins." She pointed across the square at the Community Congregational Church. "You attended the wedding at the church, remember?"

Paula shook her head. "I never can tell you girls apart. Didn't Ben volunteer to fight for the Union with one of the Herbruck boys?"

"Yes, he joined with John Herbruck and Herman Stratman."

Paula put her hand on her heart. "I hope there hasn't been bad news. Didn't those boys fight in that battle in Virginia?"

Jem didn't like her fears vocalized, especially by one of the biggest gossips in town. She nodded. "Yes, Mrs. Stone."

"Do you have any news?"

"No." Jem didn't explain why she had hurried to the store. Ben always wrote his letters on Sunday and mailed them early Monday. Sometimes she received them on Tuesday but nearly always by Wednesday. Ben's last letter had been dated July 14, 1861, two days before the troops marched out of Washington. His next letter was due today.

The door opened, ringing the bell in its path. Matt Wheeler carried the mailbag inside. Matt was an awkwardly thin boy of fifteen but strong in spite of his appearance. The boy dumped the contents on the counter.

Marcus sorted the mail and deposited the letters in

the proper slots marked for each household.

Jem hovered at the counter, trying to read the names on the envelopes. "Anything from Ben?"

He raised a letter. "This one is for Mrs. Herbruck." He turned it over. "It's from John."

"That's good news." John's letter to his mother had arrived. So where was Ben's letter? She waited as he finished sorting. Nothing from Ben.

"The mail can be unpredictable at times," Marcus said. "I'm sure you'll receive your letter tomorrow."

But Ben's correspondence arrived like clockwork. Like her, he was organized, prompt, and reliable. Jem stared at the letter in the slot to Martha Herbruck. She wanted to know what was written inside. "I could drop off the letter for Mrs. Herbruck. I'm sure she's waiting for it."

"She's probably anxious to hear something." He handed her the letter, and she tucked it in her handbag. "The *Summit County Beacon* doesn't arrive until tomorrow, but I doubt it will contain any news of the battle."

The weekly paper usually had fiction stories and poetry on the front page. Any news story was on the second page and at least one week late if not longer.

Logan handed her a newspaper from his satchel. "Yesterday's copy of the *Cleveland Morning Leader* has news of the battle."

Jem opened the folded newspaper printed Tuesday, July 23, 1861. She may have to rethink her opinion of Logan Pierce being a rude, obnoxious ogre.

Jem stood near the window reading the report of the battle near Manassas railroad junction. Under a column labeled "Telegraphic," the heading announced

Our Great Victory. In the adjoining column, the heading announced *Fearful News* followed by *Our Army Forced Back*. The Battle of Bull Run had turned from a morning victory to an afternoon disaster. The story had no news of the First Ohio. It concentrated on the retreat.

"Panic was so fearful that the whole army became demoralized, and it was impossible to check it either at Centreville or Fairfax Court House," she read.

Federal loss was as high as three thousand. "How could so many die in one day?"

"I hope they're counting wounded, too, but the battle didn't go the way planned," Logan said. "I guess it takes more than ninety days to train an army."

Paula paid Marcus for her purchases. "How difficult can it be to march in a straight line?"

"It's not the marching that's difficult," Logan said. "It's standing your ground when you're being shot at by the enemy."

The news about Ohio's two regiments was on the second of four pages, but it was about the commanding officers and positions during battle. Jem paused her reading. "Were you at the battle?"

"No, but I was in Washington City when they marched out. Most of the men were anxious to beat the Rebels."

Paula gathered her smaller packages. "Then why did they lose?"

"I think Mr. Lincoln is asking the same question, ma'am."

"What's your name, young man?"

"Logan Pierce."

"Pierce? Any relation to Franklin Pierce?"

10

Dimples in his cheeks deepened. "No, ma'am. I have no presidents in my ancestry."

"Do you need a place to stay? I have the finest inn in town. It's across the street. Meals are included in the rent."

Logan looked at Matt, who was examining fishing poles against the wall. "I believe Matt delivered my trunk."

"The porter gave me five cents," Matt said.

"I'll have your room ready. We eat at six."

Marcus signaled Matt to carry Paula's larger packages.

Logan opened the door for them.

Marcus put away the string he had used to wrap Paula's bundles. "May I help you, young man?"

Logan was holding the door, waiting for Jem to finish tying the bow in her bonnet ribbon. "I need directions to Glen Knolls."

Jem spun around in the doorway. "Why?"

A single eyebrow rose above fawn-colored eyes. "I'm sorry. I was having a personal conversation with this gentleman."

His manners *hadn't* improved. She turned her back.

"Miss Jenny can show you the way to Glen Knolls," Marcus said.

"Is she a guide?"

"Her sister is married to Tyler Montgomery and lives at Glen Knolls," Marcus explained.

Jem had reached the middle of the street when a hand cupped her elbow.

"Careful, a reckless driver is terrorizing pedestrians."

Logan revealed dimples in his cheeks with a smile

that begged forgiveness for his bad manners. She steeled her resolve not to fall for his charm. "Why do you want to go to Glen Knolls?"

"I have business with Tyler Montgomery."

"He might be at his office in Akron."

The deep dimples disappeared. "I visited his office in Akron, but Sam Morris said he was home at Glen Knolls."

Chapter Two

Sam was Tyler's law partner. Tyler was a Harvard-trained lawyer who had arrived in Darrow Falls a year earlier searching for a runaway slave. The Beechers were abolitionists, but her sister, Courtney, had fallen in love with Tyler and married him. She didn't bother to ask what business Logan had with Tyler. Cory would confide the news. "I'll take you to Glen Knolls, but I need to visit the blacksmith's house first."

He paused by the buggy. "Your horse lose a shoe in the race to the store?"

She wasn't going to confess to any wrongdoing no matter how much his humorous remark made her smile. "You're tenacious."

"In politics, that's a compliment."

Jem grabbed a medical bag from the back of her buggy and crossed the square.

He wrestled the bag from her. "A horse sick?"

"I can be secretive, too."

"My business with your brother-in-law is official. I'm not at liberty to discuss it with anyone but Mr. Montgomery."

She stopped in the middle of the road. "You're not trying to enlist him? My sister wouldn't like that."

"No." He studied her. "Mrs. Stone said you were one of the Beecher sisters. How many sisters do you have?"

"I have five sisters. Courtney, me, Colleen, Jessica, Cassandra, and Juliet."

"No wonder Mrs. Stone can't remember your names." He touched his finger to his forehead. "You're not related to Harriet Beecher Stowe?"

Jem recognized the disbelief in his voice. "She's a distant cousin."

"Lincoln blames her for the war."

"Lincoln is dimwitted."

"I'll tell him your assessment when I see him."

Jem tilted her head so the brim of her bonnet didn't block her view. Was he telling the truth? "How would you know the president?"

"I'm one of Salmon Chase's secretaries."

"Governor Chase?"

"News *is* slow in Darrow Falls. He *was* governor of Ohio. Lincoln appointed him secretary of the treasury."

"I know that," she defended. "But I liked Mr. Chase when he was governor. He supported women's rights and public education."

"As one of the Beecher sisters, don't you support him because of his stand against slavery?"

"That, too." She dismissed his criticism with a wave of her hand. Salmon Chase had run for president, but she was confused by his current position. "Didn't he run against Lincoln for the Republican Party nomination? Why would Lincoln choose him for his cabinet?"

"Mr. Chase supported him afterward, but Lincoln's choices for his cabinet have baffled many."

The blacksmith shop was on the corner of River Road and Darrow Falls Road. Smoke billowed from the chimney, and heat radiated from the fire as they passed the open double doors. Metal clanged against metal in a steady beat. Jem continued to a small house next to the livery. A porch shaded the front from the eastern sun. A young girl waved from the stone step bridging the porch to the small lawn.

Jem waved back. "That's my sister, Cass."

Cass had dark hair worn in two braids tied with pink ribbons that matched her pink and white checkered dress. The girl helped a toddler safely to the ground. They were both barefoot. "This is Adam." Jem patted the head of a little boy with dark curls and light brown skin. Adam carried a wooden block and wore a short dress and diaper made from flour sacks.

Cass waved at a stack of blocks on the porch. "We were building a house."

"Bock!" Adam waved the block in his hand.

"This is Mr. Logan Pierce. Do you mind entertaining him while I go inside and check on Tess?" Jem turned to Logan. "She had a baby Monday."

"I helped deliver her," Cass announced.

Jem smoothed a loose strand of hair into her sister's braid and retied her apron. "You did a wonderful job. You'll make an excellent midwife."

Logan pointed at Cass. "You delivered a baby? How old are you?"

"Twelve."

Logan turned to Jem. "Isn't she a little young for delivering babies?"

She took her medical bag from Logan. "I started helping Papa when I was about her age."

"Papa?"

"Doctor Sterling Beecher." Jem entered the house.

****

The children returned to the porch, and Logan sat on the stone step. Jem and her younger sister bore little family resemblance, and Cass appeared serene compared to her fiery sibling.

Cass helped Adam stack the blocks into a tower.

"You need to even the sides." Logan ran his hands along the pillar to align the wooden squares to form a tall, stable structure. "See, that's how you should stack blocks."

"It doesn't matter." Cass turned to Adam. "Go ahead."

With a swipe of his arm, Adam leveled all of Logan's work.

Logan jumped as the blocks crashed across the wooden porch. "Why did you let him destroy my work?"

"The purpose of the game is to knock them down. That's why I don't worry about making the stack perfect. Adam will destroy it no matter what it looks like."

"Why don't you teach him something constructive?"

"Like this?" Cass placed a block on top of another. "Stack them, Adam."

He took a block and placed it on the stack Cass had started. He had stacked five blocks in a tower before it toppled. Adam snorted and bounced on his butt. He threw one of the blocks.

Logan dodged the missile. "He has a bit of a temper."

"He's two," Cass explained. "He thinks it's the block's fault it fell over."

"Shouldn't he apologize for nearly hitting me?"

"Nearly doesn't count." Cass frowned. "Don't you like children?"

"I'm sure children are lovely creatures once they grow into adults."

Cass studied him with hazel eyes. "Adults have to work. What's your job?"

"I'm a secretary."

"What does a secretary do?"

He did whatever Treasury Secretary Salmon P. Chase ordered. "I meet with people and try to convince them to support the war."

"Like being a soldier? Ben is a soldier."

"Ben is your sister's husband?"

Cass nodded.

"She was expecting a letter."

"Ben always writes. But the soldiers fought a big battle Sunday, and Jem is worried."

Logan moved one of Adam's teetering blocks before it fell. "Why do you call her Jem?"

"Her name is Jennifer, but when my sister Courtney was little, she called her Jem." She hummed the m. "Cory gave us all nicknames—Jem, Cole, Jess, Cass, and Jules."

"What do you think she'd call me?"

Cass studied him and giggled. "Dimples."

Adam walked to the edge of the porch, turned, and lowered his leg to the step. Logan placed his hands in position to catch him if he fell, but he reached the ground safely and ran toward the blacksmith shop. "Da, Da, Da!"

A large black man was splashing water on his head, face, and neck at the trough in front of the building. He removed his leather apron and hung it on a nearby post. The toddler hurried toward him and smiled. He scooped Adam into one of his massive arms, exposed above the rolled sleeves of his linen shirt.

"You're doing a fine job watching him, Miss Cassandra." He extended his hand toward Logan. "Noah St. Paul. I'm the blacksmith in town."

"St. Paul." He had been Tyler's client last year. He shook his hand. "Logan Pierce. I'm waiting for Mrs. Collins."

"Is your wife expecting a child?"

"I'm not married. Mrs. Collins is taking me to Glen Knolls."

"You're a client of Tyler's?"

The blacksmith was on familiar terms with his past lawyer. "I have some business with Mr. Montgomery."

"I can call him Tyler because he's my brother-in-law." Cass danced around Noah as she entertained Adam.

"You shouldn't have to wait too long." Noah looked toward the house. "My wife had a baby girl on Monday. Mrs. Collins delivered her."

"And I helped!" Cass stopped dancing. "I heated the water and warmed the blankets. And I cut the umbilical cord."

"What?" He looked to Noah for an explanation.

"I stayed in the other room." He pointed at Adam's stomach. "The cord is the bellybutton, right?"

"The umbilical cord is attached to the afterbirth, which was attached to the womb. The blood flows from it. Jem says it's important to examine it, or a mother can bleed to death."

Childbirth was high risk. His friends were young,

and Logan had attended two funerals in the past year for mothers who hadn't survived. In one case, the child had died as well. "I'm glad I'm a man."

"Being in the room next door was close enough for me," Noah agreed.

Adam squirmed. "Down."

Noah lowered him. Adam grabbed a barrel hoop big enough to fit inside.

"Roll!" he urged Cass. She rolled it across the yard, and Adam chased it.

"He doesn't tire. Tess can dress a baby girl in ribbons and lace. If she puts nice clothes on Adam, they're ruined in five minutes. The flour bags make good play clothes for a boy."

Logan's mother had recycled cotton sacks for undergarments for him and his brother when they were children. "What did you name your daughter?"

"We're calling her Addy."

"After Miss Adelaide," Cass interjected. "Sorry. It's not polite to interrupt." She rolled the hoop again for Adam to retrieve.

"Is Miss Adelaide someone famous?"

"Miss Adelaide Thomas owned Glen Knolls before she sold it to Tyler. She helped us when we had some trouble with chasers last year."

Chasers were hired by slave owners to retrieve runaways. Logan had seen plenty of them in Cincinnati when he was a boy. They had dogs, shackles, and whips and showed no mercy to the slaves or the people helping them. "You were a slave?"

"Tyler gave me my freedom."

"Mr. Montgomery owned you?" Tyler was from Virginia, but the men living in the western part of the state usually didn't own slaves. They had been pressured to secede from the union. Their discontent with eastern Virginians was key to his mission.

"Legally his mother, Miss Olivia, owned me. Tyler and I were raised by Quakers. They didn't believe in slavery, but they believed in hard work. That's how I learned to be a blacksmith." Noah studied him. "Where did you say you were from?"

"Washington, but originally I'm from Cincinnati."

"Lot of abolitionists in Cincinnati."

He nodded. "Don't worry. I'm on your side, but what are you doing in Darrow Falls? I know about the St. Paul versus Vandal case. Aren't you afraid of chasers?"

"If you're familiar with the case, then you know my wife and son were slaves."

Logan looked at Adam who had returned to the porch with Cass. They joined them in the shade. "You were caught helping your wife and son run away from their owner, Edward Vandal. Tyler Montgomery argued your case and kept you out of jail."

"But Edward won custody of Tess and Adam. We fled to Canada like other blacks," Noah related. "But we wanted our baby born in the United States. Tyler wrote and said Edward was occupied with politics, and the chasers were too busy keeping slaves in the South to capture those in the North. After the war started, Tyler said it would be safe to come here. Darrow Falls needed a blacksmith."

Cass looked at the two men. "Lou died last winter."

"Lou was the blacksmith," Noah said. "He was old."

Cass stacked some blocks for Adam. "Older than

the flood."

Noah laughed. "That was Lou's favorite description of himself. He'd be amused to know someone named Noah took his place."

"You're not worried about the risks?"

"I hope we don't have to flee to Canada again." Noah surveyed his home and blacksmith shop. "The North can't lose this war."

"I'm hoping Mr. Montgomery can help us win it."

Noah frowned. "What do you want with Tyler?"

The threatening tone was subtle but present. Noah was protective of Tyler. "Nothing that would harm him. I'm offering him a job, but I'm not at liberty to discuss it with anyone but Mr. Montgomery."

"He won't leave Darrow Falls."

"I'm not asking him to leave." Logan sighed as Noah relaxed. He wouldn't want to be in a fight with Noah. He doubted he would survive, let alone win.

Noah stood as Jem and another woman appeared at the door. It had to be Tess. The black woman was petite with a small bundle in her arms.

Noah hurried to his wife's side. "Should you be out of bed?"

"It's not my first baby."

Noah hovered until she sat in a wicker rocking chair on the porch.

"Mama." Adam climbed on her skirt.

"No, no, son." Noah lifted him to his knee after he sat on a bench next to Tess. "You have to be gentle with your sister."

Tess uncovered the baby. Addy was fair skinned like her mother with a cap of black hair. She was swaddled in a small cotton blanket. Tess freed her hands from the material.

"Baby!" Adam shouted.

"Shh! You'll wake her," Noah warned.

Tess looked at her husband. "Don't be so protective. She won't break."

He stroked the back of Addy's hand. "She's so little."

"Compared to you or normal people?" She turned to Adam. "Do you want to hold her?"

Noah's eyebrows shot up. "Do you think he should?"

"Sit still on Daddy's lap," Tess instructed Adam. "You can help him hold the baby." Tess put Addy in Adam's arms with Noah cradling both of them.

Addy stretched.

Noah had a look of panic on his face. "She's moving."

"She's fine." Tess looked at Jem. "I had to take care of Adam all by myself, but I'm determined Noah is going to learn how to take care of Addy."

"We should leave him on the porch and go shopping."

"Don't you dare!" Noah cried.

"I'm sure Logan can help you." Jem turned to Tess. "Mr. Pierce is from Washington City and important."

Logan backed away. "I don't hold babies, and I didn't say I was important."

"You must be a bachelor," Tess said with a light musical laugh.

"Until my dying day. So I have no need to learn anything about those little bundles."

"You've never experienced unadulterated love until you've held a baby in your arms." Tess looked at

Noah. "She's captured his heart."

Noah was built like an ox but held his newborn daughter in a gentle embrace. But it was his loving expression that confirmed Tess spoke the truth. No one else existed as he gazed at his daughter.

Adam wiggled out of his father's lap and snuggled against his mother's leg. She stroked his hair. "I can't pick you up, yet, baby."

"Why don't you and Cassie play a game?" Jem suggested to Adam.

"Game?"

Cass helped him off the porch. "Do you want to throw the beanbags?"

"He doesn't stay still for long," Logan remarked.

Jem tied her bonnet. "He's two." She turned to Tess and Noah. "I have some errands to run, but I'll fetch Cass on my way back home." Jem lifted a cloth bag filled with beans Cass had dropped and returned it. "Gather your possessions and be ready when I return."

Cass handed the bag to Adam, and he tossed it at an empty half barrel. The bag flew inside, and Cass clapped. "Say hello to Cory for me."

Logan took Jem's medical bag. "Do you have to stop at the Herbruck place to deliver John's letter first?"

"John wrote?" Tess asked.

Jem scowled at Logan. He'd said something he shouldn't.

"I promised Mr. Wheeler I'd drop it off. She's probably anxious to hear from him."

Tess glanced at Noah and then back to Jem. "No word from Ben?"

"I'm sure I'll receive his letter tomorrow."

Cass threw a beanbag hard enough to send it flying

over the barrel. "He never should have left you to fight in a war."

Jem tickled her sister's nose with the end of one of her braids. "President Lincoln can't win the war if nobody fights."

"Then why do you cry at night?"

Jem's lip trembled. "I miss him." She tugged on her gloves. "I'll be gone a couple of hours but don't wait until the last minute. We want to be home for supper."

"I'll be ready." She smiled. "I bet Ben is fine."

"I know, Cassie. He's probably been too busy to finish his letter."

"Or he ran out of stamps."

"He's always giving his belongings to others." Jem smiled and waved before crossing the street with Logan on her heels.

Logan had to hustle to keep pace. Her emotions were as transparent as her skin. The rosy blush telegraphed her anger in spite of her cheery farewell. "I'm sorry about mentioning the letter. I don't think you should worry about your husband."

"Of course I'm worried about my husband. I love him." Jem turned on him. "But I don't want others to bear my burdens, especially Cassie. She's sensitive and worries too much for someone so young."

Especially when she hears her older sister crying at night.

Chapter Three

Jem took a deep breath to steady her nerves. She had lost her temper to a stranger. So what if Logan had mentioned the letter? Paula would make it common knowledge to everyone at the inn, and the news would spread throughout town. She had to stop acting like a frightened, nervous woman when Ben was mentioned. But why had Martha received a letter from John and she had not received word from her husband?

Logan loaded her bag behind the seat and offered his hand to help her board the buggy. She grabbed the dash rail to hoist herself, but her hand slipped, and she fell. Logan caught her.

"Are you always this clumsy?"

Clumsy? "You try maneuvering a tiny step in a skirt so wide you can't see your feet."

His dimples deepened, but he didn't laugh.

She boarded more slowly. Logan took the reins. "Don't you think I can drive my own buggy?"

"You nearly ran me over in the middle of the street."

"You shouldn't have been in the middle of the street," Jem said.

"Now you admit you nearly hit me."

She dismissed his accusation with a wave of her hand. "I noticed a blur."

"That was me flying through the air."

The man must have been on a debate team. "You're never going to let me forget I nearly killed you."

"I'm worried you might succeed."

"You can drive," she conceded. "Glen Knolls is north on Darrow Falls Road."

"Pretty town."

Jem pointed out the businesses surrounding the town square. Besides the livery and blacksmith shop, Darrow Falls Road was home to a tailor, cobbler, baker, and butcher. The buildings and homes were spaced farther apart as they left downtown, and the landscape was dotted with farms.

"Do you enjoy living here?"

"I've lived here my entire life."

"Bored?"

She loved Darrow Falls. "I have no dreams of leaving home to seek adventure." Had Ben been bored? She shook off the onset of doubts that had plagued her since her husband's departure. "Where are you from, Logan?"

"I was born in Cincinnati, attended Ohio University in Athens, and worked for Mr. Chase in Columbus before he returned to Washington City."

"Harriet Beecher Stowe lives in Cincinnati. Have you met her?"

"Once when I was eighteen. My parents were fans of her book and attended a lecture."

"Didn't you like her?"

"When I was introduced, I couldn't think of anything to say." He shook his head. "I stood silent like a fool."

"I'd be intimidated if I met her."

"You've never met?"

They had descended from John Beecher, the first Beecher to come to America, but the branches on the family tree had spread far and wide through the subsequent generations. "I don't know any Beechers but my sisters."

"But it must be a bonus to share the Beecher name."

"My name is Collins. I'm afraid the family name will die with my father. He has no sons."

"Does that bother him?"

Jem pondered his question. "He's never complained about having six daughters, but I think most men want a son. The Beecher name has existed in this country since 1637 when John Beecher arrived on the *Hector*. Other relatives will have to carry on the name."

Who would carry on Ben's name if he were gone? She had wanted to have children. She'd been disappointed when her flow had arrived on its monthly schedule after he left for war. She shook off her fears. She would have plenty of time to have children once Ben returned home. "You said you wanted to remain a bachelor. Are you against marriage?"

Logan's dimples appeared. "How many husbands do you need?"

"One is enough, but I have four single sisters."

He chuckled. "You want to play matchmaker? I like Cass, but isn't she a bit young to wed?"

"The family calls her Cass."

"She explained how Cory named all of you. She said my name would be Dimples."

Jem covered her mouth to suppress a laugh. "Cass

and Jules are too young, but you might like Cole or Jess."

"I'm sure they're lovely ladies, but I'm not in the market for a wife."

Jem attempted to maintain a straight face, failed, and laughed. "They're monsters."

Logan's handsome face distorted in horror. "And you want me to marry one of them?"

"I'm sorry. I had a moment of insanity."

"Do you have these relapses often? Instead of running me over in a quick death, you want to marry me to an ugly sister who will torture me for the rest of my life. What have I done to deserve such a fate?"

"My sisters are not ugly."

"They can't be as pretty as you."

Jem hadn't received a compliment from someone other than Ben for months. She was flattered but married. "Thank you, but they are beautiful. Cole has ginger curls, and Jess is a blonde."

"So why the difficulty in finding husbands?"

"Right now they're on Grandpa Donovan's canal boat singing bawdy sea shanties and challenging the other crews to any number of contests."

He shook his head. "They work on the canal?"

"Grandpa is a canal captain. A couple of his grandchildren help summers as he transports goods from Akron to Cleveland and back again. Grandma Donovan runs an inn in Peninsula. That's half way between the cities. We would spend the night."

He frowned. "You worked on the canal, too?"

"We each take our turn for a couple of summers." She shrugged. "Mama was raised on the canal boat, and she married a doctor."

"Ben didn't mind marrying a barefoot, sunburned canal gal?"

"With my hair, I wore a wide-brimmed bonnet, and by the time I met Ben, I nearly always wore shoes." She lifted her face to the sunlight. "Summers on the canal were fun."

"Sounds like a marvelous childhood."

"You lived near the Ohio River. Didn't you play on boats or go fishing?"

"I built a raft one summer with my brother, Derek. He was five years older and could walk on water in my eyes. We spent every waking hour on the river until fall, when he left to attend a preparatory school. I'll never forget that summer."

"That's why I think children are wonderful. You can recapture some of your fondest experiences through them."

"I have my memories. I don't need to relive them."

"But what about sharing life's lessons? Don't you want to take a little boy fishing or make a raft with him? Does your brother have children?"

Logan slapped the reins on the horse's hindquarters. "No. He's dead."

"I'm sorry."

"You didn't kill him."

Jem was curious but didn't ask. What or who had killed Derek Pierce?

After a silent pause, Logan spoke. "Why won't anyone marry your sisters?"

"Plenty have asked. They won't say yes."

"They like being spinsters?"

"Cole is nearly seventeen and hardly an old maid. She's having too much fun being courted to put an end to it."

"And Jess?"

"She's fifteen and can outride and outshoot any man. She'd rather compete against a boy than kiss one." Jem shook her head and sighed. "I don't understand it. Cory and I couldn't wait to marry, but Cole keeps half a dozen suitors crowding the parlor on Sunday afternoons, and she won't commit to any of them."

"She'd make a good politician."

Something in his tone hinted at cynicism. "Don't you like politics?"

"I believe in our government. I'm disappointed with its leaders."

"If you don't like politicians, why work for Mr. Chase?"

"My family has worked for Mr. Chase for a long time. My father worked for him when he was a lawyer, my brother worked for him when he was a senator, and I began working for him when he was governor. I'm the last Pierce. I feel an obligation to finish what my father started."

"It must be difficult now that he's secretary of the treasury. Doesn't he have to figure out how to pay for the war?"

"Yes, and it doesn't help when the soldiers throw away their packs and guns when the battle is over." He pointed at his leather satchel. "You read the story in the Cleveland paper about the retreat from Bull Run. The United States has kindly equipped the Confederacy with free supplies."

She smiled to diffuse his anger. "Do you think Jefferson Davis sent a thank you note?"

Logan laughed. "He should have."

"It sounds like you have an important job."

"I help carry out policy operations, but I like being behind the scenes. The unknown name among the famous ones."

"Most men crave fame."

"Fame is a two-edged sword. You're everyone's darling one moment and a pariah the next. Those men who fought should have been heroes. Now the reporters are calling them cowards."

Jem twisted her skirt with her gloved hands. "Ben is no coward."

"Publishers will print anything to sell papers." Logan shook his head. "I don't understand how they lost the battle. I was told McDowell had a sound plan."

"I don't care how we lost the battle. I want to know what happened to my husband."

"Mrs. Herbruck's letter could have some answers."

"I'm hoping she reads it to me."

Logan pointed at the reticule in her lap. "Why not read it yourself?"

Jem grabbed her bag before he snatched it and tore open the letter. "It's not my letter."

"I've never known morality to hinder a woman's personal pursuits."

"What sort of women do you socialize with?"

"Washington City is filled with heartless women with ambitions rivaling any politician."

Before she could question the meaning of his words, Jem pointed to a stone pillar with a wooden sign marking the entrance to the drive from the dusty road to a house. "Glen Knolls. We're here."

****

Logan followed two parallel paths worn in the

31

grass along the side of a yellow two-story farmhouse. Four large pillars supported a triangular portico similar to the design of Greek temples. Large sectioned windows were evenly spaced on each side of a doorway framed with faux fluted pillars.

Jem pointed to a gray weathered bi-level bank barn. "Go to the back near the barn. Tyler is chopping wood."

Tyler Montgomery was almost as big a man as Noah. The axe rose and fell with an easy rhythm. Cords of wood were stacked next to the chicken coop beneath an overhang. Freshly splintered chunks were scattered around the chopping block. Tyler drove the axe into the stump and waved.

Logan had expected a scholarly man. He had researched Tyler's history for Salmon Chase. Tyler was a graduate of Harvard Law School, and although he had only been practicing law for a year, he had made a name in the courtroom. Mr. Chase had been impressed with his logic and reasoning.

Tyler helped Jem disembark the buggy. "Cory will be happy to see you."

"This is Logan Pierce. He has business with you."

Logan removed his satchel from the buggy.

"Let me put the horse in the pasture."

"Oh, don't bother," Jem said. "I plan to visit Martha Herbruck."

"Then I'll put him in the shade." Tyler led the horse to a hitching post under an elm tree.

Jem paused at the pump in the yard and washed her hands and dampened a kerchief to swipe her face. She offered Logan the wet cloth.

He wiped his dusty face. "Thank you."

Tyler ignored the handkerchief and splashed cold water from the pump onto his face and neck. After removing the tie holding his long dark hair away from his face, he ran his fingers through the thick curls. He unrolled his sleeves as they headed for the back door of the farmhouse.

"Mr. Montgomery, I've come on behalf of Mr. Chase, the secretary of the treasury."

Tyler paused, a worried look on his face. "Let's talk in my office."

They entered through the back door. The kitchen had a large fireplace on the outside wall with a low Franklin stove in front. A woman removed biscuits from the oven and placed them in a linen-lined basket on the table. She had dark hair with a hint of red highlighting the wavy tresses gathered in a loose chignon. She turned and held a perfectly browned biscuit. "Look. Not burnt."

"The way I like them." Tyler took a bite of the hot biscuit.

"Then why do you always make me burn them?"

He finished off the biscuit and kissed her. Instead of a quick peck, it was a long, passionate exchange.

Logan looked in the neighboring room. "Dining area?"

"As a bachelor, you must not be accustomed to public displays of affection between a husband and wife," Jem said.

They were making love in the kitchen. "How long have they been married?"

Cory struggled out of Tyler's embrace. "Why didn't you tell me people stood behind you?" She looked around Tyler's massive chest. "Jem!" She gave her sister a hug, bumping her with a belly rounded from her advanced pregnancy.

Jem made the introductions. Cory smoothed loose strands of her hair into her chignon. She brushed some flour from her apron and wiped her hands clean. Logan grasped her extended hand, studying the exquisite features of her face and the strong resemblance to Cass and Jem.

Tyler placed his arm around Cory, resting his hand on her belly. Logan had forgotten to release Cory's hand. He couldn't blame Tyler for being protective. When a man married a rich woman, he gained a fortune. When he married a beautiful woman, he gained competition.

Jem removed her bonnet and hung it on a peg by the door. Ben Collins should not have left his attractive wife unguarded, especially around someone named Pierce.

"Noah and Tess said you should visit and see Addy," Jem said. "She's so precious."

"We plan to stop by this evening. I can't wait to hold her."

"You may have to wrestle her from Noah. He had a firm grip on her when we left."

"Did you hold her, Mr. Pierce?" Cory asked.

Logan raised his hands. "Not me. I might drop the squirming creature."

"See, I'm not the only man afraid to hold a baby." Tyler released his wife. "This way to my office."

Cory handed Jem a tray with biscuits, ham, cheese slices, and apple cider. "Can you serve them? Tyler hasn't eaten."

Logan waited for Jem as they entered the dining

room which overlooked the back yard. The walls were stenciled with a tulip pattern. A fireplace on the interior wall was shared with another fireplace in the front parlor, visible through an arched doorway. The federal Hepplewhite furniture included a long polished mahogany table, shield-back chairs with embroidered seats, and a hutch for displaying china and storing linens.

Logan looked around the elegantly furnished room. "You must be doing well."

"The previous owner gave me a good deal on the furniture."

"Tess' baby is named after her, Adelaide Thomas," Jem explained.

"Noah mentioned her," Logan said. "Was this house part of the Underground Railroad?"

Jem glanced at Tyler, but neither answered.

"I'm from Cincinnati. My parents' home had a tunnel from the river to the cellar." Logan wanted to gain their confidence. "They risked their lives hiding slaves."

"Are they in trouble?" Tyler asked.

Tyler had assumed his visit was for legal help. "No, they died from influenza two winters ago."

"I'm sorry for your loss."

Logan didn't want to think about his family. They were gone, and he was alone. "Noah said you were raised by Quakers in Vandalia, Virginia." He paused. "That's in western Virginia?"

"Near Charleston."

The men stepped aside in a long hallway that ran from the front to the back of the house and allowed Jem to enter Tyler's office. An oak desk was the central focus with two padded chairs facing it. Logan looked around at the shelves filled with books. A stack of papers was piled on a narrow table beneath the window. Tyler moved them to make room for the tray Jem carried. As she closed the door, Tyler asked, "So, what business does Mr. Chase have with me?"

Chapter Four

Jem joined Cory at the kitchen table and chose a biscuit. She broke it apart and applied freshly churned butter. "Do you have time to go with me to call on the Herbrucks?"

"Any news about John?"

Jem withdrew the letter from her handbag. "John sent a letter to his mother."

"How did you obtain it?"

"I told Mr. Wheeler I'd deliver it. Logan suggested I open and read it."

Cory glanced toward the doorway. "He doesn't sound like an honest man."

"He's a politician." She didn't mention his low opinion of women.

She dropped her butter knife. "What does he want with Tyler?"

Cory was worried. War had wives nervous and frightened, especially since the North had lost the battle. Would Tyler be tempted to enlist? Would Ben re-enlist? "He wouldn't say." She nodded toward the hallway. "Do you want to listen at the door?"

Cory's smug expression was her answer. "Tyler will tell me everything after their meeting." Cory stabbed the air with her retrieved knife. "He better not be here to recruit him for the military. I can't take care of a baby and the farm."

"What would you do if Tyler joined?"

Cory lowered her biscuit and chewed on the bite she had taken. "Tyler has too many friends in Virginia. He said he wouldn't fight against them."

"What if the war goes beyond Virginia?"

Cory didn't answer.

Jem grabbed her hand. "I shouldn't make you worry. Especially with the baby due in a couple of months."

"If the war lasts a long time, I know I won't be able to keep him from fighting. He'd feel obligated to take a stand for his beliefs, but I'm selfish enough to keep him home as long as possible."

"We won't let Logan recruit him for anything dangerous."

Cory frowned. "You don't like Logan?"

Jem bit into a biscuit. "He seems harmless as the messenger, but he works for a politician. I blame them for starting this war because they couldn't figure a way to end slavery. Why are men so stubborn and think they're always right? What about the different options? Couldn't they agree on one?"

"Fight the enemy until he agrees to your terms," Cory replied. "That's how a man solves a problem. Why compromise when you can beat him into submission with a war?"

"Ben couldn't wait to go off and fight."

"It was good they lost at Bull Run. He'll be glad to come home."

"I hope so." She studied the letter she had placed on the table. "I'm hoping Mrs. Herbruck reads the letter aloud." She chewed on her lip, waiting as Cory finished her biscuit.

"Now?"

"The horse is ready, and I promise we won't stay long."

Jem shoved the letter into her handbag, arranged her bonnet, and tied the ribbons. She followed Cory into the hallway where her sister gathered her bonnet, reticule, and gloves from the sideboard.

Cory knocked on Tyler's office door. "I'm accompanying Jem to the Herbruck's farm. I won't be long."

Tyler's footsteps echoed on the floorboards. He entered the hallway and kissed his wife. "I love you."

"I love you." Her hands lingered on his body.

Jem studied her reflection in the mirror above the sideboard as they exchanged words of intimacy in low whispers. Ben had never been comfortable with shows of affection, especially in front of others. His letters had contained talk of war, his fellow soldiers, and longings for home, but no words a wife longed to hear from her absent husband. She put on her gloves and followed Cory out the front door.

Jem loved all her sisters, but only Cory was married. She waited until they were on the road toward the Herbruck farm before she voiced her fears. "I don't think Ben is coming home."

Cory covered her mouth to suppress a horrified gasp. "How can you think that?"

"Oh, I don't mean he's dead." She whispered a quick prayer for his safety. "I think he's going to re-enlist."

"Wouldn't that be for three years?"

Jem had been married a mere month when Southern troops fired on Fort Sumter in South Carolina.

Ben had enlisted, packed a bag, kissed her, and boarded the train. She had pleaded with him to change his mind, but her tears had steeled his resolve. He didn't want to miss the excitement of war. "I was upset when he volunteered for ninety days."

He hadn't even discussed the matter with her. He didn't need her permission to join. He was a man, but it would have eased the transition to talk about the changes it produced in their lives. He'd announced he'd enlisted and defended any arguments by saying he was *doing his patriotic duty.*

He hadn't joined the army to make a fortune. Ben earned more at the mill than the thirteen dollars a month the Union paid its volunteers. They had been living temporarily in two rooms above the mill where Ben worked, but she had no choice but to return home after he left. She helped her father with his patients and her mother with the chores around the farm as if she had never married. "His last letter talked about fighting until the end. Now that they've lost, doesn't that mean he wants to remain in the army?" Jem swiped at a tear. "Three years is a lifetime."

"The war won't last three years," Cory reassured her. "It can't."

"The South is defending their homes. Would you surrender if soldiers attacked Glen Knolls?"

Cory met her gaze. "I'd fight to the death."

"Three years might not be long enough." Jem tightened her grip on the reins but didn't urge the horse faster. The sun was too hot for speed.

"What did Ben write in his letters?"

"He talks about everything but what matters." Jem choked back tears.

Cory put her arm around her. "Do you regret marrying Ben?"

"I love Ben, but he wasn't ready for marriage."

"Papa didn't point a gun to his head. If he wasn't ready for marriage, he shouldn't have proposed."

"I wonder if he loves me as much as I love him," Jem said. "He writes every week, but his letters contain no intimate words of affection. He calls me *Miss Jenny* and signs the letters, *your devoted husband, Benjamin.* Benjamin? I've always called him Ben."

"Some men have trouble being romantic," Cory said.

"Tyler doesn't. How long did it take him to kiss you after you met?"

"Are we talking hours or minutes?"

"Ben didn't kiss me until the day he proposed."

"Don't act smug. Tyler married me even if I did allow a few liberties."

Jem looked at her belly. "You didn't waste any time."

"You never were good at math. We were married in October, and this is July. Nine months, and I have two to go."

"I wish I was expecting a baby."

"You and Ben have plenty of time. Losing the battle is the best thing that could have happened. He'll want to come home. You can start your family so this little fellow will have cousins to play with."

"Are you hoping for a boy?"

"I tease Tyler it'll be a girl like all the Beechers, but I think he wants a boy."

"Wait until he sees Noah with Addy. He might change his mind."

They turned off Darrow Falls Road onto Herbruck Lane. Martha Herbruck had four sons and a daughter. John was the oldest with Ed, Art, and Harry in descending order. Jed Herbruck was a veterinarian and often gone to tend to the sick livestock in the county. Their hewn log farmhouse was box shaped with a stone fireplace along the north wall. Jem left the horse beneath a tree and helped Cory.

She gripped the side of the buggy and lowered her altered body. "I feel so clumsy."

"I took a tumble into Logan's arms this morning, and I don't have your excuse."

"Logan caught you?"

"If he hadn't, I would have hit the ground. I was in such a hurry to arrive at the Wheeler's store, I missed the step on the buggy and fell. Logan said I almost ran over him in the street in my haste to see if Ben's letter had arrived. I called him a liar, but I think I did nearly trample him."

"And he accompanied you to Glen Knolls?"

Jem laughed. "Brave fool."

"Is he married?"

With four younger sisters, they were constantly looking for potential husbands for them. "I told him about Cole and Jess but warned him they were monsters."

"Now why did you do that? He's a handsome man. Deep dimples." Her mouth widened in a smile. "If I wasn't married, I might consider him for a husband."

"Cory! What about Tyler?"

She tilted her head and winked. "I can admire another man and love my husband at the same time."

"I'm beginning to understand where Cole obtained

her roving eye."

"Cole looks like Mama. She doesn't have to work hard to attract admirers."

Jem had inherited her father's height and thinness and envied her sisters who had their mother's voluptuous figure. She had worried about finding a husband who wasn't a discard of Cory's, but Ben had ignored her sister. Jem had gawked at Tyler, briefly, but Cory claimed him, and no one challenged her. Tyler was the love of her life, so why was Cory looking at other men? "Are you happy with Tyler?"

"Absolutely," Cory confessed. "I love him more each day."

Jem removed her soft leather gloves and tossed them on the padded buggy seat. "How can you love him more than you did when you married him?"

"When Tyler was going to leave and never return, Mama explained how love can grow or die. In a marriage, there are highs and lows, but even when we argue, I can't stay mad for long. He's so delicious."

What did she mean? "Delicious?"

"Before you arrived I was watching him chop wood." Cory sighed and ran her hand along her face and neck. She toyed with the button on her dress. "His body moved with such force and rhythm. I would have greeted him in nothing but my apron if you and Logan hadn't arrived." She removed her fan from her bag and waved it back and forth.

Jem recognized the wanton lust in her voice. Had she achieved fulfillment of her passion with Ben or was there more? "But you're expecting."

"I don't understand it, either. All he has to do is look at me, and I'm dragging him into the bedroom.

The more we make love, the more I desire him. I'm insatiable."

"Does Tyler share your voracious appetite?"

"He's young, strong, and doesn't mind sweating." Cory laughed. "I know it's shocking. I never imagined the forbidden fruit would be so appetizing. No wonder the Reverend Davis preaches abstinence before marriage."

"At least you have a man to satisfy your needs. I don't know how many nights I wanted more after Ben fell asleep. Do you think he was dissatisfied with me?"

"Men are always satisfied. They can pay a stranger and fulfill their wants and desires. Women are the ones disappointed in the bedroom."

"You?"

"A few times at first. Then I instructed him on what I needed."

Jem's jaw dropped. "You what?"

"How else is he supposed to know? He can't read my mind."

"But don't men learn how to do it from other women?" Jem lowered her voice. "Isn't that why they go to prostitutes?"

"Keep this a secret," Cory whispered. "Tyler was more inexperienced than I."

"How is that possible?"

"He always had his nose in a book." She smiled softly. "Thank goodness Tyler is a fast learner."

They walked toward the house. "Didn't he propose to Reggie Johnston?"

"He wanted to stop her from marrying Edward Vandal, but he wasn't in love with her. He and Edward have a long-standing feud from childhood. He's never going to forgive Tyler for helping Tess and Adam escape to Canada."

"Did Edward forgive Reggie for helping Tess escape?"

"I was worried at first, but he was elected to the Virginia House of Delegates." Cory slipped her arm through Jem's. "Sarah Yoder wrote Reggie is expecting a baby."

The Yoders were the Quakers who had raised Tyler and Noah. "It seems as if everyone is creating a family."

"Don't be so anxious. Your time will come." She looked around the quiet farm. "I don't see any of the boys around."

Jem pointed to a large field of tall grass and clover. "Looks like they're cutting hay."

"Tyler cut hay last week. He was covered in bits of grass and beads of sweat. I had to wash his hair and scrub his back." Her voice was husky. "It took hours."

"Do I have to throw a bucket of cold water on you?" Jem paused in front of the house. "Remember, Martha is fire and brimstone religious. She doesn't allow the boys to swear, drink, or dance."

"Following a bunch of rules doesn't make you religious, and enjoying your husband's affections doesn't make you a sinner."

Jem knocked on the door.

Lara Herbruck, who was fourteen, answered the door. She was a tiny girl with dirty blonde hair worn in a single braid. She wore a plain brown dress too large for her petite frame. She had a serious expression, which had earned her the name of Sourpuss from other children.

"Is your mother here?"

"She's in the kitchen." Lara led the way. The house was compact with a parlor on one side, a bedroom on the other, and a kitchen and pantry in back. A sick room off the kitchen served as Lara's room. The boys slept upstairs in a loft or out in the barn during the summer.

Jem inhaled. "It smells delicious in here."

"We made blackberry pies." Martha removed her apron. "I'm afraid all the baking has made the house too warm. Why don't we sit in the yard?"

"I hate the bugs," Lara complained.

"The Lord made the bees and the beetles. Be thankful most of your work is inside." Martha sliced the pie and loaded a tray with plates. She handed it to Lara. "Don't drop it. That's my good china." She gave Jem a pitcher of lemonade and Cory a tray of empty glasses. Martha spread a tablecloth on a wide board placed on sawhorses beneath a maple tree. They sat on the benches and chairs scattered around the tree.

"Pick whichever one is most comfortable." Martha served the pie and poured the drinks.

Jem waited until Martha was settled. "I stopped at Mr. Wheeler's store. I was expecting a letter from Ben."

Martha paused her fork in midair. "Has he written? We haven't received word from John in two weeks."

"That's why I'm here." Jem removed the letter from her reticule. "I promised Mr. Wheeler I'd deliver it."

Martha dropped her fork and reached for the letter. Opening the envelope with her finger, her hand shook as she removed the missive and unfolded the paper. "John's penmanship is barely legible. I hope I can read it."

"You don't mind if we hear what he says? I was hoping he mentioned Ben in his letter," Jem confided.

Martha nodded and cleared her throat.

"Greetings, Ma. I hope to be home soon. I can't wait to see you and Pa, Ed, Art, Harry, and Lara. The officers want us ninety-day soldiers to enlist for three years, but I said no. I've had my fill of war after Sunday's battle and can't wait to muster out. The Lord must not have liked us fighting on the Sabbath because we ought to have won. The Rebels routed our troops, but before the retreat, I took a hit to the leg. Ben wrapped it with a bandage, but it wouldn't stop bleeding. They took me to a wagon, and I rode back to Washington City during the night. I haven't seen Herman or Ben, but I was so exhausted I slept most of the day. My friend, Sid, is mailing this letter for me so you'll know I'm alive and well. As soon as I can, I'm heading home. Your devoted son, John."

Jem pointed at the letter. "He was wounded?"

Martha scanned the letter. "In the leg."

No mention of Herman and Ben after the battle. What happened to them? "When was the letter written?"

"It's dated Monday, the day after the battle." Martha clutched the letter to her breast. "He's coming home."

Lara gathered the dirty dishes. "Is Ben coming home?"

Was Sourpuss insensitive, cruel, or both? "I don't know."

"Didn't Ben write a letter?"

Martha pinched Lara. "Hush. I'm sure Ben will

write."

Was John's the only letter from the three of them? "Has Herman's mother received word?"

"I don't think Juanita has received any letters from her son in the three months he's been gone," Martha said.

Jem placed her plate and glass on the tray Lara carried. "How can Herman ignore his mother and not write?"

"He didn't like her marrying Randall McFarland so soon after his pa died."

Henry Stratman had suffered a stroke more than two years ago. Jem had accompanied her father to check on his progress. He had slowly deteriorated each month. Juanita fed him, bathed him, and tended his sores. He never said a word, never acknowledged her existence. "She took good care of him," Jem defended. "Papa said he never suffered."

"John said Herman was upset she sold the farm."

Sterling Beecher had revealed the bank foreclosed on the farm because Juanita couldn't pay a loan Randall had authorized for Henry. Randall had delayed collection until after Henry's death so they would have a roof over their heads. "She needed a home, and Mr. McFarland is a successful banker."

"She should have waited an appropriate amount of time," Martha said. "Two months is hardly a respectful mourning period."

"What about the two years she mourned the loss of what had once been her husband?" Jem defended.

Cory touched her hand. "It doesn't matter now. She appears to be happy with Mr. McFarland. Let's hope Herman doesn't begrudge her a bit of happiness and forgives her."

Cory had gained diplomacy from her lawyer husband, but it wouldn't help her debate widowhood and marriage with Martha. She claimed God had cleansed her sins but had difficulty overlooking the sins of others.

"He can't forgive her if he's dead," Lara remarked.

"Lara! If Herman is dead, it's God's will."

And Juanita has to live with her guilt. Jem tried not to judge them. They were judgmental enough for the entire town. "I'm sure Herman and Ben are well. John was the one wounded, not them."

"Lara is too young to know about war," Martha excused. "Please don't pay any attention."

"I am old enough," she argued. "Harry said the side that kills the most men wins, so the Rebels must have killed lots of men."

"God doesn't reward those who murder."

Lara tilted her head to one side. "Is John a murderer?"

"Of course not," Martha said.

"But the Reverend Davis says killing is wrong."

"War is different." Martha added her plate to the dirty dishes.

"I don't see how it makes any difference. Killing is killing."

"Fetch the Bible, and we'll pray for Ben, Herman, and your brother."

Lara headed for the house but not before sharing her opinion. "I think war is stupid."

"One battle can't solve all the problems of secession and slavery," Cory said. "And all the fighting and killing won't. It's a diversion from both sides figuring out a solution they can live with."

"Women shouldn't discuss politics," Martha said. "Leave that to the men."

"War affects us as much as them," Cory said.

"But it is God's will that men make the decisions. Women are to submit. After all Eve was deceived in the garden and partook of the forbidden fruit."

"And Adam took a bite knowing the consequences. So much for his decision making."

Jem recognized the dangerous tone in her sister's voice. Women were as divided about their own rights as men were about the war. Martha preached submission, but she ruled her household with a tight grip on her sons.

Chapter Five

Martha took the Bible from Lara and prayed for the safe return of all three men. She also prayed for Juanita to see her error in marrying Randall, President Lincoln would shave his beard instead of hiding behind it, and slaves would submit unto their masters so the war could end. Cory nudged Jem on the last comment.

They said goodbye. Martha blocked Jem from following Cory to the buggy. "Your sister shouldn't be out in public in her condition. As soon as I was in a family way, I remained at home."

In her experience as a midwife, few women needed bed rest during a normal pregnancy. Old-fashioned matriarchs like Martha insisted women hide themselves while expecting a baby. "Papa said having a baby is a perfectly normal condition for a married woman. If he doesn't object, I don't see why anyone else should."

Martha made a grunting noise Jem took for disapproval. The Beecher sisters had never followed rules that lacked common sense. Their parents banned corsets from their wardrobes until they finished school, and they were never laced so tightly, they couldn't breathe. They worked the farm, which meant they wore work boots and shorter skirts than young women whose work was restricted to the kitchen.

"If you feel so strongly about it, you should discuss the matter with Mr. Montgomery."

Martha dabbed her forehead with her kerchief. Even though it wasn't ladylike, Jem ran to help Cory into the buggy.

"What did Martha want?"

"The old biddy didn't think you should be showing your belly in public."

"What?" Cory twisted around. "How dare she criticize me!"

"I said if she had a problem with your condition, she should talk to Tyler."

Cory settled in her seat. "What did she say to that?"

"Nothing." Jem laughed as she put on her gloves. "She looked like she was going to faint."

"Maybe she remembers how Tyler punched Edward at last year's Independence Day picnic and broke his nose."

Jem urged the horse forward. "There's no love lost between them."

"Another reason for Tyler to stay out of Virginia." Cory sounded worried. "Edward and his chasers would love to make Tyler pay for besting them."

"Do they know your role in helping Tess escape?"

"I hope not. Clyde and Buck Cassell have no respect for women."

Jem reviewed the words in the letter on the ride to Glen Knolls. "John didn't say much."

"He didn't want his mother to worry," Cory excused.

Was he hiding something? "If he was wounded, Ben and Herman must have been under fire, too."

"That happens in a battle."

"I read in Logan's newspaper the retreat was chaotic. Do you think that's the reason John wrote he hadn't seen Ben or Herman since the battle?"

"Probably." Cory patted her knee. "If he wrote the letter early in the morning, he didn't have time to search for them. I'm sure they're together now."

Unless they were dead or had been taken prisoner. Which fate was worse? "I was expecting Ben's letter today."

"The mail is unreliable, especially from the soldiers. Ben's letter will probably arrive tomorrow."

"What if it doesn't? Should I wait another day and another? What if I never hear anything?"

"They have to know what happened to the men," Cory argued. "Don't they keep a list or something?"

"Ben signed a roster, but said if you're not sick, you line up and drill. They never know how many men will take the field."

"I'm sure they keep good records. After all, they have to pay the men."

"If I don't receive a letter tomorrow, I'm going to Washington City."

"Alone?"

"It's not a pleasure trip. I'll find John and hope he has news about Ben."

Cory raised her chin. "Tyler can go with you."

The offer was sincere, but she wouldn't allow the sacrifice. Tyler was spending more time at the farm because the work was too difficult for Cory as her pregnancy progressed. Besides, Ben was her husband. Finding him was her responsibility. "You need Tyler at home. I'll find someone to travel with me."

"Isn't Mr. Pierce from Washington? He could accompany you."

When they met, neither had been cordial. She

didn't want to ask him for any favors, but he could recommend a place for her to stay once she reached Washington City. "I'll talk to him before I drop him at Darrow Falls Inn."

"I should invite him to stay with us."

"Oh, no."

"Why not?"

Tyler and Cory were noisy lovers. She had spent a couple of nights at Glen Knolls after Ben left with Herman and John. "He already has a room at the inn. Mrs. Stone is expecting him."

****

Tyler and Logan had finished the food, exchanged pleasantries, and were ready for business.

"Salmon Chase was interested in the St. Paul case," Logan said.

"I lost."

"You kept Noah from being charged with federal crimes. He was not technically aiding runaway slaves but his wife and child. That was brilliant."

Tyler had a lopsided grin on his face. "My wife gave me the idea."

"Does your wife know anything about the law?"

"No, but she was a teacher. I'm her private student now."

Student? "What can a woman teach a man?"

Tyler leaned forward. "Doesn't Mr. Chase argue for women's rights?"

"I don't have to agree with everything he supports." Logan opened his satchel and withdrew some papers. "Salmon Chase wants to enlist you."

Tyler raised his hands. "I don't believe in slavery, but I won't fight against Virginia."

"I'm not recruiting you for the army. Mr. Chase needs your help."

"Why?"

"I should warn you Mr. Chase probably isn't currently popular with Mr. Lincoln," Logan confided. "He recommended McDowell for command of the Army of Northeastern Virginia. The president will need someone to blame for the loss."

Tyler frowned. "Was McDowell's military plan poorly designed?"

"McDowell is known for being meticulous with detail. His plan could have been too complex for the men. The politicians argued for a fight before the ninety-day enlistment expired," Logan said. "McDowell was reluctant to fight. He warned Lincoln the men weren't ready."

Tyler returned the Cleveland newspaper Logan had shared. "This says the men panicked, but nobody can predict what soldiers will do when the enemy starts shooting at them. I wouldn't want to die. I have too much to live for."

Logan put the paper in his satchel. "I don't trust what the correspondents in Washington write. They talk about courage and panic in the same sentence. I hope to find the truth when I return to Washington City."

Tyler leaned back in his desk chair. "I hope Lincoln isn't ready to wave the white flag."

"Lincoln is more than a man of words. He believes in action, or he wouldn't have attacked." Logan shook his head. "He's probably most surprised by the outcome."

"What about all his talk about freeing the slaves? Are the Republicans going to keep their promise, or was it made only to elect Lincoln?"

"I don't think Salmon Chase would have supported Lincoln if he wasn't sincere about freeing the slaves, but politics is a game of chess. He can't free the slaves while the Union is losing. He needs to take a few of his opponent's pieces before he can emancipate the slaves."

"I support emancipation."

"Mr. Chase has other plans for you." He took papers from his satchel. "Some men from the Commonwealth of Virginia are talking about creating a state from the western portion."

"I've heard rumors," Tyler said. "Why don't you enlighten me on the facts?"

Logan broke into his sales pitch. "After Virginia seceded in April, the delegates from Northwestern Virginia marched from the convention hall in protest," Logan said. "John Carlile of Clarksburg is rallying public support to break away and create a new state."

"Out of an old state?" Tyler rose and searched his law books. He chose one containing the U.S. Constitution and read from Article IV. *"New States may be admitted by the Congress into this Union; but no new States shall be formed or erected within the Jurisdiction of any other State...without the Consent of the Legislatures of the States concerned as well as of the Congress."*

Logan was familiar with passage. "We're trying to work around that."

"Work around the Constitution?" Tyler demanded. "Didn't Waitman Willey already denounce it as triple treason against Virginia, the United States, and the Confederate States of America?"

"We have another plan," Logan said. "The pro-

Confederate leaders won't consent to ceding the western part of the state to the Union, but they're no longer in Washington. They've abandoned the Capitol Building for Richmond."

"So the only representatives in the Capitol are loyal to the Union," Tyler said.

"Last month a more practical plan emerged. Political leaders from Northwestern Virginia formed the Reformed Government of Virginia in Wheeling. The pro-Union government of Virginia can grant permission for the formation of a new state from within its boundaries."

"Will the courts uphold it?"

"Don't know. It's never been tried before."

Tyler leaned forward on his desk. "So what do you need from me?"

"We need to build support before the people vote on the issue of a new state. As a lawyer and a Virginian, your statements would carry weight."

"So two governments exist in Virginia now," Tyler summarized. "One supports the Union and sends representatives to Washington. The other supports the Confederacy and sends representatives to Richmond, the new capital of the Confederacy."

"John Carlile and Waitman Willey were named U.S. Senators in Washington," Logan said. "They represent Virginia in the Capitol."

"I read that the editors of the *Wheeling Intelligencer* didn't like Willey and his eagerness to compromise."

"That's why we need men like you to write letters to the *Wheeling Intelligencer* and other newspapers before August 6 when the delegates return to Wheeling and create the state of Kanawha."

"Kanawha? Spell that."

Logan shook his head as he searched for a paper. "I can't."

"Neither can most of the people in Virginia," Tyler said. "So, if Kanawha is formed, it'll be a free state."

Logan hesitated. He needed Tyler's support. "Not exactly. Making Kanawha a free state could be problem."

"What's the purpose of forming a separate state if it's still a slave state?"

"Politics again," Logan explained. "Lincoln needs the support of Western Virginia, especially the support of its coal. He's willing to compromise on the slave issue."

"Lincoln is a backwoodsman con artist. I can't support a slave state."

Logan leaned in close. "It's one of the issues they hope to work out in Wheeling next month. Some of the proposals are fair."

"I know some of the proposals, and they're not fair," Tyler replied. "The children and elderly will be freed, but slave owners keep the worker slaves so they don't lose any money."

"It's been the same argument for the entire South. The financial impact of freeing all slaves will bankrupt their economy."

"I argued the same point with a man who believed in colonization. What do you do with four million people?" Tyler stabbed his finger in Logan's face. "But that was before the war. Who cares about bankrupting the South when they've seceded?"

Logan patted the satchel containing the Cleveland

newspaper. "Congress passed a resolution Monday stating the war was to preserve the union and not abolish slavery. Bankrupting the South won't reconcile them."

"What about the problems partial freedom creates?" Tyler demanded. "What will they do with the freed children if the parents are slaves?"

"The larger problem is freeing all the slaves and making Kanawha a free state."

Tyler returned his law book to the shelf. "How is that a problem?"

"Think about it. Kanawha becomes a free state surrounded by slave states," Logan said. "If slaves run away to Kanawha, how long before Confederate soldiers or chasers follow? It'll make bloody Kansas look like a Sunday picnic."

Tyler stared out the window. "Politicians are cowards."

"Politicians need to be elected. Even those who don't support slavery don't believe in making blacks equal. Congress took slavery out of the equation and forces Southerners to choose between supporting the Union or rebelling against it."

Tyler faced him. "I won't support a slave state."

"Then argue for Kanawha to be a free state in your letters." He placed a list of newspapers and politicians on his desk.

Chapter Six

Logan looked around Tyler's office. He was a successful lawyer, owned a farm anyone would envy, was married to a beautiful woman, and would soon be a father. He didn't need to help, but his signature on a letter might convince those undecided to support the Union's plans.

"Why is Mr. Chase involved in this?"

None of the other men he had talked with during the past week had connected Salmon to the creation of a state. "By helping create a new state, Mr. Chase will receive support for his projects, and he needs friends for raising funds for the war. That's how things work in Washington. Do you want any favors?"

Tyler raised a single eyebrow. "Can I argue for a different name?"

Logan laughed. "If you write the letters, you can argue for anything you like."

Tyler studied the list. "I only recognize a handful of these names."

"Then you'll help?"

"I want to talk to Cory about it."

"Why? She's not writing the letters."

"You're not married, are you, Logan?"

"I inherited some money from my father, I have a steady job with Mr. Chase, and a circle of friends I find amusing. I have no need for a wife."

"I believed the same thing a year ago. Then I met Cory, and everything changed. She is the most important person in my life. I won't make a decision that involves our future without discussing it with her," he explained.

"It's only a few letters."

"We both know it's more than that. The men who support a new state are the enemies of the Commonwealth of Virginia. John Carlile and Waitman Willey must find it difficult navigating a way home with the Southern Army in the way."

"You know the risk so why does her opinion matter?" Tyler's wife was passionate but couldn't he give him an answer without her approval? "Other men ignore their wives."

"Are they happily married?"

"Define happy. In Washington City the majority of marriages are based on economic or political gain. If a wife locks the bedroom door, a man finds pleasure elsewhere."

"If you know the case of St. Paul versus Vandal, you know a bit of my personal background."

"You were raised by Quakers," Logan said. "They believe in equality between men and women."

"True, but I was referring to my mother. Edward Vandal declared in court that Olivia Montgomery ran the Dunking Witch, a whorehouse and saloon in Vandalia, Virginia. A man can claim a woman's body for a couple of dollars or through marriage. But true physical intimacy is not possible without love, trust, and respect. I don't take my wife's love for granted, and I won't offend her by belittling her worth. I doubt if she will object to my writing a few letters, but nevertheless,

I'll wait to give you an answer after I've discussed the matter with her."

"How long will that take?"

Tyler brushed aside the window curtain. "I see the buggy approaching the barn. You'll have your answer soon enough."

Logan followed Tyler outside. He strode toward the buggy which Jem had turned in the yard. Before Cory could disembark, Tyler scooped her into his arms.

"Put me on the ground. I'm too heavy for you to carry."

"Are you questioning my strength?"

Cory wrapped her arms around his neck and whispered in his ear.

Logan helped Jem out of the carriage. Her hoop caught on the step. Logan sighed as he worked it free. "Are you doing this on purpose?"

Jem wrenched her skirt from his hand. "I am not clumsy."

Logan almost laughed but caught himself. He didn't flirt with married women.

Tyler put Cory on the ground, his hand resting on the small of her back. He smacked Logan on the shoulder with his free hand. "My wife agrees with your plan."

Jem looked at Tyler and Logan. "What plan?"

No one answered. Cory looked from her husband to Logan. "May I talk about it?"

The initiative to create a new state had been public for more than a month, but Logan didn't discuss matters with others about government business. Tyler had insisted upon telling his wife, and Cory would probably share the news with her sisters. "Go ahead."

"I'm being recruited for a political mission."

Jem looked at Cory and lowered her voice. "Don't they hang spies?"

"He's not going to be a spy," Cory said. "He's writing letters to encourage the support of a new state in Virginia."

Jem washed at the pump. "How do you make a new state out of an old one?"

"The plan is to create a separate state from Virginia," Logan said. "It will be in the northwestern portion of the Commonwealth."

She removed her bonnet and wiped her brow. "You're going to split Virginia in two?"

"If a Southern state can secede from the Union, a section can secede from the state," Tyler said. "I think it's legal."

Cory jabbed his chest. "Don't you know? Isn't it in one of your big, heavy law books?"

He embraced her. "Never been done before, my love."

"How will your letters help?"

"My words will encourage voters to support it."

Cory turned to Logan. "Why did you choose my husband?"

"He's a Virginian and a lawyer," Logan said.

"Mr. Chase was impressed by my arguments to free Noah."

Cory leaned against his chest as his arms encircled her. "Will the new Virginia be a free state?"

"Not guaranteed, but I'm hoping my letters will influence whether it's free or slave."

Jem moved the handle of the pump. "What about Mr. Chase's stand against slavery?"

"No one wants to create a free state in the middle of the South," Logan said. "Slaves will run to it for freedom, and soldiers will follow to capture or kill them. Freedom will come to all slaves, eventually."

Jem wrung out her handkerchief. "What are they going to call this slave state?"

"Kanawha."

"What?" both sisters asked.

Logan threw his arms in the air. "I'll suggest a different name."

Cory took Jem's dampened handkerchief and wiped her face. "You're welcome to stay for supper."

Logan turned to Jem. "I believe you wanted to be home for supper."

"I warned Cassie to be ready. Mama will have supper ready for us," Jem said. "Some other time."

Cory handed Jem the kerchief, which she placed along the opening of her dress. The dress was modest, but Logan's eyes lingered on the damp opening where the bodice crossed over the layers of underclothes. It wouldn't take long to dry. The sky was cloudless, and nothing could escape the heat of the late afternoon. The horse had finished drinking at the stone trough and was munching grass.

Tyler shook Logan's hand. "It was a pleasure meeting you."

"Likewise." He helped Jem board the buggy and took the reins. "I'll send word about any developments with the state." Tyler and Cory walked arm in arm to their house. Salmon had asked him to assess Tyler for a commission in the army. He'd make a good officer, but he had too much to lose. The army would have to succeed without him.

Jem settled into the seat. "If splitting Virginia is like splitting the country, won't Virginians fight to unite the state?"

"Western Virginia has always been culturally different from the east. They've complained for years they weren't properly represented. But it could start a war within the state. Let's hope it doesn't."

"Does the South know about your plan?"

"It's been in the papers, but we're hoping to create the state while the rest of Virginia is busy with the war. Their victory Sunday makes it more urgent we act quickly."

"Won't it be fruitless if the South wins the war?"

She was beaten, and Logan spoke to rally her spirit. "Would the men of Darrow Falls allow Ohio to be a slave state?"

"No, but some of those men lost the battle at Bull Run," Jem said.

"Is that what John Herbruck wrote in his letter to his mother?"

"It was brief. John said he was wounded, and a friend mailed the letter Monday. He didn't know anything about Ben or Herman." She took the damp handkerchief from her neck and dabbed at a stray tear.

Logan ignored women's emotional outbursts most of the time. One minute they were laughing, and the next they were crying. It made no sense. He needed to distract her. "Tell me about your husband. How did you meet?"

Jem's worried expression transformed into a wide smile. He tried not to stare. When her head was tilted toward him, the brim of her bonnet framed her face in an image he would not forget.

"I was invited to a winter dance at the church on the square. I made this beautiful blue velvet dress with crème lace on the cap sleeves and matching lace scalloped along the hem."

Logan nodded. She had lost him at cap sleeves. And how was lace scalloped along the hem? But the tears had disappeared from her blue eyes, and she seemed excited talking about fashion, a favorite topic of women in Washington City.

"My skirt was wider than this buggy, and the bodice was a bit daring." She blushed.

Logan doubted it was as immodest as the gowns worn in the East where women gained attention by baring more than their souls.

"The dance was at Christmas, and I was near the fire talking with Cory and another girl. Ben was with John and Herman. He looked sad. Ben's father had recently remarried and moved to Pennsylvania. I inquired how he liked being on his own, and we talked."

Her face was animated as she told the story. Most people created a passive expression of indifference they hoped others translated as a look of importance or intelligence. His reaction was boredom, but he couldn't keep his eyes off Jem. Her eyes sparkled with excitement. Her mouth opened and closed in rapid movements as she told the story. Could he capture her lips with his own and silence her? He shook his head. She was talking about her husband. He turned his attention to the road. She flung her arm across his chest.

"Without any warning Ben threw punch on my dress. I was so startled I forgot to scream. Then he took off his coat and started beating it against my skirt." She raised her hands and pounded the air.

"He didn't like your dress?" he teased.

"I had backed into the fireplace and caught my dress on fire. Luckily, the cage prevented the flames from burning my skin, but my poor skirt was nearly gone. I had to borrow a tablecloth to wear home."

He laughed, and she joined him. "And you claim you aren't accident prone?"

"A little," she conceded. "Ben's coat was all sooty and burnt. I promised I'd make him another for saving my life. I used the blue velvet remaining from my dress to make the lapels and cuffs on his coat. He wore it the day we were married."

Her expression was tender. He forgot to watch the road, and the carriage lurched to the side as the wheels sank into a long rut. Jem slammed against him. "I'm sorry," Logan apologized. "The road is rough here."

Jem held onto the side of the seat. "It's not your fault. We had rain last week. The roads turn to mud and then the ruts dry out. About the time they're beaten smooth, it rains again."

"You ought to see the roads in Washington when it rains. With all the soldiers, mud is tracked inside all the buildings. It's a mess."

"I'd like to see Washington City."

Was that a hint? "I wouldn't recommend it."

"John Herbruck wrote his mother he was wounded. He might need medical attention."

"They have doctors and nurses."

"For thousands of wounded?"

She was tenacious. "If John has any news of your husband, he'll write."

"What if John is bedridden? I think the best way to

find out what happened to Ben and Herman is to go to Washington."

"I think the best strategy for you is to wait until Ben or his commanding officer writes. Stay home."

Jem's bottom lip trembled. "What if no one writes? What if Ben can't write?"

"If he's dead, someone will inform you." Logan should have been more tactful, but he wanted to dissuade her. Washington was no place for an innocent like Jem Collins, and if she were seen with him publicly, they would be ruined.

"How can you be an insensitive clod?" A lone tear marred her cheek.

He fought the urge to take her in his arms and comfort her. "Washington is overcrowded with soldiers. If your husband isn't with his company, how do you expect to find him? He's probably licking his wounds, whether physical or emotional after Sunday's defeat. You can't expect him to give you a detailed history of his every waking hour, especially after a battle. Give him time. He'll come home."

****

Jem couldn't believe the man. Did he think she was planning to attend social events? Her husband was missing or hurt. He needed her, and she had to learn whether or not he wanted her anymore. Her last letter was written in anger. Was silence the response to her ultimatum?

"I don't expect you to escort me around town," Jem said. "All I need is a recommendation for a boarding house and a simple map to find my way."

"There are more than thirty thousand men in Washington. It will be easier for your husband to find you. Stay home." He stopped the buggy in front of the livery. Cass was stroking a horse while Noah nailed a shoe to his back hoof.

Jem grabbed the reins from Logan's hands. "Mrs. Stone won't wait supper on you if you're late."

He gathered his satchel and hat. "Thank you for taking me to Glen Knolls."

"Thank you for your advice," she replied.

He walked in the middle of the road to Darrow Falls Inn like he owned the town. Jem had to fight the urge to run him over. This time she'd do a better job.

Cass climbed into the seat vacated by Logan and reached into her apron pocket. "Look. Noah paid me half a dollar."

"That's too much money."

"I pay my debts." Noah handed her a silver dollar. "That's for delivering Addy."

"The doctor is paid a dollar. I normally receive half."

"I say it's a fair price for my daughter."

"Noah," Jem called when he turned to leave. "When Tess and Adam left the Silver Pheasant farm in Vandalia and headed north, did anyone tell you not to follow them?"

Noah's pleasant expression turned somber. "No, but it wouldn't have mattered. She was my wife. She needed me."

"But it was dangerous. You were thrown in prison," she reminded him. "Not to mention beaten and dragged through the street by the Cassell brothers."

"Didn't matter. I couldn't breathe worrying about her. Couldn't work. All I could think about was Tess and Adam."

Jem nodded. "I understand."

He stepped closer and rested his hand on the frame of the buggy. "We imagine the worst. Usually we're wrong."

Jem met his gaze. "But not always."

Chapter Seven

Cass yawned as Jem turned the horse into the drive to the white farmhouse they called home. The main entrance was beneath a protruding portico similar to the one at Glen Knolls and flanked by two wings. The family resided in the rooms on the left and used the door on the porch. A similar entrance on the porch to the right was used by patients of Dr. Sterling Beecher.

Jem drove around the house to a carriage barn. She maneuvered the buggy next to a newer one used by her father. They kept the wagon outside during the summer. Both girls worked together to unhitch the horse, and Cass led the gelding to the nearby barn. Jem placed a bucket of water on a hook and removed the bridle while Cass filled the feed tray with oats. Cass brushed one side while Jem brushed the other.

Jem studied her little sister over the hindquarters of the horse. "You were quiet on the ride home. Did Adam wear you out?"

"We wore each other out. I helped Tess bathe and feed him." Cass paused her brushing. "You looked angry when you arrived."

"I wasn't angry with you. Logan Pierce is insufferable."

"Did he have bad news for Tyler?"

"No, he wants Tyler to write some letters," Jem explained. "I'm angry because Logan wouldn't help me."

"Isn't a gentleman obligated to help a lady?"

"He's no gentleman." Jem placed the brushes and bridle in the tack box. "I shared my plans about visiting Washington, and he did everything to discourage me."

"Why do you need to go to Washington?" Cass was worried.

"I need to find Ben."

"Is he lost?"

Jem fought back tears. "I don't know."

"Didn't John Herbruck's letter help?"

Cass had their father's insight. She had understood John's letter was important when Logan had revealed her mission to deliver it. "John was wounded and wrote he hadn't seen or heard anything about Ben or Herman."

"Is Ben dead?"

"Cassandra, don't dare think that."

She sniffled. "I'm sorry."

Jem hugged Cass. "We need to hope Ben is safe and coming home. I'm sure his letter will arrive tomorrow."

"But what if it doesn't?"

"Then I'm going to Washington." Saying it aloud didn't make it happen. She'd have to make plans. She'd already gone through a list of people who might be able to travel with her and discarded each one. They had other obligations, and this was her problem. But could she do it alone?

Jem and Cass entered through the back door to the kitchen. "Supper is on the table," their mother announced. "I had almost lost hope you were coming home."

Maureen Beecher had ginger curls like most of the Donovan clan, and her blue eyes had a mix of green from her mother, Caroline Josephine's German roots. She had a timeless beauty for a mother of six. Her daughters had inherited a mixture of hair color ranging from Grandma CJ's blonde hair to the Beecher's dark hair.

Sterling was seated at the head of the table eating a slice of blackberry pie and drinking coffee. His dark brown hair was beginning to gray. She recognized a look of concern in his hazel eyes as he studied her. She glanced away. She was too old to climb onto her father's lap and have him erase all her fears.

Maureen placed plates filled with ham, beans, and cornbread before them. She filled their glasses with milk. "The butter and maple syrup are on the table."

Jules sat opposite Cass and Jem. She was ten and the youngest Beecher sister. Jules had strawberry blonde hair, which was tied away from her face with a big blue bow. "I was wondering when you were going to return. I had no one to play with." She drank the last of her milk.

"Someday we'll all be married and gone," Cass said.

But Jem was married and living at home. She didn't mind helping her father with his patients and her mother with the chores, but when would she resume her role of wife?

"Not me," Jules announced. "I'm going to live here with Papa and Mama forever."

Sterling sipped his coffee. "Comforting to know someone will be around to take care of us in our old age."

"I may be around for a while," Jem admitted. "Ben's letter didn't come."

Sterling lowered his mug. "Nobody has any news from the soldiers?"

"John wrote his mother." Jem's fork shook as she placed it on the plate. "I delivered the letter for Mr. Wheeler. Cory visited Martha Herbruck with me."

Sterling took her hand and squeezed comfortingly. "Was it bad news?"

Hot tears stung her eyes, but Jem didn't want to cry about an unknown. "John was wounded in the battle. His leg," she explained. "He doesn't know what happened to Herman or Ben."

"Local papers didn't have much news," Sterling said. "Grandpa Donovan gave me a paper he bought in Cleveland. Would you like to read it?"

"Logan Pierce had a copy of the *Cleveland Morning Leader*. Victory turned to defeat."

Maureen poured more coffee into Sterling's cup. "Who is Logan Pierce?"

"He's a politician who wanted Tyler to write some letters to create a new state out of Virginia."

"He has dimples," Cass added.

"A politician with dimples who wants to create a new state." Sterling studied his daughters. "I may need to meet this young man."

"Jem said he wasn't a gentleman," Cass said.

Sterling put his cup down. "Did he behave inappropriately?"

"No, he discouraged me from seeking information about Ben."

"It may be too early for news," Sterling said.

"John wrote sporadically to his mother," Jem

argued. "Ben religiously wrote me and mailed a letter every Monday morning. If word doesn't come tomorrow, something is wrong. He's either dead or a prisoner."

Maureen dropped an empty pie tin she was drying, which rattled on the floor before falling silent. "Jennifer Caroline, you shouldn't say such words." She made the sign of the cross even though she was Protestant like her mother, and her father, Michael Donovan, had stopped practicing Catholicism when he left Ireland in 1820.

Jem left her chair and retrieved the pan. "Not state the worst? I've always looked at problems in a practical way. I returned home after Ben joined because it was the logical thing to do." She handed the pan to her mother. "I'm hoping for the best, but what if nobody knows what happened to Ben? No one is going to care more about finding the truth than his wife."

"How are you going to do that?"

Jem met her mother's gaze. "I need to go to Washington."

Maureen looked at Sterling. He stood. "When would that be?"

"Tomorrow." She had to convince them. "John wrote in his letter that the ninety-day volunteers were mustering out soon. I won't be able to talk to anyone if they go home before I arrive. That's why I need to leave as soon as possible."

Sterling carried his plate and empty cup to the dry sink and dropped them into the soapy water basin. "What if a letter comes tomorrow?"

"Then I'll save myself a trip."

"I don't think I can leave tomorrow," Sterling said.

"I'll need time to make arrangements for my patients to see another doctor. How long do you think we'll be gone?"

Her father was willing to drop everything and go with her. For that, she loved him. Jem squared her shoulders. "I don't expect you to go. I'm a married woman, and other women have traveled to Washington. I can do this."

He frowned. "It's a long trip to take alone."

"I could go with her," Cass volunteered.

"Me, too!" Jules added.

"As much as I appreciate your willingness to help, it won't be a pleasure trip," Jem said. "Besides, Papa will need you to help him with patients." She turned from Cass to Jules. "And Mama needs you to help her."

Maureen cleared the remaining dishes on the table. "When you were young, Courtney was full of ideas, but you put them into action. What are your plans?"

"I'll visit John first and talk to the other men from Ohio. Someone has to know what happened to them," Jem said. "The story in the paper claimed thousands were killed, wounded, or captured. How could there be so many?"

"The number is probably a bad estimate," Sterling said. "Men tend to exaggerate exploits of war. Ignore the rumors and find out the facts." Sterling headed toward the hallway by the staircase. "You'll need money."

"I have some saved."

"We can spare some," Maureen said.

"You can have what Noah paid me," Cass volunteered.

Jem looked around at her family. She had feared,

like Logan, they would talk her out of the trip. "You don't know what it means to have your support."

"I can help you pack," Jules added.

Jules' idea of packing was to throw everything in a bag. "You can help me unpack if Ben's letter arrives."

"When Ben's letter arrives." Maureen took the dish Jem was drying. "I'll finish these. You join your father."

The kitchen was in the back of the house with a fireplace and stove next to the pantry. The room was large enough to accommodate a table and chairs and eliminated the need for a separate dining room. A hallway ran from the back door to the main entrance in the front along the staircase to the second floor. If the doors were open, a breeze flowed through the house to cool it. The formal parlor for entertaining guests was to the right. The door to the left opened to the music room where an upright piano was positioned against an inside wall. Comfortable sofas were arranged for family gatherings. Two rooms were off the parlor. Dr. Beecher's office was behind the door on the left. The other door led to a room for convalescing patients. A bench was placed between the doors for patients waiting to be seen by the doctor.

Jem knocked on her father's opened office door.

"Come in."

A large oak desk was situated to one side. Her father sat behind the desk in a matching oak chair. His books for recording births and deaths, his ledger, and other reading materials were stacked in a neat pile on the corner of his desk. The rest of the room contained cabinets and drawers for medicines and supplies. Jem was familiar with the bottles of blue, brown, and clear glass. She replaced supplies when they ran low. She'd remind Cass to do the same when she was gone.

Sterling counted several silver dollars and placed them on the desk. "They may not honor paper money from the local banks. Too many of the bills are counterfeits."

Jem put the coins in her reticule. "I'll pay you back."

"I don't pay you enough for your nursing work. Nothing against your sisters, but you have a talent for medicine." Sterling leaned forward. "As a father, I want to protect you. The easiest way to do that is to keep you at home and wait for news. But being a parent is never easy. Neither is being a wife. If you stay home, you may never know what happened to Ben. But be careful. The world is a dangerous place, especially for a young, beautiful woman."

"I know a few tricks to keep unwelcome admirers at bay," Jem said.

"Don't take any chances." He placed a sheathed knife on the desk. "Most people are decent, but it only takes one evil man to hurt a woman."

Jem examined the knife before putting it in her pocket. "I'll be careful." Logan had said there were more than thirty thousand soldiers in Washington City. Darrow Falls had barely six hundred residents. Nearby Akron had a population of less than five thousand yet seemed crowded. Would she be able to find Ben? "I'm sure John will help me find Ben if he hasn't already."

"I like Ben, but I didn't approve of his abandoning you when he enlisted," Sterling said. "Herman and John were bachelors. They had no responsibilities."

Jem agreed but didn't want her father to think less

of her husband. She'd chosen him. She opened a book on the desk and flipped through it. "I don't know why he had to join."

"I do."

She stopped turning the pages.

"He wrote me."

Jem closed the book. "When?"

"He was in Harrisburg, waiting to march to Washington. He said he would never be a doctor or a lawyer, and he wanted to do something important in his life. He wanted to be able to look back with pride and brag about his deeds to other men. Ben needed you to admire him."

This was news. "He didn't have to prove anything to me."

"Men are peculiar creatures, Jennifer Caroline. We challenge ourselves with feats of strength, acts of courage, and daring deeds, but all we want is the love of a good woman."

"I loved him. I still love him," Jem amended.

"I know, but Ben wanted to be worthy of your love."

He was worthy even if she had written otherwise. "That's why I have to find him."

"What if…"

"If he's dead, then I would rather find out in person than through a letter written by his commanding officer."

Sterling lifted the book Jem had flipped through. "I finished this book, *A Tale of Two Cities*. Why don't you take it with you to read on the train?"

She shared her father's love of reading and trusted his instincts. "You don't think his letter will come tomorrow?"

"I hope it does. I only wish the best for my daughters. You've helped me enough with my patients to know we can't save every life. Whatever you find, good or bad, your family will be here waiting for you."

Jem hugged him. "Thank you, Papa."

****

Jem spent a restless night. She dreamed different scenarios of her husband's fate. In one, Ben was alive and well but had been too busy to write. He was amused by her concern, kissed her, and told her to wait so they could return home together.

In another, Ben was wounded, unconscious, and unable to write. She diligently nursed him back to health. Those were the good dreams. In her nightmares Ben was mutilated, his face mangled by weapons of destruction. Then he was blind, calling her name, searching in a darkness that would never see light. Lastly, he clawed at the dirt, buried alive, trying to touch her. She screamed.

Bare feet pattered on the floor, and the ropes supporting the mattresses of hay and feathers creaked as someone nestled against her. Arms encircled her neck. "Don't cry, Jem. Please don't cry."

Jem held Cass and stroked her hair. "I'm sorry. I had a nightmare."

"Was it about Ben?"

"Yes," she gasped. "I love him so much. I don't know what I'm going to do if he's gone."

"We love Ben, too." Jules climbed into bed on the other side of Jem. "He would walk on his hands and play games with us."

When all six sisters had lived at home, they shared

the three beds in the large upstairs bedroom. When Jem had returned home, she slept alone, but her little sisters would stay with her tonight, offering comfort with their presence and keeping the nightmares away.

****

Jem waited fifteen minutes after hearing the morning train whistle before heading to town. She wanted to give Matt time to deliver the mailbag and allow Marcus to sort it. Her hands trembled on the reins, and she fought the impulse to urge the gelding into a gallop. She nodded to a few people on the porch of Darrow Falls Inn. Logan wasn't among them.

Jem entered Wheeler's store and grabbed a newspaper off the stack near the door. Marcus was removing a bolt of fabric from a shelf and turned. He met Jem's gaze and shook his head. No letter had arrived from Ben.

"I checked twice, Miss Jenny." He waved his arm toward the counter. "I left them in a stack so you could look."

Jem took her time examining each letter. "None from Ben or Herman."

"I'm sorry." Marcus took the letters and sorted them into the cubicles behind the counter.

"It's not your fault, Mr. Wheeler." She paid him two cents for the paper even though it contained little about the battle, the scant news delegated to the inside second page.

"The letter may arrive tomorrow. Something could have delayed it."

"I can't wait."

"What are you going to do, Miss Jenny?"

"I'm going to Washington. I need to find out what

happened to Ben."

"Is Doc Beecher going with you?"

"No. We talked about it and agreed I should go alone."

He handed her a hard piece of lemon candy, her favorite. "When do you leave?"

"The afternoon train."

Chapter Eight

Jem filled her small trunk in silence. She packed five sets of chemises and bloomers. Dresses were worn more than once, but undergarments needed changing daily, especially in the heat of summer. She added stockings, an extra petticoat, a nightgown, robe, and knitted slippers. She packed three dresses and would wear a fourth.

One dress was a one-piece work dress she used for nursing. The mustard gown had a black diamond pattern to hide stains. Narrow sleeves could be folded back, and the front buttons and deep pockets were practical. She added a long apron to wear with it.

The second dress was the yellow dress she had worn yesterday. She could wear it to church or for calling on officers or at hospitals to find Ben. The final gown was for evening wear, and she debated whether to take it. Grandma Donovan had sewn it. The blue and white checkered gown was trimmed with black braiding in a castle pattern on the skirt and sleeves. Jem had spent hours pinning and hemming the six yards of skirt fabric to fit over a large wire and cloth frame she borrowed for the Independence Day dance last year. The wide hoop proved impractical on the crowded dance floor. Not only did Ben have to keep at arms' length when holding her, the crinoline tipped and exposed her drawers whenever she bumped into another dancer.

The admiration and approval of others had been important, but now she was more practical. The smaller crinoline provided some fullness but would not be cumbersome on a train or in a crowded hospital. Her traveling outfit consisted of a tan skirt made of lightweight wool and a short matching cape she could use if nights were cool on the train. Her blouse was crème colored with a high neck edged with lace and long full sleeves. A short gathered ruffle was sewn from shoulder to shoulder, dipping on the bodice. She chose a straw bonnet fitted snug against her head but with a broad brim in front to shade her face. She wouldn't have to remove it on the train, giving the appearance she wasn't traveling far. She tossed her wide brimmed bonnet on top of the dresses she had packed. She put her handkerchief, fan, and a few coins in her reticule and gathered her gloves. She had already hidden the silver dollars in her corset cover.

What am I doing? If she waited, someone would write about Ben's fate. In a few days or a few weeks. But what if no one wrote? What if no one had news of his fate? Could she forgive herself for not trying to find the truth?

Her father carried the trunk to the family wagon. Her mother and sisters were seated on the benches along the sides in the back. They had promised not to cry, but Cass sniffled before Sterling slapped the reins on the back of the pair of draft horses. Jem sang "Oh, Susanna" to cheer them. They created their own lyrics after the first verse of the popular Stephen Foster tune. The second verse was considered offensive by abolitionists.

When they reached the depot, Sterling helped everyone out of the wagon and carried her trunk to the depot platform.

Cass hugged Jem tightly. "How long will you be gone?"

"Not more than a week." She hugged Jules and her mother. "I'll try to send a telegram, but I'll write, too."

Maureen had packed a rectangular basket with sandwiches, a jar of lemonade, blueberry muffins, peaches, carrot sticks, and raspberry pie. She wouldn't starve. She closed the hinged lid and draped the handles over her arm.

Her father bought her ticket and instructed the porter to load her trunk in the baggage car. She stared at the big black steam engine as it puffed smoke into the summer sky. The coal car, passenger cars, baggage car, and caboose would transport her more than four hundred miles. A trip alone far from home had risks, including assault, rape, and death. Her knees trembled beneath her hoop skirt. She reached in her pocket for the knife her father had given her. Could she defend herself? What if more than one man attacked her? Was she making a mistake?

She turned to her family. Home meant safety. They would understand if she didn't leave. But what about Ben? Would he forgive her? Especially after her last letter.

A well-dressed couple arrived in an elegant carriage with inlaid wood decorating the front and side panels and tassels hanging from the cloth canopy. The man helped the woman descend but stayed with the carriage as she approached the Beecher family. She was dressed in a dark blue silk gown with a black lace parasol and lace gloves. Jem stepped aside to allow her to board, but she grabbed her hand. "Mrs. Ben Collins, I'm Mrs. McFarland."

Jem had known her as Juanita Stratman. She was Herman's mother. The change was more than her clothes. She looked healthier and happier than the woman who had nursed her dying husband for two long years.

"I was in Mr. Wheeler's store, and he said you were traveling to Washington to seek news about your husband."

Jem nodded.

"Could you ask about my boy, Herman?"

And if she found him alive and well, she'd chastise him for not writing his mother all these months. Juanita loved her son, worried about him, and sought news like her. "I will."

"Marcus said Martha Herbruck received a letter from John." Her face was anxious. "You delivered it. Do you know what he wrote?"

"John is wounded, but well. He doesn't know what happened to Ben or Herman."

Juanita glanced toward Randall waiting quietly by the carriage. "Herman said I was being disloyal to his pa's memory by marrying Mr. McFarland, but he's a good man. I love him."

Her confession was startling because others had said Juanita married Randall for his money.

"It's not that I didn't love Herman's father. I married him when I was sixteen. He wasn't much older. Those were rough years with fighting, cruel words, and tears. When you're older, you look back and wonder why you wasted so much time disagreeing. Marriage should be a partnership. Randall and I didn't want to wait another year or two to satisfy someone else's timeline for mourning. I'd been mourning Henry's loss since the stroke. I couldn't ignore a second chance at happiness. I think Herman joined the army to spite me," Juanita concluded. "I've written, but the only news I received was from your husband."

"Ben wrote you?"

"Your husband is a good man and a good friend." She withdrew a letter from her purse. "I was going to mail this, but if you're going in person, I'd appreciate you giving Herman this letter. Try to make him read it."

Jem put the letter in her handbag. "Herman is a mule, but I'm sure he regrets being stubborn."

"He's like his father, butting heads and for what?"

Jem patted her hand. "I know you took good care of Henry. My father said you were an excellent nurse." She glanced toward Sterling waiting nearby.

Juanita threw her arms around Jem's shoulders. "Thank you. Please tell him I love him. He's my son." She dried her tears. "And if he didn't make it through the battle, I'd appreciate you delivering the news. Not knowing his fate is worse than knowing he perished."

"I will," she promised.

"Please take this." She shoved a coin purse into her hand.

"I don't want to take your money."

"You'll have expenses. And if you don't need it, give it to Herman," she said. "He'll refuse to take it, but you figure out a way to put it in his hand. They don't pay soldiers much."

Jem was familiar with the pay. Ben had made seven dollars a week at the Darrow Falls mill. He'd left his job and her to pursue life as a soldier for thirteen dollars a month. She put the purse in her drawstring handbag.

"Young men have so much anger in them. Hard work tends to mellow some. I pray he doesn't hate me anymore."

"Men deal with death and change differently than women," Jem said. "We accept it, and they fight it."

Juanita studied her. "Why did Ben join?"

Jem was caught off guard and stammered a reply. "He joined because John and Herman did. They were best friends."

"He was the leader," Juanita said. "They admired Ben. They were envious when he married you."

Ben had chosen her over them, at least for a short time. But if Ben didn't like marriage, why didn't he say something? If he wasn't ready to be a husband, why had he married her? She'd given him time to change his mind. They were beginning to settle into life together when he uprooted their lives to join the army. Her letter had given him an option. Had he taken it?

Juanita rejoined her husband. She burst into tears, and Randall gathered her close. He was a good husband. Why couldn't Herman accept that?

"Here's your ticket." Sterling placed it in her hand. "You have your pocket friend?"

"Ready to defend me."

"Anyone gives you any trouble, don't hesitate to use it. You have your medical bag if he warrants repairing."

The bag was in her trunk. "I won't take any chances."

The train whistle blew a long blast, and the steam

billowed from the smoke stack. "Time to go."

Sterling helped her board. She turned at the top of the step and waved. Her family waved and forced smiles. What was she doing? Her stomach convulsed, and panic seized her at the prospect of being on her own. But before she could jump to the safety of the depot platform, the train jolted forward.

For better or for worse, she was heading to Washington City. Jem entered the passenger car and peered through the windows as her family disappeared. She wanted to cry. She loved them. More than Ben. Was that wrong? Ben was her husband. But Ben had only been in her life a few years compared to an entire lifetime with her family. Yet, Ben was her husband. She was legally bound by wifely duty to find him. She took a calming breath and looked around the rows of seats facing her.

Logan Pierce was seated near the front of the car. He scooted toward the window to make room. Jem made a point of passing him and sitting across the aisle in a seat behind him. He had refused to help her. She would accomplish her task without him.

The sash window was open, and Jem lowered the inside pane to prevent the smokestack's soot from blowing inside. She arranged her belongings on the seat beside her and enjoyed the ride. After growing tired of the tree-filled scenery, she removed her father's book, *A Tale of Two Cities* by Charles Dickens, from the basket. *It was the best of times, it was the worst of times, it was the age of wisdom, it was the age of foolishness, it was...*

Jem had read a third of the way through the novel before the train car had filled. A woman sat next to

Logan. He had offered her the window. They made eye contact before a man stepped between them.

"Hello, miss. I hope you don't mind some company." Before Jem could protest, the man turned to lower himself into her seat. Jem snatched her basket and cloak to safety before he sat on them.

He was short with a paunch. "Buster Goodman at your service." He removed his hat. He had long greasy hair, a droopy mustache, and scraggly beard, leaving blood-shot eyes and a bulbous nose as his only exposed features. "I've been on the road. Nearly wore out the soles on my shoes. Good to sit." He removed a checkered handkerchief from his pocket and wiped his brow. "It's hot today. Do you mind if I open the window."

"The soot blows in."

Buster leaned over her and shoved the window open.

His clothes were stained, and by the offensive odor assaulting her nostrils, he needed a bath. She turned away, and a gust of wind blew back her bonnet.

"Red hair," he announced. "I like redheads."

And I liked being alone. The man behind her frowned as the breeze blew in his face. "I'm sorry. I'll close the window."

"Nonsense. Nothing better than some fresh air." Buster inhaled and pounded his chest.

While Buster introduced himself to the men behind them, she lowered the pane in the window. She adjusted her bonnet back around her face and arranged her belongings on her lap. From her handbag, she removed a nosegay of flowers in damp moss and sniffed the fragrance to disguise Buster's odors. It didn't help. She should have left the window open.

"That's a mighty pretty dress you're wearing. Did you make it?"

"No, my grandmother made it."

"Your grandmother!" he howled. "You're not in short skirts and pigtails." Buster studied her. "But I bet it wasn't long since you were."

"I'm a married woman." She showed him the narrow gold band on her ring finger.

"Married! Now, I can't believe that. Not that you aren't a fair miss. I like redheads. You aren't a true redhead. I mean, not like a carrot top. You have a darker shade of hair. Like copper or bronze. What color is your hair?"

"Auburn." Jem inhaled the nosegay. Buster's breath reeked of onions and bitter beer. Would it be impolite to ask if he would mind finding another seat? She looked around. Her gaze met Logan's. His dimples were deep, his smile wide, and laughter danced in his fawn-colored eyes. "You seem crowded. I could find another seat."

"I'm as comfortable as a butterfly in a cocoon."

"Chrysalis," Jem corrected.

"What?"

"A butterfly hatches from a chrysalis. A moth exits a cocoon."

"Is that so? You a teacher or something?"

"No, I'm a nurse. I've studied biology."

"Biology? What is that?"

"It's the study of living organisms."

"You ain't one of them atheists who believes in Darwin's lies? I don't care for none of that talk about man coming from monkeys."

"I am not an atheist, and if natural selection creates new species, then why aren't monkeys evolving into men now?"

"Are you calling me a monkey?"

Jem wasn't sure how to answer.

Buster rattled on about Darwin as if he was an expert on the man whose book on evolution had created an uproar among churches. Jem would have argued some of his points if he had given her an opportunity to reply, but his constant dialogue was one sided. Although rude, she opened her book to continue her reading.

Buster snatched it from her hands. "What are you reading?"

"It belongs to my father." She reached for it.

"Excuse me, I'd like to sit with my wife."

Logan stood in the aisle. What had he called her?

Buster's bushy eyebrows shot up. "I didn't know she was married."

Jem showed her ring hand. "I said I was married."

Logan displayed his dimples. "Jem, darling, is this man bothering you?"

The endearment stunned her from answering.

"I didn't know your husband was on the train." Buster stood and handed Logan the book. "You weren't sitting with her."

"I'm sitting with her now." He relaxed against the seat and pointed. "There's an empty seat in the front."

Why hadn't Logan come to her aid sooner? "Am I supposed to be grateful?"

He leaned forward to stand. "I could call him back."

"No!"

Buster relocated a safe distance away.

"This doesn't mean I can't take care of myself."

"No doubt, but I'm tired of people talking *On the Origin of Species by Means of Natural Selection* when they obviously haven't read it." He looked at her basket. "Your parents know you're running away from home?"

He could be charming when he wasn't rude. And he was better company than Buster. "I am not running away. My family supports me in my endeavors. Papa gave me a book to read."

He looked at the cover before handing her the book. "Dickens. I've read it."

"Don't tell me the ending. I hate that."

He tapped his finger on the cover. "You like reading about politics?"

She gasped as she flipped through the pages. "Isn't it a romance?"

"You can't tell the difference between a political essay and a romantic romp? Why would your father give you a book you don't understand?"

Typical male. She wasn't done playing with him. "What makes you an expert on politics?"

Logan pointed at his inflated chest. "I earned a degree from Ohio University to learn how governments work or why they fail. I've studied the history of civilizations. I've studied every word of the Constitution of the United States. I think that qualifies me as an expert."

Her laughter interrupted his tirade. "Do you think London and Paris are similar to Washington and Richmond? Let's hope the South doesn't build a guillotine. And I think a novel in which two men are in love with the same woman qualifies as a romance."

He stared. "I don't like intelligent women."

"How unfortunate you sat next to me." She resumed her reading.

Chapter Nine

Jem silently counted, waiting for Logan to share his opinion.

"You think the South is like France?"

She placed her marker in the page where she had been reading. "The French royalty were indifferent toward the starving masses. They ignored the problem, and the poor rioted in a bloody rampage. Isn't that what Southern slave owners fear the most? A violent rebellion from the slaves?"

"The war isn't about slavery. It's about preserving the Union."

"Hogwash. The North was gaining support to abolish slavery and, I thought, elected a president willing to do it. The only way the South could maintain slavery was to break away from the Union. If President Lincoln doesn't resolve the issue of slavery, the Union won't exist."

"Part of being a politician is to say whatever is necessary to gain support." He looked around the car. "Lincoln could free the slaves today, but the slave border states would secede and cut off Washington from the free states. He's playing a balancing act. One misstep and our government could tumble. He has to be cautious. Not everyone is an abolitionist."

"Whether you're an abolitionist or not, slavery is wrong. How can politicians evade the problem for so long?"

"A politician depends on the support of his constituents," Logan said. "He has to vote for the legislation they support."

"Politicians have their own agenda," she said. "They vote to advance their careers not to represent the people. I don't know how you can be part of a corrupt system of government."

"Nearly a century of checks and balances control the corruption. Our government is complex, but it works better than any other form of government." He tapped her book. "Better than the monarchy in France." Logan was sincere.

"You believe that."

"I wouldn't be in politics if I didn't."

"I may have to revise my opinion of you." She studied him closely. "You're an idealist and a reluctant rescuer of women."

"Mrs. Collins, remember you're married."

Was she? Or was she a widow yet to be informed of her husband's death? She wouldn't entertain the notion. "Did the South take many prisoners?"

Logan frowned, lines of worry creasing his brow. "Do you think your husband was captured?"

"If I don't find Ben among the wounded, he's either a prisoner or dead. How do I find out?"

"I don't know." He crossed his arms. "We weren't going to lose."

"Hopefully by the time I arrive in Washington City, John will know something about Ben or Herman."

"The letter was from John. Who's Herman?"

"Ben, John, and Herman have been best friends for years. They did everything together. I don't know who had the idea initially, but when Lincoln asked for volunteers, they signed the roster together."

"You didn't object?"

She didn't answer. Ben hadn't consulted her about joining. They had talked about the chance of war, especially after states seceded from the Union. First, South Carolina in December and then in January, Mississippi, Florida, Alabama, Georgia, and Louisiana broke away from the Union. After they were married, she couldn't imagine he would abandon her, even for three months. She pleaded to let other men without responsibilities fight the war, but he wanted to do his duty. He had signed the roll and wouldn't go back on his word. She had cried, but her tears didn't stop him from leaving.

She waited, hoping he had changed his mind, but his first letter spoke of his resolve to fight if necessary to restore the Union and put an end to slavery. She dried her tears, returned home, and wrote him about her decisions. She stored his belongings in the Beecher barn and resumed her role of daughter. Her letters were filled with news about her family, but she never mentioned her broken heart, her doubts about their marriage, or the fear her love would turn to bitterness and resentment. Until her most recent missive.

She'd seen other women disappointed with their husbands. Men who were drunkards, wife beaters, or cheated with other women. Divorce was not common, but laws were changing to make it easier to obtain one. She hadn't considered divorcing Ben, but she wanted to be important in his life. She wanted him to love her as much as she loved him. And if he didn't, she wanted to part while they were friends and not disillusioned enemies.

"Are you all right?" Logan looked worried.

Jem shook off the foreboding feelings and forced a smile. "I was thinking about Ben."

Logan settled back into the bench seat. "How long have you been married to the fire beater?"

"Four months."

He bolted forward. "But he's been a volunteer for three months."

Not much of a honeymoon. "We've known each other for years. We attended the same parties. I taught Herman how to dance. My sisters and John's brothers would join us on outings. We had a wonderful time together," she defended.

"So why didn't they ask you to come along on their latest adventure?"

They'd abandoned her because she was a woman, and they were best friends. She was Ben's wife, but she was second place in his heart. The hurt festered.

"Don't look so serious. I was joking," Logan said. "I don't remember the Ohio boys arriving in the city in April with the other troops."

"After hearing about Maryland's civilians greeting the Sixth Massachusetts with rocks and curse words when they changed trains in Baltimore, they stayed in Harrisburg for a couple of days. Only days turned into weeks. Ben wrote the men were glad when they finally received their uniforms and munitions and marched into Washington in late May."

"How often does he write?"

"Every week." She wanted to explain her decision. "I know you think I'm being foolish traveling to Washington City when I could wait for news at home, but I have my reasons." What if Ben mistook her ultimatum for not loving him? She wanted to save their marriage, not abandon it. She put her book on top of the basket. "Tell me about Washington City. What's it like?"

"It's crowded, dirty, and surrounded by ugly forts and tent camps." He looked at the town they were approaching. "You have time to turn around."

"Don't worry about me. I have a plan."

"A plan?" His dimples deepened. "Does it come with a map and secret passwords?"

Jem turned her back. "I'm not a child."

He flicked a ribbon hanging from a thick braid wrapped in an intricate weave at the base of her neck. "What's the plan?"

She turned. "You're not going to laugh?"

"Of course not." His dimples didn't disappear.

Men never took a woman seriously. She removed a small notebook from her handbag. She showed him a list. "First, I'm going to find a cheap but clean boarding house. Then I'll visit John and learn what he knows about Ben. I hope he knows more than what he wrote in his letter." She chewed on her bottom lip. "If John doesn't know anything, maybe the other men in his company can help me. That's why I wanted to go to Washington before they muster out."

"What regiment does Ben belong to?"

"The 1st Regiment, Ohio Volunteer Infantry."

"A colonel is in charge of a regiment, but the captain of his company would have a better idea of what happened," Logan said.

"If they don't know, I can visit the wounded and see if Ben is among them."

"That's not a bad plan."

"Don't sound surprised," Jem said. "My sisters say I'm practical. I make lists."

He withdrew a paper from his coat pocket. Every item on the list had a mark through it.

"Everything is crossed out," she said.

"Mission accomplished."

They had something in common. They made lists. "You said you wouldn't help me, but could you recommend a boardinghouse?"

"I refused help to dissuade you from the trip," he explained. "Since I failed, I'll assist in any way I can."

"Thank you." She opened her basket. "Are you hungry? Mama packed plenty."

****

Logan studied Jem, who had fallen asleep on his shoulder. Her bonnet had fallen back, and he could see her face clearly. Her nose was strong, cutting a striking profile framed by her auburn hair. Long dark lashes rested against delicate pale skin, lacking any sign of freckles common in redheads. He should never have come to her rescue. Her femininity ignited an overwhelming protectiveness, and he battled a growing desire to be more than a casual acquaintance.

After his brother's death, he made it a rule never to associate with married women in social circles where gossip could flame an innocent gesture into a notorious scandal. Six years ago, he had been attending Ohio University, and Derek Pierce had been the young secretary serving U.S. Senator Salmon Chase.

It was common for young men in Washington to escort the wives of officials. Senators, representatives, and other politicians were too busy with important deals and liaisons to attend social events with their spouses. Derek had loved Washington and all the back room dealings. He'd written him in college about all the important people he'd met. Then he started writing about a woman named Hannah. She was young, lonely, and the wife of Senator Lewis Smith. Derek was obsessed with her.

Affairs were common among the rich and famous, but lovers were cautioned to be discreet. His brother and Hannah were reckless in their trysts. Her husband discovered the affair and fatally shot Derek in January of 1855.

The police pressed no charges against Senator Smith even though Derek was unarmed, and the newspapers extolled his virtues for defending the sanctity of his home and the honor of his young wife. They painted Derek as a seducer of women and a destroyer of decency.

Derek was dead at twenty-five years old. All his dreams and ambitions gone because of a careless affair. After Logan graduated two years later, his father had helped him obtain a position with Ohio Governor Salmon Chase. Within a year, his parents' death left him without any family.

Salmon was the one link he had to Derek and his father. He had enjoyed working in Columbus and hoped to avoid the intrigues of Washington, but others talked about the scandal. With another Pierce in Washington City, they were waiting to see what mistake he would make and whether he would fall victim to the same fate as his brother. Logan had vowed never to become involved with a married woman. So why was he helping Mrs. Benjamin Collins?

Even if he wanted an affair of the heart with her, she claimed to be happily married. But was she? Why would a man leave his wife after one month of marriage?

****

A baby's cry woke Jem. She was resting against a man's side, her hand clutching the lapel of his jacket. Ben? She lifted her head from Logan's shoulder and gazed into his warm brown eyes. "How long have I been sleeping?"

He removed his arm from around her shoulder and stretched. "A few hours."

A woman in front of them calmed her baby. She had two small children with her. "I'm sorry to disturb you," she apologized.

The girl knelt on the seat and faced them. "Hello."

"Hello," Jem said. "What's your name?"

"Inga." She had dark blonde hair and light brown eyes. Her faded lavender bonnet matched her well-worn dress. She smiled, exposing a gap in her top row of teeth. "This is my brother Odin."

Odin looked over the back of the bench and stuck out his tongue.

"Stop that," his mother warned. "Turn around."

"I'm not offended," Jem said with a laugh. "I have four younger sisters. They're always misbehaving."

"Boys are worse," she said. "I'm Ellen Strasburg."

"Jennifer Collins."

"I'm Logan." He nodded.

"I'm going to Washington City to care for my husband," Ellen said. "He was wounded at the battle in Manassas, Virginia." She furrowed her brow. "Only I think it's called Bull Run."

How was she going to tend an injured husband with three children in tow? "How badly was he hurt?"

"I don't know." Ellen had brown hair, brown eyes, and a brown dress. She was a sparrow on the edge of her nest begging for help. "His captain is a friend and telegraphed me. I left as soon as possible." She rubbed her finger on her baby's gums. He was about eight months old and revealed eight tiny teeth. "He said Thornton was taken to a temporary hospital in Arlington Heights. Do you know where that is?"

"It's in Virginia," Logan said.

Ellen looked surprised. "Isn't that enemy territory?"

"We occupy the part around Washington."

"Thornton is in the Second Wisconsin. We live outside of Milwaukee with my father. He has a dairy farm. We make cheese." She was rambling.

"That's nice." Jem glanced at Logan, who was grinning. Another damsel in distress for him to rescue.

"I gathered the children and boarded the train. My father said I was a fool." She put her arm around Inga and Odin. "I couldn't leave the children with him. When he drinks, he's mean."

Ellen wasn't censoring any of her life story. Jem had cared for the victims of drunkards. The emotional pain was sometimes worse than the physical abuse.

"It's difficult, but Thornton said he had to join. I can't blame him. My father worked him like a slave and refused to pay him. He said room and board were payment. Thornton said with the money he earned in the army, we could buy our own farm." Ellen paused, her brow creased. "I hope he's not too badly injured."

"I'm sure his wounds are minor." Jem lifted her

basket from the floor. "Would you like something to eat?"

"Oh, no. We couldn't take your food," Ellen objected.

"But I'm hungry, Mommy," Odin announced.

"I would feel guilty eating in front of you, and we have plenty. My mother always packs too much." Jem handed her two sandwiches and sliced a peach with the knife she withdrew from her skirt pocket. She ignored Logan's look of curiosity. "It's juicy." She handed each child a piece. She handed Ellen and Logan a slice before biting into one.

The baby continued to fuss. "He must be hungry, too." Ellen looked around the crowded car.

"You can nurse him privately in the back."

She stood. "Would you mind watching the children? I won't take long." Ellen took the baby.

Inga and Odin stared at Logan. He stared back. "I hope she returns."

"Mommy isn't going to leave us like Daddy did, is she?" Inga asked.

Jem frowned at Logan. "Now see what you've done."

"What?"

"You've upset them." She smiled at Inga and Odin. "Why don't I tell you a story?"

"What kind of story?" Odin asked.

Jem leaned over the seat. "Are you comfortable?" She grabbed her cape and arranged it around them. "The story is about a doll named Janie."

"A doll?" Odin whined.

"Hush," Inga said.

"Janie had a body made of linen and hair made

from walnut-dyed yarn. Her green eyes and red mouth were embroidered with silk thread. She had a red and white plaid dress and a little white apron. One day she was put in a box. The box was dark, and she couldn't see anything. Strange sounds and voices whispered outside. Someone shook the box. She fell against the side. What was happening?"

Inga cowered under the cloak. "Was she scared?"

"A little. Most people are scared when strange things happen. We don't know if we'll like the changes. A light appeared in a crack above Janie. A little girl named Cassie opened the box. She had wished for a doll for a long time. Cassie lifted Janie and hugged her. She kissed her face and promised to love her forever."

"Did she?" Inga asked.

"Yes, and Janie became her special doll. They were always together and even today, she sits on Cassie's bed in a place of honor."

"I wish I had a doll like Janie," Inga said.

"Someday you will." They had fallen asleep by the time Ellen returned.

She took a seat next to the man across from Logan. "We traveled from Milwaukee by coach, then by boat, and now train. If I fall asleep, can you make sure I don't drop Thor?"

"You need to sleep," Jem said. "Logan can hold him."

Logan's eyes widened. "I don't…" Before he could finish, Ellen placed the sleeping baby in the crook of his arm. "What if I drop him?"

Jem arranged the blanket around the baby. "I won't let you."

"What if he wakes up?"

"He ate. He'll sleep for hours."

"What if he does something else? This is a store-bought suit."

"Relax."

"I'm not enjoying this."

"I'm not taking him." Jem opened her book but glanced frequently at Logan, who studied the child cradled in his arm. She had expected him to surrender Thor, but he took possession much like Noah had owned Addy. Ben had enjoyed entertaining her sisters with stories and games, but he had never held a baby. She had imagined children with Ben's dark hair and gray eyes in her future family. She sniffled back a tear and turned the page.

Chapter Ten

The conductor tapped on a man's shoulder. "Baltimore, I believe that's your stop." The man snorted and gathered his belongings. He bumped his head on the lantern hanging on the wall as he stood.

Jem closed her book. Her handkerchief was twisted and soaked. She blew her nose.

"It's in my pocket."

She turned to Logan. "What is?"

"My handkerchief. Yours is soaked by all the tears you've shed."

"You said it was a political book." She removed the kerchief from his coat pocket. "It was awful."

"Politically it shows how ordinary men can commit atrocities in the name of justice. It's meant to have an impact."

She blew her nose. "I meant romantically it's horrible. He loves her and dies."

Logan raised his finger in the air. "But the husband lives."

"At what price?" Jem burst into a fresh round of tears.

"You claimed you were practical." He looked around, hushing her. "You're an emotional train wreck."

"It's not me. It's Dickens. This isn't like his other books. Papa reads *A Christmas Carol* every Christmas, and *Oliver Twist* was about a boy who overcomes poverty."

"Most of his books are about the working class," Logan agreed. "*A Tale of Two Cities* is no different. He focuses on the elite more, but it's a struggle between the rich and poor."

"And out of all the suffering and poverty, a shred of decency emerges only to be destroyed." She wiped her nose.

"Scrooge becomes generous, Oliver finds a home, and a drunk aristocrat named Sydney Carton nobly sacrifices his life for the woman he loves."

Jem gasped, fought to control her tears, and lost.

"Is something wrong with your wife?" the conductor asked.

"She wants her mother to live with us. I said with three children, we couldn't make the room."

What tale was Logan spinning?

"Don't compromise," the conductor warned. "I have more relatives living with me than I can count. That's why I ride the train."

After he moved away, Jem caught her breath. "Why did you tell him that bucket of lies?"

"You're not the only one who can weave an entertaining story."

Jem wiped her face, placed the book in her basket, and looked at the baby. "He's awake."

"He's been staring at me for the last fifteen minutes. Do you think he's plotting something?"

She took a sniff. "I think he's accomplished his task."

Logan inhaled, made a face, and handed the baby to Jem.

She held him at arms' length. "Wake his mother."

Logan shook Ellen, who woke with a start. "Have you been holding him all this time?"

"And he's ripened."

Ellen took him, checked the children who were beginning to stir. "Do you know when we'll be arriving?"

Logan looked out the window. "We're heading into Washington City now."

Ellen handed Jem her cape and instructed Inga and Odin to follow her to the washroom.

They rejoined them as the train slowed to a halt at the Baltimore & Ohio Station at the foot of Capitol Hill.

Jem peered out the window. A huge building of white marble was built on a rise, towering above the town. The building was under construction with scaffolding and cranes protruding from the roof in the central area. "What's that?"

"That's the Capitol," Logan said. "Congress outgrew the old building. Thomas Walter is the architect. He probably wishes he had never entered the competition to design wings for the building."

"I would think it would be an honor."

"It's been a disaster. He had to rebuild the exterior with marble because the sandstone was falling apart. Then he had to restore the Library of Congress in the Capitol's west central section after a fire in 1851, and like any government project, others suggested changes, including President Pierce."

She tilted her head as she tied the bow on her bonnet. "No relation?"

"Unlike you, I have no famous relatives."

She pointed out the window. "What's happening in

the middle?"

"Congress wanted a cast-iron dome instead of wood. They had to reinforce the Rotunda walls. Then the Statue of Freedom going on top was too tall. Walter had to redesign the dome to support the larger figure."

"Too bad the war stopped the work."

"It stopped on the wings but not the dome. Walter hired Kirtland and Company to finish the dome, and they aren't letting a little thing like a war stop them."

"Where does Congress meet if the building isn't finished?"

"Their chambers are completed. The House of Representatives was finished about three years ago, and the Senate began meeting two years ago. Currently, they're meeting in special session because of the war, but they'll be going home soon. Then the soldiers will overrun the place."

"Won't they ruin it?"

"Walter covered most of the valuables not small enough to store." Logan stood and made room for Jem to precede him. "The damage is in wear and tear. Washington City is built on a swamp, and it doesn't have to rain for men to find mud. And a bunch of drunken men like to tear apart everything in sight. I hope the battle loss has mellowed the rowdier ones."

****

Jem stared at the Italianate-style depot with its arched windows and wide arched doorway opening at the foot of Capitol Hill. The nearby countryside was barren except for a few wooden sheds. In the distance she could see small red brick houses and white churches. Ellen and her children joined her. All her belongings were in a large carpet bag.

Logan found a black hack carriage for hire, and they headed south on First Street before turning west on Pennsylvania Avenue. The cobblestones were broken and uneven, making the ride bumpy. On the north side, hotels and shops began appearing like a row of children's drawings. None of them belonged to the others. Some were wood or brick while others were ornate marble. Squat one-floor offices were next to three-story buildings. No plan or reason explained any of the structures in town.

Jem sat next to Logan with the Strasburg family across from them. "Where are you planning to stay, Ellen?"

"I don't know. I was hoping Thornton could make arrangements if we have to spend the night. He always took care of details."

Logan waved toward the right. "The finer hotels are on the north side of Pennsylvania Avenue."

"I can't afford any fancy place," Ellen said. "I don't have much money left after coming all this way from Milwaukee. The trip cost more than I expected."

"The south side has several affordable boardinghouses."

"Why don't you come with me while I obtain a room? You can store your bag, and if you like the place, you can rent a room if necessary," Jem suggested.

"I'll have to talk to Thornton first, but I don't see any harm in storing my bag."

"You said your husband was in a hospital in Arlington Heights," Logan said. "I know the army took over the Washington Infirmary on E Street and turned the Union Hotel in Georgetown into a military hospital, but I don't know of any others. Did he mean the regimental hospital?"

"What is that?"

"Each regiment has a tent hospital. If a soldier is sick, he reports to the regimental doctor who decides when he can return to duty," Logan said.

"The Wisconsin regiment is in Arlington Heights." Ellen looked around. "How do I reach it?"

Logan pointed in the distance across the Washington Canal and mall. "Arlington Heights is across Long Bridge."

"The Ohio Camp is in Virginia, too." Jem patted Ellen's arm. "We'll go after breakfast and ask the soldiers about the hospital."

Ellen nodded.

"Is that a castle?" Inga pointed at the solitary structure of the Smithsonian Institute on the mall. The only other structure was the unfinished Washington Monument in the distance on the edge of the Potomac River.

"It's a research institute run by Joseph Henry," Logan said. "He lives there."

"Is he a prince?"

"No, he's a secretary like me," Logan said.

Inga stared. "You look like a prince."

Logan blushed and pointed to the large buildings in the distance on the right. "That's the National Hotel and ahead is the Brown's Hotel."

Ellen looked around. "I've never seen so many huge buildings."

"They were built to impress visiting dignitaries," Logan said. "But I'm still awed by the grandeur."

The carriage halted as several wagons blocked their

path. Jem looked around. "What are all these wagons doing in town?"

"They provide supplies for the troops. The army is bigger than three large towns. The government hired teamsters to haul food to the different camps." The carriage wedged into an opening and continued. Most of the boarding houses had signs indicating *no vacancies*. Between them were saloons, brothels, and restaurants. Jem spotted a sign, *rooms for rent*. She ordered the driver to stop at the two-story building. The house had fallen into disrepair with a missing shutter from one window and gray weathered boards showing through the whitewash.

Logan didn't move. "Are you sure?"

"It looks affordable."

Logan told the driver to wait. He carried Jem's trunk and Ellen's bag.

Jem pointed to a large sign hanging from the frame of the door. "Southern Belle?"

"That would explain the empty rooms. Most of the clientele have left town."

Inga yanked on the rope attached to a small bell. A short, plump woman answered. She scanned the group and ushered them inside. The front of the house consisted of two rooms. One was a sitting room and the other a dining room. A kitchen was visible in the back.

"I'm Annabelle Sharpton." She folded her hands in front of her apron. "What can I do for you?"

Jem smiled. "I would like a room."

"For all of you?"

Jem looked at Ellen. "Why don't you plan to stay at least for tonight? Your husband may not be ready to travel."

Ellen agreed to her suggestion.

"What about him?" Annabelle pointed at Logan.

"That's her husband," Ellen said.

"No, he's not." Jem recalled their introductions. Logan had not given his last name.

"What is he then?" Annabelle demanded. "I don't allow unmarried couples to board under my roof."

"I have a house I rent," Logan said. "I won't need any accommodations."

"Mr. Pierce works for the secretary of the treasury. He's our guide," Jem clarified.

"He isn't your husband?" Ellen whispered. "He acted like your husband."

"My husband is Ben Collins. He's with the First Ohio. He's missing."

Annabelle pointed at Logan. "Is he your husband's replacement?"

Jem lifted her trunk. "I don't think I'll stay here after all."

"Only place with a vacancy. The town is crowded with mothers and wives taking care of the wounded."

She dropped the trunk. "We'll take two rooms."

Logan handed her some money.

Jem shoved it back. "I don't need your money."

"It's for the food we ate and them." He nodded toward Ellen and the children. "You're far too generous, Jennifer Collins."

If people kept giving her money, she'd make a profit from the trip. She turned to Annabelle who was watching the exchange of money. "How much for a single room and a room with a double bed and trundle?"

"Twenty cents a night, and I don't accept any paper

money."

"Does that include meals?"

"Breakfast and supper. I serve sandwiches for dinner, or you can take them with you if you're going to be away."

Jem counted a dollar from Logan. Who was far too generous? She handed the money to Annabelle. "I plan to stay for a week." She looked at Ellen. "We'll know later today how long Mrs. Strasburg will be staying."

"My husband is with the Second Wisconsin. I believe he's in Arlington Heights."

"Probably squatting on the Robert E. Lee plantation."

"Lee resigned his commission and abandoned his home," Logan said.

"Major General Lee is a loyal Virginian," Annabelle said. "I was good friends with Mary Custis Lee."

"Custis?" Jem repeated. "Why does that name sound familiar?"

"Didn't you attend school? George Washington married Martha Custis. He adopted Martha's son, John, and then his grandson, George Washington Parke Custis, who was Mary's father," Annabelle said. "She edited his writings about Washington. She had to flee Arlington House when McDowell made it the headquarters for the Army of Northeastern Virginia."

"If Lee had accepted President Lincoln's offer to lead the Union Army, she could have remained," Logan reminded her.

"He wouldn't fight against the Commonwealth of Virginia."

"He served in the United States Army for thirty-five years. Who does he think he's fighting now? He's a traitor to his country."

"Don't you dare call Lee a traitor!"

Jem shoved Logan toward the door. "I think you've helped enough. We'll be fine."

"I have to report to my supervisor." He lowered his voice. "Don't trust her."

"She'll have to torture me to find out any state secrets."

Logan looked around. "This isn't funny. Spies are a serious problem, and she doesn't hide her loyalties."

"Where is Long Bridge located?"

"Cross the mall at Seventh Street and follow Maryland Avenue." He looked at Ellen. "Hire a hack. It's a long walk in this heat, and those children are tired."

It would be the last time they talked. "I appreciate what you've done, Logan. I'll repay you somehow."

"We rode on a train to the same destination. I didn't do anything." He nodded, turned, and headed for the hack.

Jem waited by the door until he boarded. He didn't acknowledge her wave and seemed preoccupied. What was wrong with the man? The coach lurched forward, and he was gone.

Annabelle led them upstairs. She stopped at the far end of the hallway and unlocked the door. "This is for you and the children." The room had a double bed with a trundle. "I'll fetch a cradle for the baby." Ellen ushered the children inside.

"When is breakfast served?"

"I'll start on it now."

Jem listened for any noise. "Where are the other

guests?"

"Last one left before the battle."

"Why didn't you leave?"

Her stern visage broke into a frightening grin. "They'll be back."

Was it a warning of a Southern invasion?

Annabelle showed Jem a room next door with a single bed. Jem lifted the feather mattress to reveal another mattress beneath. "When was the straw changed?"

"Last week."

Jem bounced on the bed.

"Are the ropes tight enough?"

"It'll do."

"The chamber pot is under the bed, and the washstand is in the corner. No dresser. You can hang your clothes on the pegs on the wall. I have an iron in the kitchen if you need to remove wrinkles. I do laundry on Mondays." Annabelle lifted the pitcher from the washstand. "I'll fetch some water."

After Annabelle left, Jem fell back on the bed. She'd reached Washington City. Now the hard work began. She rolled off the bed and unpacked. She had finished hanging her clothes on the posts when Annabelle returned with the water. She removed her traveling dress and undergarments to bathe. The cold water removed the soot and dust from her trip and refreshed her body as she ran the sponge over her arms and legs.

She dressed in a clean chemise and bloomers. She usually had a sister available to help lace her corset, but it could be done by reaching back and tugging each row of laces from top to bottom until it was snug. After tying the laces, she added the corset cover. Her work dress was wrinkled, but she didn't want to waste time ironing. She tossed on the mustard gown with the black diamond pattern. She buttoned the narrow sleeves instead of folding them back. She tied a white apron around her waist. She shoved a handkerchief, fan, and small leather purse in one of the deep pockets on the dress.

Jem removed her midwife bag from the trunk. The hinges opened wide on the leather bag and was similar to her father's bag but smaller. She checked some of the glass bottles. Nothing had broken during the trip. She placed her brush, matches, and a few personal items on a small table near the bed.

She frowned at her reflection in the small mirror nailed to the wall above the table. Her hair was a frizzy mess. She removed the combs and undid the braids. Static electricity crackled as she ran her brush through her hair. She dipped her brush in the water in the basin and smoothed the strands, braiding several sections and interweaving them into a chignon at the back of her neck. She plucked two short strands from the neat coiffure to frame her face.

A bell rang at the bottom of the stairs. "Breakfast is ready!"

After eating scrambled eggs, ham, biscuits, and fried potatoes, Jem, Ellen, and the children hired a coach to take them to Arlington Heights.

A train of wagons and vehicles made crossing Long Bridge a laborious task. Walking would have been faster, but Ellen and the children would have been trampled by the sea of soldiers pressed among the wagons.

The men were dressed in a variety of uniforms to represent their state militias. They were unarmed, rifles forbidden in Washington City, but the sheer number entering the city was intimidating.

Jem searched each face of the men passing their open carriage. She should have been tired after the long trip, but her anxiety to learn about Ben had revived her spirits. After crossing the bridge, the driver said the camp for the McCook regiment where Jem would find out about Ben was in the other direction from Arlington Heights.

Chapter Eleven

Jem grabbed her medical bag and paid the driver. "I'll join you later at the hospital." Jem made her way along the road, caught in the current of the endless flow of soldiers. She turned to a man walking beside her. "Do you know where the men from Ohio are camped?"

He pointed west. "Over yonder hill."

She thanked him and walked beside a worn path in the grass, following it toward a flat field planted with canvas flowers. She found a sign for Ben's company in front of a row of tents separated by a wide pathway. Most were wedge tents with a peak from front to back about twelve feet long and ten feet wide, room for six men sleeping side by side. A few of the tents were conical shaped with a central pole and the canvas pegged to the ground. Inside, a tarp was spread on the ground with blankets, bags, and other supplies scattered in the living quarters. Along her path rifles were stacked in groups, the shiny bayonets interlocked, ready to grab if an alarm was given.

She was in Virginia, the South. When the war first broke out, many worried Washington City would be taken by the Confederacy. But now fortifications and cannons surrounded the perimeter of the city, offering some protection. With the loss at Bull Run, sentries were on alert for an attack.

Ahead, a few men played cards in the shade

beneath a lone tree. Planks placed on barrels created a table, and crates or storage boxes served as chairs.

A coffee pot hung from a metal hook over a fire pit created with a ring of rocks surrounding a hole in the ground. Several logs had burned to black and white embers beneath a metal grate for cooking. A few tin plates and cups were discarded in a basin filled with soapy water. Breakfast had been served.

A few of the men wore the light blue pants and dark blue jackets of Ohio soldiers. The others wore wool shirts with a single button and collar. "Do you know where I can find Ben Collins or John Herbruck?"

A man wearing spectacles stood and removed his circular kepi hat with a flat top. "John is in our tent." He wore an unbuttoned short shell jacket. His light blue trousers were stained with dirt, grass, and what could have been blood. "I'm Corporal Sid Wilson. "

"I'm Jennifer Collins. If you know John, you must know my husband, Ben Collins."

He chuckled. "The good looking kid who can juggle."

"That's him. Is he here?"

His fallen expression gave her the answer. "No." He stared. "You're Miss Jenny. He said your hair rivals the morning sun."

Ben had mentioned Sid in his letters. "You're good friends with Ben?"

He stopped by a conical tent. "We've been living together for the past three months. I was a poor farm boy who didn't know the gun barrel from the trigger. He taught me how to shoot."

"Ben loves to hunt." Jem touched his sleeve. "What has he told you about me?"

"Mostly he reads the letters you wrote to us around the campfire at night."

What did he mean? "Those were personal."

He smoothed his hair back, revealing a receding hairline. "He didn't read all of the contents. Only the parts about your sisters, visits to your neighbors, and helping your father with his patients. We were happy to hear about home."

"Didn't you have anyone writing to you?"

"No. I don't have any family. I looked forward to your letters."

Her letters made them friends. She expected the truth. "Do you know what happened to Ben or his friend Herman Stratman?"

"The First Ohio didn't see much fighting until the retreat. A couple men were seriously wounded and about five are missing. Ben and Herman are two of them."

"Out of the hundred in the company? The newspaper made it sound like more were killed."

"I was giving the numbers for our regiment. We have nine hundred men in it."

"Then the papers exaggerated the losses."

"Not for the other regiments. There are more than a thousand wounded and nearly two thousand dead or missing." Sid entered the tent. "Hey, John. You have company."

"John?" Jem looked around the circular surrounding. Like a clock, each man had staked out an hour in the circle. John was near the opening. Two spots next to his were empty, unclaimed since the battle, waiting for Ben and Herman to return.

John was propped against a storage box, reading a

Bible. His right pant leg had been ripped from ankle to knee and exposed a dirty bandage wrapped around the lower part of the leg and foot.

"Miss Jenny." John closed the Bible and attempted to stand.

"Stay seated." Jem knelt beside him.

John had a week's growth of beard, but she recognized the deep set eyes and long narrow face of the Herbruck's clan. "Are you sick, John?"

"A little tired."

He was more than tired. The sweat on his brow could be from the heat, but it was early in the day. Why was he inside the tent instead of outside with the rest of the men? She rested her hand on his forehead. He had a fever.

The battle may have killed hundreds of men, but more soldiers had died from illness spread from one man to the next in the crowded camps. Ben had written about those claimed by dysentery, smallpox, and measles.

His fever was the only symptom, and she turned her attention to his wound. "You wrote your mother you were hit in the leg. How bad is it?"

"It was a little scratch. The doctors were too busy during the battle to bother them about it, but it's swollen and hurts to stand on it. Do you think someone should take a look?"

The bandage was filthy, and he had a fever. "The wound could be infected."

John drew his knee close to his body and put his arm around his wounded limb. "I don't want a surgeon touching me. You know more about medicine than these sawbones. Would you mind?"

"No, but you have to promise to see my father when you return home."

"Now why would you want to return home to a soft bed and your mother's cooking?" Sid sat on his bedroll opposite the doorway. "Don't you like our company?"

"They're trying to encourage us volunteers to stay." John grimaced as he lowered his bandaged leg.

Jem looked at Sid. "Did you re-enlist?"

Sid removed his spectacles. "Can't quit and let the Rebels whip us."

John pointed to his leg. "I don't know if I can walk let alone march. My days of fighting are over."

"After a few months of being home, you'll change your mind." Sid waved his arm at their surroundings. "You can't beat the food and accommodations."

Jem didn't think much of the smell a dozen men created living in a tent. "Do you know when you're leaving for Ohio?"

He rubbed his head. "I'm so confused I don't even know what day it is. Why are you here, Miss Jenny? Did you receive word about Ben?"

Was her trip futile? "The only news I've had was the letter you sent your mother. She read it to me. Have you learned anything more?"

John looked at the empty spaces beside him. "Nobody remembers seeing Ben or Herman after we retreated. Once my leg healed, I had planned to ask around the other camps. I'm sorry I don't know more."

"Some men are making their way back to camp after heading to Alexandria after the battle." Sid chuckled. "No sense of direction."

Sid was trying to give her hope. Ben might be alive, hiding out until he could return. He could be wounded and in one of the makeshift hospitals scattered around town. Or he was dead. She might never know. She had to think of something else. She looked at John's dirty bandage. "When was the last time you changed the wrapping?"

His eyes widened. "I didn't know I was supposed to change it?"

"This has been on for six days?" What would she find under the bandage?

"I was hit with shrapnel from the Confederate artillery," John said. "Ben had a bandage in his haversack and wrapped the cut."

"You saw Ben?"

"We were together on our line. I wanted to stay, but the blood seeped through the bandage with every step. Ben and Herman put me in an ambulance wagon heading back to Centreville. That's the last I saw them."

Jem opened her midwife bag. She needed hot water. She turned to Sid. "May I boil some water on your fire?"

"Sure, ma'am. I'll add some wood before it burns out."

"I have a pan in my haversack," John volunteered. He rolled to his side and began removing items from a large bag with a strap. He produced a quart pan with a long handle.

"Do you have a smaller flat pan, too?

He removed a pie tin. "Will this do?"

She took it. "That bag contains everything a person needs."

"I didn't leave mine on the battlefield like some men."

He hadn't left his bag, but he left something more important behind—his friends. She carried the pan to Sid, who was tending the fire. "Where can I find clean water?"

"The rain barrel is the closest." He offered his hand. "I'll fill the pan for you."

"Thank you, Sid. Let me know when it's boiling."

"My pleasure, Miss Jenny. It's been a long time since we enjoyed the company of a lady."

Jem returned to John, who was searching through his bag. "What are you looking for?"

John rubbed his growth of beard. "My razor. I haven't shaved since the battle."

"That can wait, but don't wait until you return home. Your mother doesn't approve of whiskers."

John stopped fumbling with his belongings. "How is she?"

"She misses you. I didn't visit with your brothers, but I'm sure they miss you, too."

"Are they completing the chores?"

"They were gathering hay when I visited." Jem removed a towel from her bag. He missed home and his family. "Why did you join the army, John?"

"I was bored," he admitted. "Farming is the same year after year, and Herman made the army sound exciting."

"Is that why Ben joined?"

"No, Miss Jenny. He didn't want to join."

That couldn't be true. "What do you mean?"

"Herman and I didn't want to go without Ben. We took him with us to the camp to sign the roster and shamed him into joining. We said he was an old married man who couldn't have any fun beating the

Rebels. I'm not proud of it now. I hope nothing has happened."

He was responsible. So was Herman. Ben had joined for his friends and the fun of comradery. They couldn't leave Ben alone with her. They had to drag him into a war.

"He wouldn't back out once he signed," John continued. "We said he should, but he was too honorable. He said it's only ninety days. Miss Jenny will wait for me."

Why was he so sure she'd wait? Other men had courted her before she had committed to Ben. Some men found excuses to talk with her after his departure. One man had kissed her at the Independence Day celebration. She had excused it to his intoxicated state, but his actions frightened her. Ben should have been home to defend her honor, to protect her from unwanted advances. If he had loved her, he would have kept his vows of marriage.

"What should I do?"

Jem had lost herself in thoughts of Ben. She looked around the tent, warm but private. If his leg was infected, she didn't want to attract a crowd of curious gawkers. "Do you have a clean blanket?"

He gave her a rolled blanket he used for a pillow. She spread it on the ground and arranged her scissors, forceps, razor, and other items on a towel she had placed on the end of the blanket. "Where is the wound located?"

"Back of my leg."

"Roll over on the blanket on your belly." No telling what she would find under the bandage. Hopefully, he wouldn't be able to see if it was gangrene.

Jem used her scissors to cut the fabric behind the knot near his knee. She slowly unwrapped the bandage, but it was stuck to the wound. She cut along the length of the bandage and peeled it back to expose what was underneath. The site was swollen and oozed yellow pus from a curved slit along the calf that gaped in the middle.

John rose on his elbows and turned to look. "That don't look good." He gagged.

"Turn away," Jem warned. She didn't want to clean away vomit. She had to fight her own nausea at the sight of the infection. Although the wound was red and swollen, nothing indicated blood poisoning. She had arrived in time.

"Am I going to lose my leg?"

"No, John."

He settled on the blanket.

"I better check on the water." She stood and shook her finger at John. "Stay still and don't touch anything."

Sid was watching the pot on the fire. Four soldiers remained under the tree playing cards. "Do any of you have a bottle of liquor?"

Sid held his hand out to the man dealing. "I know you have a bottle of whiskey."

He removed a bottle from his coat. "It cost me ten cents."

Jem removed money from her dress pocket and paid him. The whiskey would help sterilize the wound, but she also needed it for John Herbruck's low tolerance to pain. She removed several thorns from his foot once, and he hollered so loud she'd almost given up. The alcohol might dull his pain, but none of the Herbrucks drank liquor. She pointed at the coffee pot on the hook. "Any coffee left?"

"Plenty." Sid took a tin cup from a wooden rack. "You want some?"

"Half a cup."

Sid grabbed a rag to lift the pot and poured.

Jem opened the whiskey and added enough to fill the cup.

"I suspected you were Irish," Sid said. "But I didn't know ladies drank their coffee laced with whiskey."

She nodded toward John's tent. "It's for medicinal purposes."

"What do you plan to do to John?"

"I may need you to hold him. I have to open the wound to drain it, and it's going to hurt even with the whiskey."

"Why don't I wander over with two cups of coffee?" Sid suggested. "After we finish, I'll be in place to help if he starts thrashing."

Sid poured another cup of coffee. He looked at the whiskey in Jem's hand. "Could I add a little to mine?"

She poured an equal amount into his cup before corking it and dropping it in her skirt pocket. She used her apron to carry the pan of boiling water to the tent.

Sid and John drank their coffee while Jem placed her tools in the pie tin and poured hot water over them. She added a folded diaper on top to soak while John relaxed. "I need you to lie flat."

He handed the empty coffee cup to Sid and flopped on the blanket, his arms crossed to cradle his head.

"This is a hot towel. Try not to jerk." She nodded to Sid, who took position on the opposite side. She slapped the hot rectangle of cloth onto the puss filled wound. John howled and jerked, but Sid anticipated his movements and pinned him.

"Hey, what's going on?"

"Hold still!" Jem ordered. The hot water steamed the infection to the surface. Jem took her scalpel from the pie tin and cut along the wound. More pus and pink blood gushed out.

"Miss Jenny! You're hurting me, Miss Jenny!"

"She's helping you," Sid said.

He thrashed side to side but couldn't knock Sid off. "She's going to take my leg."

"She's trying to save it, you fool," Sid said. "If you don't want to go home with a stump, hold still."

Jem wadded the wet diaper against the edge of the wound, massaging more pus and blood to flow. When the blood darkened, Jem poured whiskey over the wound. "That's the worst of it. You can release him."

Sid lifted his weight, and John gasped for a breath. "That wasn't fair, Miss Jenny."

"I'm not going to stitch it until tomorrow, John. I want to make sure the infection is all drained." She removed a bandage from her bag and wrapped it around the wound. "Keep this clean and rest."

"All I've been doing is resting. I'd like to hear more about home," John said. "Can you visit with us?"

"I'll put on a fresh pot of coffee," Sid said.

The heat was beginning to build, especially in the tent. "Anything cool to drink?"

"I'll send one of the men to the spring. The water is clean and cold."

"John could use some fresh air, if someone can help him outside," Jem said.

Sid nodded. "I'll ask the men to carry John. They'll like to hear about home, too."

Chapter Twelve

Logan arrived at the U.S. Treasury at the west end of Pennsylvania Avenue. Only the Capitol was more impressive in size and architecture. Even the sand bags around the entrance didn't distract from the Greek Revival design with a triangular pediment supported by columns reaching three stories high. He climbed the staircase and walked along the marble walls and floor to the southeast corner of the third floor. He found his desk among several others in a room that was deserted.

A messenger boy, who had been staring out the window, stood. "Mr. Chase called a meeting."

Logan hurried to join the staff in the reception room outside Salmon's private office. He had eaten and changed clothes before reporting to work. He adjusted his tie and tugged on his gold and black vest. The chairs had been claimed. He stood near the door and nodded at his friend, Pete Burdett, before turning his attention to the secretary of the treasury.

Salmon was fifty-three, but his height and strong build gave the appearance of a younger man. He had a receding hairline, thick brows, and strong convictions.

It didn't matter that he had practically inherited the job from his brother, Logan admired Salmon. In Cincinnati he was known for defending fugitive slaves by arguing slavery was governed by states and not the federal government, and once a slave stepped into a free state, he was free. He opposed the Dred Scott case which argued a slave was a slave no matter where he lived.

Salmon believed in political reform and had been a member of the Whig, Liberty, and Free Soil parties. He was elected to the U.S. Senate in 1849 and was an anti-slavery champion. He helped establish the Republican Party and was the first Republican Governor of Ohio, elected in 1855. He supported women's rights, public education, and prison reform.

Women liked him but couldn't cast a ballot. After failing to obtain enough votes at the 1860 Republican National Convention, he had thrown his support behind Abraham Lincoln, who had appointed him secretary of the treasury.

"The president has called for five hundred thousand volunteer soldiers to serve for three years," Salmon stated.

Others joined him in shock over the number. In April, the president had called for seventy-five thousand soldiers to serve three months. After the defeat, he wasn't taking any chances by enlisting five hundred thousand.

"Some think the task herculean with the conflict extended and more troops, but the treasury is going to find a way to pay for the war."

"How are we doing that?" Pete blurted aloud. "I mean how is the government paying for the army?"

Salmon studied a document. "On the seventeenth, Congress voted to allow the United States to borrow a quarter of a million dollars."

Pete let out a long whistle while others kept their opinions to soft murmurs.

"But that was before the battle," Logan said.

Salmon squinted. He was nearly blind without his spectacles. "Mr. Pierce?"

"Yes, Mr. Secretary. Sorry to interrupt."

"You made a valid point," Salmon said. "If Congress thought they were generous, wait until they see the cost of the war now."

He shuffled through some papers. "Congress authorized fifty million as non-interest bearing Treasury Notes." He surveyed his staff. "We're calling them Demand Notes in order to function as currency. We'll use them to pay debts, the military, and federal employees."

"Does that include us?" Pete looked at the others. "Will the paper money be honored?"

"Even if I have to guarantee it personally. The design is different from previous notes. Two large elements will be on the front, and the backs will be green instead of blank." He handed the undersecretary a print. "The samples printed by the American Bank Note Company of the engraved artwork need approval."

When the meeting was concluded, Salmon signaled Logan to remain behind. "How did your business go?"

"I have a dozen supporters for the proposed state. Half are raising funds and most are writing letters."

"I'll let Governor Pierpont know the North is rallying support for the Restored Government of Virginia." He smiled. "And I'll expect some favors in return."

"Some of the men wanted to know if a state within a state was legal."

"Logan, anything is legal until it's challenged in a court of law."

"I didn't attend law school. Does that mean we advance with the plan until someone stops us?"

He patted him on the back. "Precisely."

"Won't Virginia try to stop the efforts of a rogue government, especially after its victory?"

"I'd welcome any distraction," he said. "The city is surrounded by its enemies. We expected an attack by the South at the outbreak of the war, and everyone is on alert after the defeat at Bull Run. We have better defenses in place now, but morale is low." Logan followed him into his office where Salmon sat at his polished walnut desk. "I recommended Irvin McDowell to lead the army into battle, and he failed me, President Lincoln, and the Union. Now, I need to figure out how to return to the good graces of the president."

"What happened? I was told General McDowell had a good battle plan."

"It's never a good plan when your side loses."

Logan looked out the window at Pennsylvania Avenue. "I've only read what was in the Cleveland paper. What happened?"

"I forgot you left town before the battle. No one seems to know. Lincoln received a message from Fairfax Station in the afternoon stating the battle was won. Later Secretary of State William Seward told John Nicolay and John Hay at the Executive Mansion that McDowell was in full retreat. He begged General Winfield Scott to save the city. Panic ensued."

"How bad is it for you?"

"I still have a job, but after listening to accounts of the battle from the generals and spectators, Lincoln replaced McDowell."

"And by your recommendation and association

with McDowell, he blames you?"

Salmon's worried expression gave him the answer. The president didn't have to like him, but he needed to respect him and his recommendations.

"In Washington we're quick to place blame. Lincoln already pinned the defeat on McDowell. He didn't waste any time replacing him with George McClellan, but I owe it to Irvin and the men who served him to find out why his plan didn't work."

"It's never one man's fault," Logan said. "How would you like me to find some answers and restore the president's confidence in you?"

"You have a plan?"

"I'd like to talk to the men who fought the battle," Logan said.

"You'll have to work fast. Lincoln wants to discharge the men who won't re-enlist."

"I know. Can you spare me a week to investigate?"

"Have someone help you. I want the report on my desk early next week. Say Tuesday."

"This is Friday."

"I need every man on my staff to campaign for the support of Congress before they vote on the Demand Notes."

"When will that be?"

"Early August. Congress has already stayed longer than usual. They want to be home in time for fall harvest."

He dipped his pen in ink. "I'll write letters of introduction so you'll have access to the officers and men, but be back in the city before dark. I don't want a nervous sentry shooting you."

Salmon handed him two letters. "You can fill in the

name of your helper."

Pete was waiting for Logan outside. "What did Mr. Chase want?"

Logan shared a house that had belonged to a Southern senator with Pete, two other secretaries, and a clerk. He considered Pete a friend, but he was aware of his shortcomings. No matter what someone said to Pete, he agreed. If his companion said the sun was red, the sun was red. If another person said the sun was blue, the sun was blue. He had no spine, but everyone enjoyed his company. Who wouldn't? He never argued, never criticized, and never told the truth. He was the quintessence of a politician. He excelled at recruiting support, which was why he was on the staff. "He gave me an assignment. Want to help?"

"I'll do anything to help, buddy."

"Good, Mr. Chase wants us to discover the reasons we lost the battle."

"The men dropped their guns and ran. You can't win a battle if you don't fight." He handed him a newspaper he had tucked under his arm. "For two cents you can read all about it."

"I want to talk to the men who fought."

"Good luck finding any," Pete said. "They're the dead ones."

"Then we might as well surrender and learn to pick cotton."

"What happened to being a lone wolf, Logan?" Pete studied his reflection in the smooth marble wall. "If you're going to socialize, pick company that matters. I'm meeting a lady at Willard's Hotel tonight. She might have a friend."

"We have a job, and Mr. Chase wants it done by

Tuesday." Logan handed him his letter. "I'm heading to the camp across the Potomac to talk to the soldiers who fought in the battle. You coming?"

He returned the letter. "These boots are new, and I don't plan on tramping around swampy camp grounds and talking to lice-covered soldiers."

"How about talking to the officers and politicians at Willard's Hotel. Your boots will never lose their shine, and you might impress the ladies with your official assignment."

He took the letter. "Why don't you join me? The ladies have been asking about you."

"If I have time." Logan avoided social gatherings. If the ladies were asking about him, it was only to discover if he was going to make the same mistakes as Derek Pierce.

****

Logan rushed to the Ohio camp. He could initiate his research with John Herbruck's story. Would Jem see through his flimsy excuse to spend more time with her? He'd proposed the research to Salmon because he genuinely wanted to know what had gone wrong with the battle, but his choice of John Herbruck was based solely on Jem.

He had left her at the Southern Belle, dismissing her from his life, but her image wouldn't disappear from his thoughts. He had to see her again.

She was seated among a group of soldiers under a tree. She had removed her bonnet, and the fiery shades of her hair framed her delicate features. She sat in the shade, but the heat of the day warmed her translucent skin to a gentle blush. She laughed at some remark, and her mouth widened. What had the man said to elicit her response? Why did he want to know? He wasn't falling in love with her. He would never make the mistake his brother did and fall in love with a married woman.

She had changed her dress. The black and yellow pattern was faded and the front buttons, lack of collar, and apron made it obvious she was dressed to work. So why was she enjoying the company of half a dozen soldiers? And why was she alone? Where were Ellen and the children? Her brows arched above blue eyes. She looked surprised by his presence. Was she angry or happy to see him?

He turned his attention to the men around her. They were young and in infantry uniforms. Was one of the men her husband? Had she found Ben Collins? No wonder she was laughing and enjoying the company of Ben's comrades. His shoulders sagged, and he opened his satchel. He could cover his blunder with his assignment. The coffee pot hung over the fire. "Do you have an extra cup?"

Jem made the introductions. No Ben Collins. She used her apron to lift the coffee pot from its hook and fill a cup. "Don't you have meetings or something?"

"Finished my meeting. Now I'm doing an investigation."

"What sort of investigation?"

He looked around at the men. "I'm questioning soldiers about the battle."

Sid and the others focused on Logan. "What soldiers?"

"I was going to begin with your friend, John."

John had been resting in a padded embroidered chair someone had procured. His bandaged leg rested on a crate.

"Do you have time to talk?" Logan showed him the letter from Salmon. "I've read what's in the papers." He shoved the unflattering account of the battle Pete had given him into his satchel. "I'd like to hear about your experience in the battle."

John wiped his high forehead with a kerchief. "I didn't see everything. You better have Sid tell you his story, too."

"I'd like to talk to as many men as possible. I want the truth." Logan removed a bound book from his satchel. "I'm taking an official statement from you. No embellishments."

Sid spat. "I don't trust politicians."

"I don't either," Logan said. "That's why I'm doing the investigation."

"I have no reason to lie," John said. "Do you want me to swear on my Bible?"

"That won't be necessary." Logan opened the journal to reveal blank lined pages. He sharpened his pencil with a knife he withdrew from his boot. "Go ahead. Tell us what happened from the beginning."

John looked at the other men and Jem.

"Go ahead, John." Jem handed him a cup of coffee. "Don't leave anything out."

He took a sip. "Rumors spread about a battle, especially since our enlistments were expiring. Our company began drilling every day, mornings when it was cooler and sometimes in the evening with our captain, Gary Mercer. Sometimes all ten First Ohio companies drilled together as a regiment."

He rubbed his head. "It was on the sixteenth when the Army of Northeastern Virginia was ordered to march west to capture the railroad at Manassas and then on to Richmond. We dressed in our uniforms and packed our supplies, including our blankets, canteen, rations for three days, a full cartridge case, and a clean rifle."

Sid removed his kepi hat and raised it in the air. "On to Richmond!"

"We were arrogant fools," one of the soldiers commented. He put his pipe back in his mouth and took a long draw. "Go ahead, John."

"We formed our lines but didn't march out of the city until the afternoon. Ben wrote you a few lines in a letter while we waited. He always wrote a little bit during the week and mailed it Monday."

Only she hadn't received the letter. Logan searched Jem's face for any signs of distress, but her focus was on John as he spoke.

"The drummers pounded a beat to match our hearts, and the bands played 'Yankee Doodle.' We were finally going to war. The ladies and gentlemen of the town waved and cheered. A woman gave me a bouquet of flowers. One of them kissed Herman on the mouth. He looked like he was going to faint."

The other men laughed but quieted as they glanced toward the tent they had shared with their missing comrades. "It was slow going at first. We were in the front, but we'd never marched as one group." John turned to Sid. "How many was it?"

"Thirty-five thousand men," Sid supplied the count. "Five divisions comprised the army, and each of them had at least two brigades."

"I need your name," Logan interrupted. He wrote Sid's name in his book.

"Sid knows all the officers," John said.

"Four brigades were in the division commanded by Brigadier General Daniel Tyler," Sid said. "Our regiment was under the command of Colonel Alexander McCook, and we were in the brigade commanded by Brigadier General Robert Schenck."

Logan listed the names in descending order of rank.

"We'd march a bit and stop for the men at the front to clear trees the Rebels had placed in the road," John said. "Then we'd march a little more. Some men wandered off to pick berries or nap. The marching wasn't nothing, but carrying all our gear in the hot sun wore us out. Some men started tossing blankets and gear. They figured they wouldn't need them in Richmond. We marched all day, camped, and by noon the next day, we arrived at Fairfax Court House."

"They wanted us to march on to Centreville, but we were exhausted," Sid said. "We camped at the court house."

"We marched to Centreville before noon the next day," John said. "The eighteenth."

"Tell them about the fighting," Sid said.

John took a long drink. "The battle was set for Sunday the twenty-first."

"Don't forget Blackburn's Ford," Sid said.

Logan turned to Sid. "I read about that in the Cleveland paper. Tell me about it."

"Tyler took some of Colonel Israel Richardson's brigade to search out the roads. He met some Confederates at Blackburn's Ford on the eighteenth. They beat us, soundly. That was a bad sign to some of us."

"Nearly a hundred men killed, wounded, or

missing," a soldier added.

"Not that many," Sid argued. "But close."

"Anything else happen before Sunday?"

John shook his head. "We waited at Centreville for the rest of the army to arrive."

Chapter Thirteen

Jem studied Logan's neat handwriting about the details of the battle. He stopped to sharpen his pencil. He wrote *July 21st* at the top of a clean page. She looked at the men surrounding them. A few more had joined the group. John adjusted his leg. "Are you all right?"

"My leg is throbbing, Miss Jenny. Maybe you should stitch the wound today."

"I want it to drain." Jem noted a small bloodstain on the bandage. "The pain will ease."

He turned to Logan. "Where was I?"

"Tell me about Sunday."

"It was dark when Tyler ordered our division to march along the Warrenton Turnpike," John said. "They had this huge gun called a Parrott rifle and didn't think Cub Run Bridge would hold it. We had to wait for the engineers to reinforce the bridge."

"Hurry and wait. Hurry and wait," a soldier repeated.

"It was nearly dawn when we finally crossed the bridge," John said. "Two divisions headed northwest."

Sid supplied their leaders' names. "Colonel David Hunter and Colonel Sam Heintzelman."

"All the Rebels were positioned to the south along Bull Run. Sid figured McDowell's plan was to go around and flank the Rebels."

"Schenck gathered his brigade south of Stone Bridge, and Colonel William Sherman set his brigade north of the bridge," Sid said.

"Your regiment was in Schenck's brigade," Logan recalled.

"That's right." John scratched at his beard growth. "We worked our way along a path to the stream where the Rebel artillery was set up. We were positioned in a cornfield but fell back into the woods while the artillery fired at each other. They recalled us to the road to wait."

Sid removed his spectacles. "We figured the artillery was a show for the spectators."

"Spectators?" Logan interrupted.

"Word arrived from Centreville people in coaches and carriages were arriving from Washington," Sid explained. "Some of them were congressmen. Others were reporters. Most observed the battle through field glasses at a safe distance, but some of the fools moved in closer. They had picnics on the hillside overlooking the battle. War is not a picnic."

"Not when the fighting started." John finished the coffee in his cup. "Tyler ordered us to attack. That's when the Rebels showed. At first it didn't seem like too many, but more and more Rebels descended upon the Stone Bridge area. They were different regiments by the uniforms. None of them were the same."

"They used flags to signal each other," Sid said. "Something was going on to the north because a bunch of Rebels headed that way."

Logan recorded John and Sid's words in his journal, identifying each speaker with his name.

"We were eating lunch when Sherman's brigade

crossed Bull Run," Sid said. "Tyler marched with Colonel Erasmus Keyes' brigade and followed Sherman. We remained in reserve at the bridge. The Rebels fell back from our location."

"Ben climbed a tree to report on the battle. He could see the Rebels regrouping on a hill southwest of our position," John said. "Keyes sent Maine and Connecticut boys to attack a house. Then all confusion broke out. Maine wore gray and so did the Rebels attacking them. We found out they were General Thomas Jackson's Virginian infantry, who were supposed to be at Harpers Ferry. They were dressed in gray, too."

Logan stopped writing. "The Confederates from the Shenandoah Valley fought at Bull Run?"

"They traveled by train," Sid said. "We didn't know what to make of the train whistles at the depot at the time."

Logan made a notation and underlined the word *train*. He looked at John. "Keyes withdrew his men toward the Stone Bridge near us," John explained. "It was quiet for a couple of hours."

John had a queer expression on his face. "I was bleeding through the bandage Ben tied around my leg, and they helped me to the ambulance."

"How were you wounded?" Logan asked.

"Cannon fire."

"A cannon ball hit you?" Jem interrupted.

"I wouldn't be here if the whole shell hit me," John said. "They're hollow and filled with powder and a fuse. When it explodes, shrapnel flies everywhere. I dove for cover from the blast, but a fragment of the shell cut the back of my leg."

"The canisters are worse," Sid said. "They pack metal balls in a can and shoot it out of the cannon. The balls spread out and break anything in its path."

"Break?" Logan looked around at the group of soldiers. "Break what?"

"The balls are about this big." Sid held his thumb and forefinger to demonstrate an inch wide ball. "They break tree limbs, bones, and rip a hole in a man."

"At the hospital, they were trying to patch the holes," John said.

"You said the doctors didn't take care of your leg wound," Jem said.

John trembled and wiped his handkerchief over his forehead. "I reached Centreville and hobbled into the house serving as a hospital. They had cleared out all the furniture except for two tables where the doctors stood. They wore white aprons only they weren't white anymore. Blood covered their clothes and hands. It dripped from the tables and pooled on the floor in big red circles. Between the tables was a pile of arms and legs, some with shoes on them."

John stared, his eyes wide with fear. "On the table, a man's foot dangled from what was left of his leg. The aide had a mask over the soldier's face. The doctor's knife circled the leg, and he peeled back the skin. He used a metal rod heated in a lamp flame to cauterize the blood vessels. The worst part was when he sawed the bone like the butcher does back home. Then he tossed the leg onto the pile with the others."

John put his head in his hands and muffled a sob. "I limped out and vomited in the yard."

Jem patted John's shoulder. "It's all right. Whenever I help Papa with an amputation, I make sure my stomach is empty. It's pretty shocking."

"I've helped my pa doctor animals, but when a horse breaks its leg, you put him down. You don't saw it off," John said. "I was afraid the doctor would start cutting."

"You're not going to lose your leg," Jem said. She meant it.

John squeezed his eyes shut. "I can't stop seeing that boot with a metal cleat on the heel with a leg inside and nothing above the mangled knee. I wonder what they did with all those sawed off limbs."

Logan lowered his voice to a whisper. "Why so many amputations?"

"When a bullet or canister round shatters the bone, it leaves a jagged mess," Sid said. "The bones won't go back together, and if an infection sets in, the leg has to be amputated anyway."

"How do you know so much about surgery?" Jem asked.

"I ask questions. I need to stop being so darn curious."

"Can you add to John's story?" Logan raised his pencil. "What happened back at the bridge?"

"The fighting was farther west near the Manassas-Sudley Road so we didn't see much," Sid said. "We could hear the guns, attack after attack. We waited, expecting victory for our side."

"The Cleveland paper announced the Union had won in the type set in the morning," Jem said. "In the column next to it was news of the retreat."

"We were winning, but about five o'clock, they started coming toward us."

Logan paused his writing. "Confederates?"

"No, our own men. First it was a few soldiers tired of fighting all day." Sid shook his head. "I had barely fired my rifle. Then larger groups followed. The Rebels continued to fire their cannons. Men screamed and yelled, surging toward us and running like the devil was chasing them."

"What happened?"

"I don't know what started it, but nothing could stop them from fleeing. We'd lost the battle. Soldiers crossed Stone Bridge and headed to Centreville." Sid looked at his fellow soldiers. "We stayed by the bridge, shooting at any Rebels, ducking when their cannons fired. They hit a wagon on the bridge over Cub Run and blocked the escape route. Civilians, who had come close to the battle, were screaming to escape across the bridge. We fired, retreated a few yards, reloaded and fired again, covering those fleeing. Whole packs, guns, and cartridge boxes were discarded in the panic. Men took the horses for transporting our cannon and fled on them."

Jem had waited long enough for news of her husband. "Where were Ben and Herman?"

"I lost sight of them during the retreat," Sid said. "The smoke was thick, and a crowd of retreating men surged around me. The entire Union Army or what was left of it was crowded on Warrenton Turnpike struggling to cross the bridge ahead of the other men."

Sid shook his head. "I looked around for the generals and colonels but didn't see them. Captain Mercer kept us together. Threatened to shoot us if we turned and fled with the crowd."

John blew his nose. "I should have been there."

Jem filled his cup with fresh coffee. "Where were

you during the retreat, John?"

"I was riding back to Washington in a wagon with the wounded when some of the retreating men caught us," John said. "They tried throwing us out so they could ride, and they weren't even wounded. I clobbered one with the butt of my rifle and sent him over the side."

"I'd done the same," a soldier said with a whoop.

John looked away. "That's all I know. It started to rain. We huddled under blankets until we reached Washington City. They took the wounded to different buildings and homes. I hobbled to camp and collapsed on the ground wrapped in my blanket under this tree." He looked up. "When I woke, the other men had returned, but Ben and Herman weren't with them. Nobody knows what happened."

Jem turned to Sid. "You never saw either one of them again?"

"We kept falling back, shooting, falling back, and shooting. At Centreville, we waited to see if the Rebels would attack. I looked around, but I didn't see Ben or Herman with us. I asked a few of the other men, but they hadn't seen them since Cub Run Bridge."

"How long did you stay at Centreville?"

"We camped for a couple of hours. Then we headed back to Washington City, guarding the rear."

Logan closed his notebook. "Thank you, gentlemen. You've helped tremendously."

Jem stood.

"Are you leaving, Miss Jenny?"

"I'll return tomorrow, John. I need to stitch your wound."

"It's good to see you." He stood, wobbling on his

good leg. Logan and Sid helped him to his tent.

Jem followed and gathered her belongings. "Where can I find Captain Mercer?"

"Don't tell him I'm wounded." John settled on his blanket. "I don't want it to delay my return home."

"I won't." Outside, she arranged her bonnet to shade her face from the hot sun.

"He has the big tent at the end of the line," Sid pointed. "Miss Jenny, when you return home, can you remind the women to remember us?"

"What makes you think we don't think of you?"

"Some of the soldiers receive jellies, honey, and stewed fruits from home." He rubbed the side of his jaw. "The single men don't have anyone who cares about sending homemade items. We don't expect it, but some little tokens would be appreciated."

"I'll see what I can do."

****

Captain Gary Mercer was seated in a wooden slot chair at a small folding table inside a large tent with straight sides and an awning in front. He had a cot for sleeping and a trunk to store his supplies. There were two other empty cots in the tent. He stood when Logan called his name and buttoned the single row of buttons on his long coat.

"I'm Logan Pierce, and this is Mrs. Ben Collins."

He turned to Jem. "Mrs. Collins?"

"My husband, Ben Collins, is one of the men missing from your company."

He lifted a letter he had been writing. "I was informing you that Benjamin Collins is designated as missing." He handed her the unfinished note.

Jem sat across from his table. Logan remained

standing by her side. "What about Herman Stratman? He was with my husband during the battle."

He searched a roster of names. "Missing. We've accounted for everyone else in the company. Ben and Herman haven't shown."

"Then they're dead." The words sounded surreal to her ears. She didn't want to believe Ben could be dead.

"I don't know," Gary said. "Please understand, we lost the fight."

Did she look stupid? "I know that."

"Do you understand all its implications?"

"I'm a poor country girl, Captain. Could you explain the…implications?"

Logan opened his journal and made a notation in it.

Gary pointed at Logan's notebook. "What is that?"

"I work for the Treasury Department." He handed him his letter of introduction.

"You were explaining the implications," Jem said.

Gary returned the letter to Logan and met her gaze. "We left our dead and some wounded on the battlefield. Some men reported seeing the Rebels bayonetting any men breathing."

"Unarmed wounded men?" Jem leaned forward. "Why were they left behind?"

"The retreat was so quick there was no time to evacuate the wounded," he said. "Some of the doctors in the field hospitals were taken prisoner as well."

"Unarmed medical staff?" Jem looked at Logan. "Why would they take them?"

"They took everyone too slow to escape," Gary said. "They took New York Congressman Alfred Ely prisoner."

Logan stopped writing. "What was he doing

there?"

"He had traveled from Washington City to watch the battle. When the soldiers fled, the spectators were caught in the retreat. We guarded the bridge and road, but in the confusion, some ran the wrong way, right into the enemy's lines."

"Were the dead recovered?" Logan asked.

Gary stared at Jem. "It's July. The Confederates buried the dead, which creates the problem of identification. We don't know who they buried and who they took prisoner."

"Won't they tell you the names of the prisoners?"

"They're trying to enlist some," Gary said. "Nobody likes to be on the losing side."

Ben would never turn traitor. "What do you know about the prisoners?"

"They took the wounded to the new Alms House and prisoners to a warehouse in Richmond. Some of the prisoners may have been shipped by train to different camps in the South by now. We're trying to obtain names, but we can't send anyone without risk of the messenger being imprisoned or hanged as a spy."

"Are they allowing wives to visit?"

"Don't you dare think it," Logan said.

Jem didn't argue. Even though Logan wasn't responsible for her, his tone indicated he would stop her if she tried visiting Richmond. "Could Ben or Herman be anywhere else besides Richmond or the grave?"

"Were they enlisted for ninety days?"

"Yes."

"They could have deserted."

Jem didn't like the captain's insinuation. "My husband would not desert. Neither would Herman

Stratman."

"Some of them didn't see going home as desertion because they'd served their time."

"He isn't home in Darrow Falls." She remembered John. "When will the men in the First Ohio go home if they don't enlist for three years?"

"Next week. Someone more important than me is working on a schedule."

"I'd like to interview as many soldiers as I can before they leave," Logan said. "I want to make a record of the battle."

"I gave my official report to McCook who gave it to Schenck who gave it to Tyler. If he gave it to McDowell, it's burned to ash." Gary spat on the ground.

"You blame McDowell?"

He stood and turned. "I have no holes in my uniform. What should I blame him for?"

"You were positioned for demonstration," Logan said. "What factors do you think contributed to the loss of the battle?"

"Demonstration," Gary repeated. "Do you know what demonstration is?"

Jem frowned. Now he was insulting Logan's intelligence.

Logan whittled his pencil. His tone was calm and controlled. "You distract the enemy so other forces can march into position."

"Distract?" Gary looked into the distance. "We may have been a fly on a horse's rump, but we engaged the enemy. Wide-eyed boys who were glad to have new uniforms were shocked to realize war wasn't a game, especially when someone shoots a hole through the man

153

standing next to you in formation. Had to teach them the right foot from the left foot and how to march with a hundred other men. Most of them had never owned a gun. Had to instruct the boys how to load the powder, lead ball, and ram it down the barrel. We didn't see much action until the end of the battle when all hell broke loose." He looked at Jem. "Sorry, ma'am."

Logan flipped back a few pages. "I heard the Ohio boys covered the retreat."

"Retreat? That word implies order. It was mass panic. My men were more in danger of being trampled than shot. I had to threaten them to prevent any from joining the fleeing masses. They only stopped because they were afraid I'd use my new Springfield rifle on them."

"What's that?"

Chapter Fourteen

Gary retrieved a rifle from a post in his tent along with an ammo pack. The gun looked like any other. It had a wood stock with a metal barrel and percussion lock. "This is a new rifle being manufactured for soldiers at the Springfield Armory. It's nothing like the muskets most men carry. With a smooth bore rifle, you could stand twenty paces away from a man and miss him. That's why we line the men shoulder to shoulder and fire in mass for the greatest effect." He handed the rifle to Logan and emptied the ammo box onto the table. He showed them a conical Minié ball. "With the bore rifles, a man with a steady hand and keen eye could hit his mark three to five hundred yards away."

Logan stared at the rifle. "How far?"

"You want to win this war, put this rifle in the hands of every soldier."

"How did you obtain one?"

"I bought it for twenty dollars."

Jem gasped. "How will soldiers afford them?"

Gary smiled at Logan. "That's Mr. Chase's problem."

Logan examined the rifle. "It doesn't seem fair for our men to have these guns and the others relying on muskets."

"Don't worry, the Rebels are working on their own version."

"The Ohio boys defended the rear during the retreat," Logan said. "Can you tell us what happened at the end of the battle?"

"The second Ohio defended the house where the doctors were tending the wounded. The First Ohio was at Stone Bridge. My company was one of the last to cross. We retreated to the bridge across Cub Run, but it was a mess. A shell had blown apart a portion of the bridge, and a wagon had to be shoved off the side. We made sure the civilians and teamsters made it out of the area and followed to Centreville."

He turned to Sid's account. "You camped at Centreville."

"At the foot of a hill west of the turnpike where we waited to see if the enemy would pursue. Luckily, they didn't. We marched to Fairfax Court House and finally Vienna. I think the front of the troops straggled into Washington around midnight. We rested in an open field until dawn to cover the rear of the columns. Couldn't have fought if we were attacked. Everything was soaked from the rain."

Logan pointed his pencil toward him. "What would you have done differently during the battle, Captain?"

"Me, nothing. But when the flank crumbled, McDowell should have regrouped and charged instead of retreated. Half the men who marched to Bull Run never fired a shot. You don't win a battle by being cautious and attacking half-heartedly."

"Thank you for your honesty, Captain Mercer."

"You can put my name on that report. I'm not ashamed of anything I said." He turned to Jem. "I hope someone has news about your husband, ma'am."

Jem stood and tied her bonnet. "Have you visited

the wounded? The missing could be among them."

"Only a couple men from Ohio were wounded."

She returned the note he had given her. "At least my visit saved you a stamp."

"Wait!" He searched through the papers on his desk and retrieved an envelope. "Since I couldn't deliver this, I was going to send it back to you."

Jem took the letter, the most recent one she had written. "Thank you." Ben hadn't read the anguished words she had penned about their future. She clutched the letter to her breast. A reprieve. Instead of telling him she was wrong and begging for a second chance at their marriage, she could declare her love and promise to wait for him, no matter how long. She hid the letter in her skirt pocket.

Logan shoved his notebook into his satchel. "Where do you plan to go next?"

"Ellen said her husband was at a hospital in Arlington Heights." She looked at the captain. "He was with the Second Wisconsin."

"They fought most of the battle. A lot of wounded." He pointed at Logan's notebook. "If you want to find out about the fighting, you should talk to them."

Jem turned to leave.

"If he's not in the regimental tent hospital, he may be in one of the outbuildings near Arlington House," Gary said. "The wounded were taken to any place with a roof and beds."

"I'll find it."

Jem asked directions twice before finding the wood frame building on a flat area overlooking the Potomac River. It had been used as a warehouse before the war and recently turned into barracks.

The heat intensified the coagulation of human sweat, blood, and urine from the bodies crowded in the single room. The building had a wooden floor with cracks between the flat boards. Puddles and stains marked where men had relieved their bladders or spilled the chamber pots between the beds. Logan covered his mouth. "What happened here?"

Dr. Sterling Beecher had always emphasized cleanliness, but it appeared as if nothing had been done since the men had been dumped in the beds early Monday morning.

Ellen stood at the end of a bed near the far door. Jem walked toward her, carefully avoiding the human waste on the floor.

The children sat on the bed. Ellen was crying.

"What's wrong?"

She couldn't answer. She struggled to change the baby's diaper.

Jem nodded at the man in the bed. "Your husband?"

"Thornton." She couldn't penetrate the diaper pin through the fabric. Jem placed her medical bag on the end of the bed. She took the pin from Ellen's shaking fingers and secured the diaper. She lifted the baby. Ellen wouldn't take him. She needed to discard the contents of the soiled diaper. She looked around the room.

"Shake it in that slop bucket by the door," Jem said.

"Or dump it on the floor with the rest of the garbage."

"Logan!" He was right about the filth. "All these

chamber pots need to be emptied and the windows opened."

Logan raised his arms. "I am not a chambermaid."

Ellen returned with the wadded diaper and shoved it into a large cloth bag with wooden handles.

"Ellen." Thornton rose on his elbows but one arm was bandaged, and he collapsed on the bed. "It's not so bad. I'm getting stronger each day."

The blanket covered one leg. Only one. The other had been amputated.

"How are you going to take care of me and the children with one leg?" Ellen demanded.

"It can't be gone. I can feel it hurting."

"That's impossible," Jem said. "It's gone."

"Look." He tossed the covers off and stared at the bandaged stump. His eyes widened, and he shook. "Where did it go?"

Ellen screamed and ran outside.

Jem shoved the baby into Logan's arms. "Watch the children."

"Why do you think I'm an expert on children?"

She found Ellen outside behind the building, leaning against a table where a pitcher and metal bowl had been placed for washing. She was weeping between gasps of air.

"Don't you want to take your husband home?"

"What husband? Nothing is left."

Jem jerked her arm to spin her around to face her. "He only lost a leg and below the knee. That's a good thing. He can walk on a wooden peg or use a crutch. Did you look at the other men? They lost more. You're lucky."

"I can't look at Thornton without shuddering." She

shook.

"Why?"

"He's deformed. His leg is missing."

"You're missing the end of your index finger."

Ellen hid her finger with her other hand. "I accidentally cut if off with a hatchet when I was a girl."

"Are you less of a person without it?"

"It's only the tip of my finger."

"It's only the tip of his leg. He's still the same man."

"How do I not cringe?" She shuddered.

"You look." Jem grabbed her hand. "The first time I looked at your finger I realized it wasn't normal. But the abnormal becomes normal with time. When your children look at your finger, do they see a disfigurement or a shorter finger?"

Ellen stopped sobbing. "But how long will it take? How do I touch him without recoiling? He'll see it in my eyes and know."

"You don't think he's in shock? He woke without his leg. He's scared, too."

"Then how can we help each other if we're both frightened?"

"He needs his bandage changed. We start with that. You talk about it. You touch it as much as you can. Soon, it won't seem so odd or repulsive. You'll accept it as normal."

Ellen swiped the tears from her face. "Are you telling me the truth? Will I ever be able to love him the way I did? And what will he be able to do with only one leg? We wanted to buy our own farm. What now?"

"Do you milk cows with your toes?"

Ellen gave her a queer look. "That would be

ridiculous."

"He has two hands. What won't he be able to do? Back home we have a man who lost both legs. He has a little cart with wheels he rides in. Nothing stops him."

Ellen looked toward the door. "Will you help me?"

"I'll change the bandage if you promise to watch."

"I think I can." She schooled her face free of expression.

Inside Logan and the children were holding their noses and making faces at each other. She laughed. For a man who claimed to know nothing about children, he had no trouble entertaining them. She looked around at the unsanitary conditions. "This place could use a thorough cleaning."

Logan looked at the beds crowded in the building. "You'd have to take the men outside."

He was right. "Who's in charge of the wounded?"

"I think he is." Ellen pointed to a man in a dirty white coat.

He had a bald cap fringed with white hair. His matching beard balanced the lack of hair on the top of his head. Jem approached him. "Are you the doctor?"

"Doctor Will Martin. How may I help you?"

"Can we carry these men outside?"

"What for?"

Jem counted on her fingers. "The room needs cleaned. The mattresses need fresh straw. Blood has soaked through some of them. And the linens need stripped and washed."

"I can't find volunteers to empty chamber pots let alone clean this entire space."

"If I find the volunteers, will you approve moving the men?"

"Do you think you'll be able to complete the work before nightfall or do you plan on spending the night?"

Routes to the city would be shut down. She'd need help to finish the work in time. "I'd like to try."

Dr. Martin agreed to her plan.

Jem returned to Logan and the others. His fingers pinched his nose. "This room is a stinking cesspool."

"Stinky!" Odin agreed.

Logan laughed. "You can say that again."

"Then you agree with my plan to clean it."

Logan looked from Odin to Jem. "What did I agree to?"

"I need you to find men willing to carry the wounded outside. We'll need stretchers or blankets to set the men on temporarily while we clean."

Logan still held his nose. "It doesn't smell so bad."

"If you don't want to help, I'll find Sid. He's a corporal."

"I'll find Sid," Logan said. "He can recruit some workers."

"He seemed eager to help," Ellen said after Logan left.

"He couldn't wait to leave and breathe fresh air."

Ellen looked around. "What should I do?"

"Stay here and talk to your husband. I'll fetch supplies for his leg."

Jem found a water pump nearby in the yard. Two women were filling buckets. Cloths were wrapped around their hair, sleeves were shoved above their elbows, and water stained their aprons. Their hands were red and nails worn short from scrubbing on metal washboards.

She extended her hand. "I'm Jennifer Collins. I

need some laundry done."

"I'm Debbie Kennedy and this is my sister, Dottie O'Brien. Our husbands are in the 69th New York."

"How much do you charge for washing sheets and blankets?"

"How many?"

Jem had counted about twenty beds in the building. "Twenty each."

Debbie looked at Dottie. They put their heads together and whispered back and forth. "Two dollars," Debbie said.

She'd forgotten the mattresses. "What about washing mattresses?"

"Twenty of them?" Dottie looked alarmed. "When would this have to be done?"

"It's for the wounded soldiers." She pointed to the building. "Another woman and I are cleaning the building. The soldiers are moving the men outside so we can have the men back in the building by nightfall."

They put their heads together and whispered back and forth. "Five dollars for all," Dottie announced.

"I'll give you two now and three more when it's done." She counted two dollars in coins.

The sisters split the money. "Deal. Our camp is in the shade." Dottie pointed to a tent beneath a maple tree. In front were four large wooden tubs, stools, and scrub boards. Two iron cauldrons were suspended above fire pits. Ropes were stretched from the tree to posts driven in the ground for drying the laundry.

"I'll gather the bedding." Jem carried the washbasin of water to the makeshift hospital. The soldiers would evacuate the wounded. Ellen would help strip the linens. The men could remove the soiled straw from the mattresses so they could be washed. She'd need fresh straw. Sid could probably locate some. The worst task was emptying the chamber pots and cleaning the floor. She'd look for supplies after changing Thornton's bandage.

Ellen was waiting by the bed. Inga and Odin were on the far side of the bed near their father's head. He put his good arm around Odin who snuggled against him.

Jem gathered some towels and joined them.

"Should I take the children for a walk?"

"They need to understand what has happened to their father." Ellen took a position near the end of the bed as she cradled the baby, who was as wide-eyed as his siblings.

Thornton struggled to sit up. "Will it hurt?"

"It's probably tender," Jem said. "But that's normal."

Jem folded the blanket to reveal both legs. One was heavily muscled with some minor scratches. The other ended below the knee. She unwrapped the dirty bandage that had been on since the amputation. She threw it in the chamber pot beneath the bed. The fresh wound was red and swollen, but had no signs of infection. Large stitches had been used to close the folds of skin around the end of the bone. Jem cleaned away some dried blood.

Thornton shivered. "The water is cold."

"I didn't have time to heat it."

Inga stared. "Where's your leg, Daddy?"

"A musket ball blew it off."

Inga walked along the side of the bed to look closer. "Did it die?"

"Did what die?"

Inga pointed at his missing limb. "Your leg."

"It was pretty lifeless," Thornton agreed.

"Did you have a funeral for it?"

Thornton laughed. Ellen joined him. The fear in her eyes was gone. Jem handed her the bandage. "Would you like to help?"

Ellen put the baby on the bed, and he crawled onto his father's lap. Ellen held a thick wad on the end of the stump as Jem wrapped another bandage around it from the stump to above his knee. "Do you have an extra diaper pin?"

Ellen took one from her dress and pinned the end in place. "That wasn't so bad."

"You're a good candidate for a prosthetic." Dr. Martin had been watching from the end of the bed. "Your local doctor can fit you with one once the stump is completely healed."

"Will I be able to walk?"

"I don't see why not." Odin had joined his sister who was staring at the stump. "I don't know if you'll be able to match this guy, but you can try." He put his hand on Odin's head. "It won't hurt to touch it."

Odin slapped his hand on his father's leg. Thornton jerked.

"Odin," Ellen reprimanded.

"It didn't hurt," Thornton excused. "He startled me. For a little guy, he's strong."

"Be gentle," Ellen warned.

"Can I touch, too?" Inga asked.

Ellen nodded.

"I feel like I have a leg," Thornton said. "Why is that?"

"Some of the other men have complained about the same thing." Dr. Martin examined the bandage. "Where did you learn to wrap a wound?"

"My father is a doctor and trained me," Jem said.

"Do you know how to remove stitches?"

She showed him her bag. "I can put them in, too."

"Tomorrow I plan to remove stitches from all these men who were sewn back together after the battle. I could use some extra hands. Can you help?"

"I'll make time."

Chapter Fifteen

Logan and Sid stood in the doorway. "Our helpers are here."

"The soldiers will dirty the floors and beds again," Dr. Martin warned.

"My father likes to read about new discoveries in medicine and science. He believes in cleanliness. He says it prevents infections."

"Then he better stay home." Dr. Martin waved his arm around the room. "This place will give him nightmares."

"Well, for a few minutes it will be clean." She turned to Logan. "Start moving them outside."

Jem and Ellen began stripping the bedding from the empty beds. She recognized the blue uniforms of the Ohio volunteers and the gray uniforms of the Second Wisconsin, but another small group of soldiers had joined the work force. Their uniforms matched Ohio soldiers in color but were dirty and worn. The kepi top had the number *69* above the infantry horn. "Who are you?"

"Timothy O'Brien, miss."

"What regiment are you with?"

"The 69th New York State Militia. My wife Dottie said you might need some help. Our enlistment ran out yesterday, but we stayed to see if we can help our wounded friends."

"Did you see much of the battle?"

"We fought the Fourth Alabama. Don't let anyone say an Irishman can't fight." In spite of the battle loss, his voice had pride and swagger.

"My grandfather, Michael Donovan, would agree."

"Your hair screams Irish."

She waved for Logan to join them and made introductions. "You were in Sherman's brigade with the Second Wisconsin?"

"Sherman gave the order to break rank and run," Timothy said. "Every man for himself. Our colonel, Michael Corcoran, was wounded and taken prisoner. We have nearly a hundred men missing and another hundred dead or wounded."

"The Irish spend all their time talking instead of working," Sid interrupted.

"Sid!" Jem scolded. "That's a horrible thing to say."

Sid turned to those in the room. "I bet the Ohio boys can carry more wounded than the Irish 69th!"

"You're on." Timothy spat in his hands and shook Sid's hand.

The men hustled to remove the wounded. Jem turned to Logan. "What was that?"

"The best motivational speech possible. I'm going to recommend Sid for general." He looked around. "What do you want me to do?"

"Once Ellen and I have the beds stripped, the men can carry the mattresses outside and empty the straw." She frowned. "Do you know where some fresh straw is stored?"

"The barn is nearby. Lee liked horses."

Jem calculated the amount of straw needed to fill

the mattresses. "You'll need a wagon to haul it."

"I bet Sid can find one."

Ellen and Jem carried the laundry to Dottie and Debbie, who soaked, scrubbed, and rinsed each piece several times before hanging it on the rope line to dry.

When they returned to the hospital, the water in a cast iron cauldron above a new fire pit was boiling. Jem had asked for hot water, and Sid had delivered. They filled several buckets and carried them to the building. Jem pinched her nose. Even with the men removed, the room reeked of disgusting odors. "Are you ready to go to work?"

"I live on a dairy farm. This is nothing compared to cleaning the piss and dung of thirty cows."

"We have six cows," Jem said.

"Isn't your father a doctor?"

"With six daughters," she added. "The farm feeds us when patients can't pay or there's an epidemic of good health."

"I found some old boots to wear," Ellen said. "They're behind the building in the wash area where we talked."

"Are you feeling better about your husband?"

"I stopped crying."

Ellen and Jem donned the oversized boots and covered their dresses with extra aprons. Jem tied a scarf around her hair and helped Ellen do the same. She carried another scarf and rubber gloves. "Your children won't recognize you."

"I hope they remember me." Ellen looked toward a tree. Underneath, Thornton and a group of men were entertaining the children.

"Looks like they're having fun."

"Let's finish this so we can join them."

Logan was waiting by the door to the sick room. He'd discarded his jacket and vest, and his sleeves were rolled to his elbows.

"I see you found straw." She plucked a stalk from his hair. He turned toward the movement, and his lips brushed against her hand. In the past only Ben's touch ignited a response. How could a man other than her husband create desire? Had her body responded from memory or was it something more? She drew her hand to her breast, and the pounding of her heart quickened beneath.

His touch had been accidental, and Logan seemed unaware of the reaction of her body to an innocent gesture. He pointed toward a cart loaded with straw. "We hauled the cart when we couldn't find any horses. Once the mattresses are dry, the men can stuff them."

Logan followed Jem inside the hospital room. The men had moved the bed frames to one side. Chamber pots, bedpans, and spittoons were scattered on the floorboards, a few had spilled a mixture of foul contents during the work.

"Phew!" Logan waved his hand in front of his face.

Jem helped Ellen tie a scarf over her nose and mouth. "We need some slop buckets."

"I'll fetch them," Logan volunteered.

Jem tied her scarf and removed a wooden spatula she had found among the cleaning supplies. She put on her gloves, looked at Ellen, and headed for the nearest pots.

Logan appeared wearing a long leather apron and gloves. He carried two slop buckets. "I'll carry the bucket, and you ladies can empty the pots."

"You don't have to do this. You have a report to write."

"Believe me, I'm going to put this in my report."

Ellen dumped a chamber pot. "You like to experience life first hand, Logan Pierce."

"Not until recently."

"We'll try not to miss and ruin your boots." Jem looked at his face. "Here." She tugged off her gloves and removed a scarf from her apron pocket. "Duck, and I'll tie this around your face."

He squatted. She covered his square jaw and sharply defined features beneath the cloth. His caramel-colored eyes peeked above the fold. She brushed his blonde bangs back before realizing how he might interpret the intimate gesture. Her fingertips lingered near his cheek.

Jem grabbed a chamber pot and emptied it into one of Logan's buckets. Ellen filled the other. When both were near the rim with a disgusting mixture of waste, he hauled them away. They finally emptied all the containers and began carrying them outside where Sid dumped boiling water into them. Timothy and his men scrubbed the pots and dumped the dirty water into slop buckets, which Logan hauled away.

Ellen found a shovel and brush normally used for cleaning ash from a fireplace. She scraped anything remaining on the floorboards. Sid tossed a few buckets of water on the floor, and Jem mopped them clean. The windows and doors were open to allow fresh air to dissipate the offensive odors and hurry the drying process. By the time Logan returned with the empty slop buckets, they were ready to repeat the process for the other half of the building.

It was dirty, disgusting, but necessary. As long as she associated the waste to mucking the horse stalls or shoveling the cow piles in the barn, it was tolerable. She'd changed diapers, mopped vomit, and disposed of afterbirth. Women cleaned the messes of the world.

It was late afternoon when Jem removed her gloves and lowered her scarf from her face. She looked around. "It's clean."

"I didn't think we would finish." Logan helped Sid tighten the ropes on the last bed.

Sid turned the rope key. "No sense in putting a newly filled mattress on sagging ropes." He stood. "They're ready for the mattresses."

Ellen had lowered the scarf around her face once the pots were emptied, but she removed the scarf covering her hair and held out her hand to Jem. "Give me your dirty clothes. I'll give them to Debbie and Dottie to clean."

Logan and Sid added their protective garments to the pile.

"When you finish that, spend time with your family," Jem said.

Outside, the clean mattresses were stuffed with straw and stacked in neat piles on a tarp protecting them from the ground. Nearby were the clean chamber pots and spittoons, drying in the sun.

"Take them inside." Logan turned to Jem. "With your permission, Mrs. Collins."

The sight of his deep dimples and wide smile made her heart flutter. "I think you've earned the right to call me Jem."

"John called you Miss Jenny."

"My friends call me Jenny or Jennifer. Only my

family calls me Jem." Why had she given him such a personal privilege? Even Ben had called her Jenny. She pointed at the empty slop bucket near the door. "I wouldn't ask a mere friend to do what you did today."

"I don't mind doing the work of a chambermaid if it wins a place in your heart."

Was he trying to win her heart? Had she done something to encourage him? She needed to think of something else. Something unromantic. "Where did you dump the slop buckets?"

"A ditch runs to the Potomac." He made a face of disgust. "Some men swim in it."

"Papa says a man will drink water out of a creek and then build an outhouse on the same waterway further downstream never thinking about the neighbor upstream who's doing the same thing."

Logan looked around at the camp. "Do you think these open ditches are making the soldiers sick? Most of them have fevers, stomach aches, and dysentery."

"You have thousands of men living in close quarters. A water pump is near here, but the Ohio boys were using a rain barrel. Who knows what the other men are doing for drinking water."

Sid joined them. "The men are cooking supper. They'd like the ladies to join them."

"I'd be happy to accept."

"You too, Logan?"

"Any place I can wash up?'

"Behind the building," Jem said. "You'll need water."

Sid dipped his finger in the cauldron they had used for heating water. "This isn't too hot for bathing."

"I'll gather some towels and soap," Jem said.

****

Jem examined her dress as she headed for the back of the building with bathing supplies. The hem was damp where the mop had splattered, but fairly clean. Her personal apron had been protected by the outer one. She sniffed and determined none of the foul excrement lingered on her clothing or body. Bending over steaming buckets of hot water had left her hair frizzy. Sweat beaded on her neck and back, and her clothes clung to her damp body. She was exhausted but didn't dare stop. Once she sat, she would collapse and never want to move.

She turned at the corner of the building. "I found some towels and soap." She froze.

Logan was stripped to his bare chest. His pants' suspenders hung along his trousers, which were perilously low on his narrow hips. He was bent forward, splashing water from a porcelain pan on his chest and back over his shoulders. The muscles of his back rippled with the movement of his arms. Ben had been strong from lifting and carrying heavy bags in the mill, but Logan rivaled him in size and strength. Why had she thought him too scholarly to be more than skin and bone?

He turned his head. "I saved some water if you want to wash."

What had her sister said about being attracted to a man who wasn't her husband? If her feelings were normal, why did she feel guilty for enjoying the sight before her? The sunlight glistened on his damp skin and highlighted the blonde streaks in his hair. She wanted to run her fingers through the silky strands of hair that fell across his forehead.

"Soap." He extended his hand toward her.

She found the small bar among her supplies and placed it in his hand. His fingers brushed hers as he clasped it. She flexed her hand, trying to dispel the tingling sensation.

He began washing his face, neck, shoulders, and chest. "I don't know if I'll ever feel clean again."

She stared, hugging the towels. She missed having a man's arms around her. The feel of his hard chest as she cuddled against him during the night. The smoothness of his skin as she stroked the muscles beneath. Her body reacted suddenly and strongly to an arousal she fought to control. She twisted the towels in her hands, hoping they hid the hardness of her nipples. Her bloomers dampened as a contraction from memories from past lovemaking overcame her. A throbbing beat began below her belly. She longed for release. "Ben." She burst into tears.

****

Logan didn't know what to do. Jem had been stoic all day. What had caused this outburst of emotion? He grabbed a towel from her and dried off. "What's wrong?"

She shook her head and placed the other towels on the table. As she turned, she bumped him.

His bare flesh tingled where her hand brushed against his chest and ignited a fire he had vowed to extinguish because of his brother's death. Married or not, he wanted to uncover the passion he sensed beneath the surface of her cool and proper behavior. She had teased him since their meeting with her beauty, intimate closeness, and now a teary-eyed pleading that awoke a response of action.

He trapped her with his arms. She gasped but didn't attempt to escape his embrace. Her blue eyes widened as she returned his gaze. He recognized the desire she did nothing to hide. She was no innocent, blushing at the bloom of passion. She had been with a man. She had experienced the pleasure two people could share with their bodies. The same pleasure he wanted to share with her. He lowered his mouth until it nearly brushed against hers. He hesitated, and when she didn't protest, he kissed her.

Logan had expected a cold, stiff reception taught to most proper young ladies, but her mouth sought his lips, eager, and warm. Her hands caressed his bare arms, traveling along the hills and valleys of hardened muscle, yielding her form against his. Her fingertips brushed through his damp hair and clung around his neck.

He deepened his kiss, building on the desire that erupted like a raging storm between them. Control was lost as wave after wave of passion crashed upon them.

Jem broke away, her face flushed from their lovemaking. She trembled. "I'm sorry. It's been so long since…" She turned her head. "I'm married," she announced. "I love Ben."

Logan's arms loosened, and she backed away, a look of bewilderment on her face. She turned and ran back toward the camp. He had forgotten she was married, but she hadn't. Married or not, the attraction was real. What had she said? *It's been so long since…* Ben Collins was a fool. Did he think his wife would remain celibate while he played soldier? Women were passionate creatures who sought lovers whether married or single. He'd be more than happy to satisfy her wants.

But he'd be careful. He wouldn't make the same mistake as his brother.

Logan maintained his distance, interviewing soldiers while Jem directed the volunteers in placing the mattresses on the beds. Jem and Ellen placed clean sheets on the mattresses while several men returned clean chamber pots and polished spittoons to the room.

The wounded remained outside for supper. Cooks in the different camps were roasting sides of beef freshly slaughtered near the unfinished Washington Monument. Fresh green beans, carrots, and corn on the cob were delivered from nearby farms.

Debbie and Dottie joined their husbands from the 69th New York. Ellen sat with Thornton, and Jem stayed close to John, who had traveled in the wagon used for hauling straw.

Logan poured a cup of coffee and joined Thornton, who had made a pair of cornhusk dolls for Inga. Ellen encouraged Odin to take another bite of green beans. He clamped his mouth tight and made a face instead.

Thornton raised his cup of coffee. "You boys from Ohio and New York are all right. Thank you for being so hospitable toward a poor cheese maker from Wisconsin."

"We thank you and your lovely family," Sid replied.

"The women reminded us of our duty to take care of our fellow soldiers," Timothy added. "Besides, some of those wounded are Irishmen."

"Here's to the Irish," Thornton toasted. "What are you, Logan?"

"I'm English and German."

"No, I meant you're not a soldier. Sid said you

were asking about the battle."

"I work for Salmon Chase, the secretary of the treasury. He's the one paying for the meal you ate."

"My compliments," Thornton said.

"I'm trying to find out more about the battle," Logan said. "Care to talk about it?"

A murmur rose from the men gathered around.

"Sid and John told me about the Ohio boys holding Stone Bridge. I'd like to hear your story, Thornton."

He looked at Ellen. "Some other time."

"No," Ellen said. "I want to hear it, too."

"What about the children?"

"They're too young to understand."

A man stopped playing a fiddle. The other soldiers grew quiet. Thornton looked around.

Logan, who had reclaimed his belongings, removed his notebook and pencil from his satchel and turned to a blank page.

"I'm no general. My story is from the battle line."

Logan nodded as he wrote Thornton's name. "That's the one I want."

"The Second Wisconsin was part of Colonel William Sherman's brigade in Brigadier General Daniel Tyler's division."

"That's the same division as the First Ohio," Sid said. "Only we were under the command of Brigadier General Robert Schenck."

Chapter Sixteen

Logan didn't need to look back at his previous accounts to make the connection. He was beginning to understand the hierarchy of command in the military. He concentrated on writing the words as Thornton began his story.

"We left Arlington Heights on the sixteenth. We had rations for three days in our haversacks. Nothing like this." Thornton wiped his plate clean with a piece of bread and popped it into his mouth. "We had some stale crackers and dried beef, which we ate in Vienna after dark. We didn't have time to pitch our tents, which had been transported in the wagons, so we wrapped our blankets around us and slept on the ground. The dew soaked through the wool to our uniforms and made marching uncomfortable the next day. In addition, the Rebels had placed trees in the road to slow us. Ten miles took all day."

Odin climbed onto his lap.

"The next day some of the men from New York, Massachusetts, and Michigan engaged some Rebels in the woods. We were ordered to march double quick in the heat. By the time we closed the gap between us, we were wore out. When the bullets and cannon balls fired around us, we ducked and prayed. We waited for the call to advance, but instead we were ordered to retreat. Heard eighty men were killed."

"Was that Blackburn's Ford?" Logan asked.

Thornton nodded.

"What about Sunday?"

"We started the day north of Stone Bridge along the woods and Bull Run. Cannon fired in the morning. Mostly our side. We were waiting to march into position to fight. Then a couple of Rebel columns double timed away from us. Something was happening farther west. Fighting lasted a couple of hours, but all we did was wait."

His story matched John and Sid's accounts of the battle.

"After lunch we traveled along the river to a spot where we crossed over. The bank was steep, but we met no Rebels. At first."

Thornton stroked Odin's hair, and the boy yawned. Inga was snuggling against her mother and nodding off as well. The baby was resting in Timothy's arms. "We formed lines and advanced on a hill and along a ridge to attack the Rebels. I don't know where the Confederacy was earlier, but they formed a line in front of us. When we were close enough, the front row knelt and fired. I was in the second row. We fired while the first row reloaded. They hit us with everything they had."

Logan stopped writing. Thornton was pale. He wasn't telling a story. He was living it.

"We had to retreat. We left the dead behind and carried the wounded." He swallowed some coffee. "Then we regrouped and attacked the hill again. Only this time we understood what was going to happen. We fired. They fired. Men in the line crumbled to the ground, blood staining the gray uniforms we wore. When we retreated to the road for cover in the ditch, our own men fired upon us."

Logan looked at what was left of his trousers. "Because you were wearing gray."

He pointed to his left leg. "Black stripe. Rebs wear yellow."

Sid smoothed his hands over his blue jacket. "You Wisconsin boys need our tailor."

"Some of the Rebels wore blue," he argued. "I still don't know who shot me: friend or foe."

Logan made a note of their banter. "The uniforms caused some confusion, but wasn't the Union winning? What happened to turn the battle?"

"We couldn't take the hill." Thornton pointed at Logan's book. "We kept trying, but our guns were hot, our ammo bags empty, and our legs buckling under us, and no reprieve. Our lips were black from chewing open cartridges. We climbed that hill fight after fight until the dead covered the ground and the living staggered from exhaustion."

Ellen laid her hand on his arm, and he calmed enough to continue. "The Rebels sent in fresh troops. We could hear the train whistle in the distance at Manassas Junction. General Joe Johnston and the Shenandoah Army is why we lost the battle."

He fought back a sob. "McDowell never committed fresh troops. I'm no expert on battles, but it seems to me the reserve should have replaced the battle-weary men."

His words were filled with anger. "What was he saving them for? We were ordered to charge Henry Hill again. That's when I fell."

Thornton rubbed his thigh above the amputated portion. "My foot was dangling in a mangled mess.

Two of my friends crossed their rifles and carried me on them. Our guns were empty by then, and the artillery wagon was nowhere to be seen. Did they expect us to throw rocks at the enemy? Other men were leaving the battlefield like they had called it quits."

"Where did they take you?"

"A field hospital on the other side of Bull Run. They gave me something to knock me out, but I remember all the blood. The floor was covered with it."

John groaned, and Jem slapped him on the back when he couldn't stop coughing. Logan turned his attention to Thornton.

"I woke in a wagon. I remember seeing the stars in the sky and wondering if I was in heaven."

Ellen leaned against his shoulder. "I'm glad you're here."

Logan looked over his notes. "How many men were in the second Wisconsin when the battle started?"

"We had nine hundred in the regiment," Thornton answered. "We thought we had lost half after the battle, but I think they updated the numbers to about a hundred wounded and another hundred dead or missing."

Thornton paused, and Ellen took his hand. "I'm glad you shared your story. I won't ever ask you to repeat it."

Thornton looked around at the men. "I see some Wisconsin boys. Thanks for helping out. Where are you camped?"

"They have some of us guarding the railroad and the rest on garrison duty at Fort Corcoran protecting the Aqueduct Bridge," a soldier in gray said. "Some of the wounded officers were taken to the hospital in Georgetown."

"I guess I won't finish my three-year enlistment."

"You take care of your family." The soldier tipped his hat to Ellen. He turned to Sid. "You Ohio boys aren't too bad. You didn't see much fighting, but you guarded our backs on the road home."

"We'll take our turn at the Rebs next battle," Sid promised.

The scratching of Logan's pencil was the only sound in the camp. The fire popped, waking them from their reverie. Several soldiers removed pipes from pockets and added tobacco. The fiddler resumed his playing. Inga raised her head. "I hear music."

"What are you playing?"

" 'Coming Through the Rye.' "

"It's not Irish, but it'll do," Timothy said.

"You know that one, Miss Jenny," John said. "You and your sisters sang it at the fall harvest."

Logan closed his notebook and stored it in his satchel. The sound of a crystal clear voice drew his attention to the singer. The sound was simple and sweet with a bit of sass as Jem sang the words of the Scottish air.

"Every lassie has her laddie, Nane, they say, ha'e I; Yet a' the lads they smile on me, When comin' thro' the rye."

The song had attracted other musicians who lent their instruments to the impromptu concert. They played a march. Odin stared at the fast beating of the drummer's sticks against the drum skin.

Inga twirled around. "I want to dance."

"The little lady has requested a lively tune for a dance." Sid bowed and offered his hand to Inga.

Other soldiers danced with Jem, Ellen, Dottie, and

Debbie. Logan rested on a blanket and watched Jem dance, debating whether it was wise to take her in his arms. Inga curtseyed in front of him. "Dance with me."

He led her in a country dance, teaching her the steps as they moved to the beat of the song. He twirled her around until she fell. He carried her to Thornton and joined him. "You have a lovely family."

"Thank you." He looked around at the other wounded. "I hope the government does right by these men."

"I'll mention it in my recommendations."

"Mrs. Collins said I was lucky." He raised his hands. "I can still milk a cow."

"You were hoping to buy your own dairy farm?"

"A man doesn't like living off his wife's family. I enlisted for three years thinking the war wouldn't last long. I was hoping to meet someone who might be willing to partner with me and start a cheese business."

"I have some money I can invest in your cheese company."

"It's only an idea now."

"You let me know when it's more than an idea." Logan extended his hand. "Thank you for serving our country."

Dr. Martin clapped his hands. "Time to put these men back in their beds."

"Wait," John said. He had been reading from his Bible. "I'm no preacher, but I'd like to offer a prayer and a passage of scripture for the men who lost their lives."

He read a psalm and prayed. A few men answered, "Amen." John looked at Jem. "Miss Jenny, would you sing a hymn? 'Just As I Am'?"

Jem nodded. She waited for the musicians to begin playing and sang the words.

The others joined in the final line of the stanzas, "*O Lamb of God, I come, I come.*"

Her voice would haunt Logan as he helped the men carry the wounded inside to clean beds. Some of the soldiers tarried by bedsides, offering to play cards or checkers with men unwilling to end the comradery.

Logan paused by the door and looked over the sick room.

"You did a good thing today," Dr. Martin said.

"I didn't do it." He looked at Jem who was distributing paper and pencils to the men so they could write home. "She did."

"She has a gift for organizing work."

"She makes lists," Logan said, watching Jem leave to answer the call of her name by John.

Dr. Martin clapped his hands. "Most of you will have your stitches removed tomorrow." He turned to Ellen who was saying goodbye to Thornton. "Will you be helping?"

"Mrs. Collins said she would show me what to do. I don't know how much help I'll be, but I'll try my best."

Thornton grabbed her hand. "You're quite capable, Ellen." She glowed from his praise.

It was a private moment between a husband and wife. An intimacy he had never experienced. Logan headed for the door.

"Mr. Pierce," Ellen called. "Will you tell Mrs. Collins I'll be out soon?"

Logan found Jem with John and Sid. John extended a piece of paper toward Logan. "Do you know where

Matthew Brady's shop is located?"

He took the paper. "Yes. What is this?"

"It's a receipt," John said. "Would you take Miss Jenny to his place tomorrow?"

Jem tied her bonnet. "I'm sure I can find it."

"I'll be happy to escort her." Logan cut off any further protest. "What is at Brady's shop?"

"He took a photograph of Ben, Herman, and me while we were waiting to march south," John said. "I found the claim ticket in my Bible. I put it inside for safe keeping before the battle and forgot all about it until today."

"A photograph might help the men remember Ben or Herman." Logan tucked the ticket in his pocket. "Someone might recognize his face if they don't remember his name." He turned to Jem. "What are your plans for tomorrow?"

"I need to stitch John's leg, and I promised Dr. Martin I would help remove stitches from the other soldiers."

"Then we better stop at Brady's first thing in the morning."

"Don't you have to work?"

"This is my current assignment. If we purchase multiple copies, I can show Ben's photograph around while I'm interviewing soldiers. I'm as anxious to find Ben as you are."

Jem blushed beneath his gaze. She understood his implications. What was he doing? If he found Ben Collins alive, he would lose Jem. Yet, he was guilt-ridden when he contemplated whether Ben was dead. What would he accomplish? Even if Ben had perished, Jem would mourn him. She would be untouchable for a year or two. Did he want to wait not knowing whether she loved him? And what if she forgot her marriage vows? She would become like all the other women in Washington who forgot their husbands while in the arms of another man.

He returned Jem, Ellen, and the children to the Southern Belle.

****

Jem was awakened on Saturday by the bugle blasts from a nearby camp. Others echoed in the distance. Jem had retired early and should have been refreshed, but sleep had eluded her. She couldn't forget Logan's kiss. She imagined Ben when she returned his kiss and surrendered to his strong arms. But then all memory of Ben had disappeared in the passion ignited by Logan's lips upon hers. What had she done? How would she explain her behavior to Ben when she found him?

Finding Ben was the solution. Once she was reunited with him, Logan would fade from her dreams. Ben was her husband. She loved him. She concentrated on dressing. She put on clean undergarments and slipped on her work dress.

She knocked gently on Ellen's door. The children were still sleeping.

"Mr. Pierce is taking me to Brady's shop, and I have to take care of John's wound. Why don't you let the children sleep and meet me at the hospital later?"

She yawned. "They are tired."

Jem ate breakfast alone. Annabelle was talkative and seemed interested in what she had done yesterday. When she asked about the camps, Jem evaded answering. She could be a spy as Logan suspected, or she could simply be curious. Someone knocked, and she put on her bonnet and gloves.

"Mr. Pierce is at the door," Annabelle said. "He's a handsome escort, don't you agree?"

Jem fumbled tying her hat ribbon. Did Annabelle suspect something? Why was she acting guilty about a harmless kiss? Harmless? Her heart was fluttering thinking about his lips on hers. Logan had invaded her dreams and now wouldn't leave. What was she going to do?

Logan stood in the doorway, the morning sun shining in his hair. She drank in the sight before returning to reality. She grabbed her belongings.

He pointed at her medical bag. "You want me to carry that?"

She led the way. "It's not heavy."

He offered his hand to board the carriage, but she grabbed a leather strap near the metal step instead. She missed her footing, and Logan caught her. She scrambled out of his arms and sat on the cushioned seat, her heart racing. He sat beside her. "Is something wrong?"

"I appreciate your help, Logan, but if you're aiding me in the hopes of a repeat of yesterday's misstep on my part, I should make it clear I love my husband and would never be unfaithful." She caught her breath and avoided his scrutiny.

"Noted, officially."

She glanced a peek. He appeared calm and unaffected by her words. Was her attraction one sided? Had she imagined the explosion of emotion between them?

Logan found Brady's office midway between the Capitol and White House on Pennsylvania Avenue near

Seventh Street in the business district. The studio was above a drugstore adjacent to Brown's Hotel. An advertisement in the window had run in the *New York Daily Tribune* and warned parents they should capture the image of their young soldier, warning "*You cannot tell how soon it may be too late.*" A cold shiver trekked down her spine. Was this the last image of her husband?

She forced her fears to the back of her mind. A photograph with Brady's nameplate below it hung on the wall above the sales counter in his studio. Brady had a sharp angular nose that was overshadowed by thick bushy hair and a mustache and short beard that jutted out in a small triangle. A young man entered from a back room. He was tall, thin, and his face bore the scars of smallpox.

"Welcome. I'm Davy Cooke. How may I help you?" He waved his hand above the display case.

Small portraits were matted on thick cardboard. Larger prints were framed beneath glass. Several photographs of soldiers were displayed on the counter.

Logan lifted a framed photograph of a soldier on the ground, his body contorted from being shot. He turned it over.

"That wasn't Ben," Jem reassured him.

"Mr. Brady is documenting the war," Davy said. "He took a wagon to Bull Run."

"A group of civilians watched the battle," Logan said. "Some of them were caught in the panic."

"Mr. Brady was lost for days after the battle but avoided capture," Davy said. "He's home with his wife recovering from the ordeal. I'm in charge of portraits in the studio."

"How do you make these?" Jem examined the black and white print that was so sharp she could see the buttons of the soldier's coat. The print wasn't a daguerreotype, a painted image, or the engraver prints in newspapers. She couldn't turn away from the young man who stared back with eyes full of intelligence and life.

"We use a collodion wet-plate process."

"What?"

"Here." He removed a glass plate from a box behind him. "Once I have a subject, I coat the plate of glass with collodion. It's a mixture of chemicals. In a darkroom I immerse it in silver nitrate to make it sensitive to light. Then I store it in a light-tight holder."

"Can you show me?"

"You can't see anything in the dark room," he explained. "Otherwise, the plates are exposed to light and ruined."

"How can you work in the dark?"

"I arrange each item so I know exactly where it is." He lifted a box. "I place the plate inside, ready to mount in my camera. Would you like me to take your photograph?"

"I was looking for a photograph of my husband," she explained. "I believe Mr. Brady took it before the army marched out of Washington City."

Chapter Seventeen

Logan handed Davy the receipt John had given him. "He's missing. The photograph might help us find out what happened. We want to purchase it and show it to his friends and anyone who might have been in battle with him."

"Now, I understand." He opened a logbook. "You said it was taken before the battle."

"The day they marched out of the city. Three men from Ohio were photographed standing together."

"The Ohio Volunteers," Jem added.

Davy scanned the entries.

Each line contained a plate number, date, a description of the subject. "You keep track of each photograph?"

"Mr. Brady insists upon accurate records by all his assistants. He wants to document the war but has to finance the project." Davy pointed to an entry. "This might be it. He left them and returned with an envelope. He removed several photographs and carefully arranged them on a velvet cloth on the counter. "Is your husband in any of these?"

Jem stared at Ben's familiar face. He had grown a mustache, which made him appear older than twenty-one. He stood between John and Herman with his hand on Herman's shoulder. She could see the gold wedding band she had placed on his finger on their wedding day.

"He's wearing the coat I made him."

Davy examined the photograph. "Was he an officer?"

"No."

"The other men are wearing the short jackets of privates." Davy handed her the picture. "You said you made this coat?"

"It was a wedding gift." The cuffs of his coat were darker where she had sewn velvet from the remnants of the dress that had caught fire an eternity ago. Ben had worn the coat when he enlisted, but he had to have been issued a short coat like John and Herman. Why had he worn this coat into battle?

She withdrew money from her pocket. "I'd like to buy this. How much?"

"Fifty cents for this size mounted."

"Can you make more copies?"

"We keep all the glass plates. How many?"

Logan looked at Jem.

"One for John and Herman's mother."

"Make it five more." Logan placed five dollars on the counter. "We can pass the extra ones around and see if anyone remembers Ben or Herman."

Jem handed the bill to Logan. "I have money to pay for them."

"We can share the costs," Logan said.

Davy took the money. "Are all three men missing?"

Jem pointed at the man on the left. "John is alive. But he was wounded before the end of the battle. He doesn't know what happened to the others."

"While you're here, you should have your portrait taken," Davy suggested. "It would be a nice gift to give your husband when you find him."

"How long will it take?"

"Not long. The camera room is in the back of the building."

Jem studied Ben's photograph. If Ben was a prisoner, she could at least give him her image. "I'd like you to take my photograph." She turned to Logan. "Have you ever had your photograph taken?"

"No. It steals your soul."

His dimples revealed he was teasing. The man could never lie. He was probably the worst politician in Washington City. "Then you can go first," Jem said. "So I know it's not a trick."

Davy led Jem and Logan to a room on the north side with large windows to allow indirect sunlight to flood the room. He had a view camera on a tripod facing a chair and small table in front of a bare wall. "Please sit." He entered a nearby room and returned with a narrow wooden case. "Place your arm on the table to keep from moving."

Davy stepped back and looked at his subject. "Tilt your head a little higher," he instructed. "Do you want me to take that satchel?"

"It never leaves his side," Jem said.

"Hold onto it then." Davy stepped behind the camera. "Now remain still." He covered his head with a black cloth at the back of the camera, disappearing beneath its dark folds.

Davy's fingers removed the lens cap from the front of the camera, adjusted the bellows to focus on Logan, and replaced the cap. His hand disappeared under the cloth, and she could hear him loading the glass plate. "Don't move." His hand removed the lens cap. He counted to three and replaced the cap before retreating under the cloth. Jem could hear him placing the plate back in its protective cover before he showed his face, his hair in brown tufts from rubbing against the cloth.

"I need to process this plate in the darkroom. I'll be back to take your photograph in a few minutes."

Jem removed her bonnet. "I wish I had worn a nicer dress." When Davy returned, she followed his instructions.

"Too bad photographs can't capture color." He blushed. "Your hair is beautiful."

"My sisters will think I'm vain," Jem said.

"When they come to Washington City, Davy can take their photographs," Logan said.

"I don't mind photographing women, but children are restless and ruin the image." He gathered the light-tight box. "When do you need your images printed?"

"Those can wait, but we need the ones of the three men as soon as possible."

Davy carried the exposed plate to the darkroom. "After I process this, I'll retrieve the glass plate of your husband and make some prints. Can you wait?"

Jem didn't answer. She was studying the photo of Ben.

"I think we'll wait, if you don't mind," Logan remarked.

Jem nodded in agreement. She had always considered Ben handsome. The scar across his eyebrow made him more attractive. He was smiling and looked happy to be with his friends. The image was so real. He had to be alive. She would certainly find him now.

Davy returned with the prints they had ordered. "I'll print your photographs later today."

"I'll pick them up," Logan said.

"How many copies?"

"One for Ben, my parents, my grandparents, and my sisters," Jem listed.

"Make it ten prints for Mrs. Collins and two of me."

"Only two?" Jem opened her reticule.

"I don't have any family." He paid Davy before Jem had time to open the coin purse in her handbag.

"I'll take one of Mr. Pierce." He raised his eyebrow. "My sisters haven't seen you. One of them could change your mind about matrimony."

"A consolation prize," he murmured.

She turned to Davy. "I can't tell you how much I appreciate this. What you do is short of a miracle."

"I wish I could capture real life," Davy said.

"But this is real life," she argued.

"Any movement and the picture is blurred. That's why we can't take photographs during the battle."

Logan lifted a newspaper from the counter. "Why don't you put photographs in the newspaper?"

"Can't. But an artist takes a photograph and draws a replica for the engraver. He reproduces it on a zinc plate which is used by the newspapers," Davy explained. "The images are more accurate but not the same as a photograph."

Jem clutched the photographs of Ben, Herman, and John. "These are invaluable."

"I made single prints of each of the men in the photograph," he said. "No charge."

"You can do that?" Jem stared at a smaller print of Ben that had been taken from the larger group photo. She hugged Davy. "Thank you."

****

John was seated in the shade reading his Bible when Jem joined him. Logan talked with Sid, who was heating coffee.

"They're sending the Ohio boys home Monday if they didn't re-enlist. And the wounded if they can travel," John added. "Word is they want to make room for the new recruits."

"That's great news," Jem said. "Your family will be happy to see you."

He closed his Bible. "Do you think I'm well enough to travel?"

She rested her hand on his forehead. "Your fever is gone. After I close the wound with a few stitches, you'll be ready to travel."

John paled. "Are you sure I need stitches?"

"The wound won't heal without them," she said. "Do you want to go home or not?"

"Will it hurt?"

"I have some pain medicine." She turned to Logan. "Can you help him to his tent? It'll be easier to stitch the cut."

She kept her back to John and Logan while she handed Sid a bottle of whiskey. Sid uncorked the bottle. "How much do you think you'll need?"

"John is a nervous patient. The more relaxed he is, the easier my job stitching the wound."

"I'll be generous." Sid added whiskey to the cup of coffee.

Logan joined them. "John is ready." He looked around. "Where are all the soldiers?"

The camp was nearly empty. A couple of men in another tent were packing.

"They're saying goodbye," Sid said. "Taking one last look around town. I'm looking forward to all the recruits. As corporal, I'll be able to boss them around."

"If you don't mind answering, why did you re-enlist?" Logan took one of the cups of coffee Sid had filled and sipped. His eyes widened. "Mighty fine coffee."

Jem took the cup. "That's for John."

Sid poured Logan a drink. "You asked why I'm staying. I figure it's better if I do the fighting than a man with a wife and little ones like Thornton." Sid wiped his forehead with his handkerchief. "And I don't like being beat. Those soldiers weren't better fighters than me or anyone else in this army. If they didn't have the high ground and a few lucky breaks, we'd be in Richmond. Besides, three years isn't so long."

To a man, but a woman's beauty was fleeting, and her childbearing years limited. Jem wanted Ben home, but was she being selfish? Would she wait three years if Ben decided to fight? "Waiting is difficult, but not impossible. If you love someone, you'd wait no matter how long." Who was she trying to convince? Could she watch her friends marry, give birth, and raise their families while her life was on hold?

Logan was studying her. She had the decency to blush.

They joined John in his tent. Jem placed a kettle of hot water on the ground.

John had retrieved the pans she had used yesterday. Jem arranged what she needed in the pie tin and poured hot water over them.

"You can put this in your Bible." Jem removed one of the photographs from an envelope Davy had given her.

John studied the photograph. "We were so happy." He started to cry. "They can't be dead. They can't."

"I don't think they are dead," Jem said. "I think they were taken prisoner. They were in the rear and couldn't escape."

John nodded as he swiped at his tears. "I think you're right."

Jem pointed at the picture. "You and Herman are wearing short jackets. Why is Ben wearing the coat I made him?"

John smiled. "He said your coat was the best in the army, and he wouldn't wear any other. He gave his short jacket to some soldier who had bought his uniform from a sutler crook. It fell apart within weeks of wearing it. Some recruits wasted their money on shoddy goods."

Sid offered one of two cups of steaming coffee. "What do you have there?"

John traded him the photograph for a cup.

"When was this taken?"

"When we were marching out of Washington. I think you were checking out the front of the line." John put the photograph in his Bible.

"I had extras made." Jem handed one to Sid. "I was hoping to show this around to the men and ask if they remember what happened to Ben or Herman."

"Let me show it around, Miss Jenny," Sid volunteered. "Some of these men don't know how to act around a lady." He tucked it in his coat.

"I'll be at the barracks' hospital if you have any news."

"I'll ask the chaplain to say a prayer tomorrow

during church service. I can show my picture around then," John volunteered.

Jem removed the individual photograph of John. "I think your mother will like this one."

John studied his photo. "I look so young."

"It was less than two weeks ago."

"A man can age a lifetime in a moment." He took a sip of coffee. "This is good."

"Do you want another cup?"

John stared at Sid. "Are you planning to pin me again?"

"I need him to hold your leg. I can't have you move."

"Better fill this again." He handed Sid the cup. "Add plenty of whiskey."

Jem gasped. "I didn't think you drank, John."

"My mother doesn't approve of drinking, dancing, or the women I courted. Why do you think I volunteered for this? I wanted to leave home."

"But you're going back."

"Home isn't so bad compared to war. Ma only made all those rules to keep my brothers and me in line. Raising four sons is difficult, especially since Pa preferred animals to people. Nothing against him, but Ma had to discipline us. I remember her praying and crying over our misdeeds. I plan to make her life a little easier."

"Sounds like you matured from a boy to a man since you left home."

Sid fetched another cup of coffee.

John rolled to his side and placed his leg on the blanket.

When Jem shoved the pant leg away to expose his

leg, the bloodstain was larger on the bandage. "What happened?"

"I forgot my crutch this morning and walked on it."

"That's why it needs stitches. But you have to stay off it and try not to bump it on the train ride home."

"I will. I want this place to be a memory."

Jem removed the bloodstained bandage. Blood had cleansed the wound free from pus. Some doctors believed pus meant a wound was healing, but her father said it was a sign of infection and needed to be cleansed.

When Sid returned, she took the bottle of whiskey and poured some over the cut.

John cried out. She waited while he drank the rest of the coffee and whiskey mixture. She added morphine to the cut to numb the area. She removed two needles from the hot water and threaded them, placing them on a clean cloth.

Sid handed John a strip of dried beef. "It's as tough as leather. Bite on it if you feel the urge to scream. I don't want half the brigade running this way if you start hollering."

John clamped on the beef jerky. Jem signaled Sid to hold the knee. Logan held his foot.

She pinched the skin on each side of the cut to close the wound and made her first stitch. John jerked, but Sid and Logan held him. Jem worked quickly, stitching and knotting the gash closed. Not her best work, but it would hold. "I'm done."

Sid and Logan released John.

"You didn't have to hold me so hard. I only twitched."

She wrapped a clean bandage around the wound.

"Keep it dry and use crutches so you don't put any weight on it. After a week, visit Papa, and he can remove the stitches."

"You should return home with John," Logan said.

Why was he eager to see her go? "If I hear news about Ben or Herman, I will."

He took one of the group photographs. "I'll show this picture around when I'm interviewing soldiers. Someone could remember them." He placed it in his satchel.

They had no future together, yet he was helping her. "Thank you, Logan." She gathered her medical supplies. "I better report to Dr. Martin. I'm sure he's wondering where I am."

****

Jem was removing stitches from a New York soldier's upper arm when Ellen arrived. She left the children with Thornton and joined her. "I'm sorry I'm late."

"Do you want to remove Thornton's stitches?"

"Can I watch first?"

"You can watch and then practice." She showed her how to tease the knot in the thread away from the skin and clip it with small curved scissors. She took tweezers and grasped the thread. "Tug."

The soldier jerked.

"They can feel it sliding through their skin." She looked at the soldier. "Does it hurt?"

"No, tickles, ma'am."

"Then we lightly bandage the wound or wrap the stump, and he's ready to go home."

"Some of them can walk, but how is Thornton going to travel home?"

Jem frowned. "I'll ask Dr. Martin if they have crutches and wheelchairs."

Ellen looked toward Thornton. "Will I be able to take care of him?"

"The problem will be helping him too much."

"What do you mean?"

"You'll want to help him, but don't," she said. "Force him to explore what he's capable of doing on his own. Think of your husband the way you do of Odin. Last night you let Odin feed himself even though he made a mess."

"But it's the way he learns."

Jem nodded. "Exactly."

Chapter Eighteen

Ellen took care of the next soldier. He had lost part of his foot. She washed the wound and examined the stitches.

"Locate the knot," Jem instructed.

"Some skin has grown over it."

Jem handed her a large needle. "Pick at it the way you would remove a splinter."

Jem removed the bandages on the next patient. If the wound was healing properly, Ellen removed the stitches. If the wound was infected or gangrenous, she fetched Dr. Martin.

By the time it was Thornton's turn, Ellen had gained the confidence to do the work on her husband.

"You're good at that," he praised her.

"No needle or thread is going to repair that uniform."

Jem looked around at the patients. "What happened to your supplies?"

"Lost in the battle. I don't even have a pair of shoes." He paused. "I mean shoe."

Most of the men were wearing rags of their former uniforms, torn apart like their bodies. She asked Dr. Martin about clothing and medical supplies for the men.

"We're short on most items. This isn't a real hospital. It was a storage building before they converted it into barracks. Because it had beds, they put the wounded in here. I had to steal or borrow what I have. Do you know someone who can trade or bargain for more supplies?"

Logan had political connections, but Sid was familiar with how the army worked. She found him outside showing the photograph to the men they had dined with the previous night. She shared her problem.

"We sometimes trade, but we don't have anything to trade anymore." Sid snapped his fingers. "A woman donates items to the soldiers. She might give you enough items to trade for what we need."

"What's her name?"

"Clara Barton."

"Where do I find her?"

Sid thought for a moment. "She's taking care of patients at the Patent Office."

"The Patent Office?"

"The big government buildings were used as barracks before we moved into tents. She turned the exhibit hall into a makeshift hospital after the battle."

"Can you find out who has wheelchairs and crutches while I visit Mrs. Barton?"

"Oh, it's Miss Barton. She's a spinster. She was a school teacher in Massachusetts before working at the Patent Office. She cared for the Sixth Massachusetts when they were attacked by the mobs in Baltimore at the beginning of the war. Folks from home send her items, and she distributes them to the soldiers. I've traded with them. She might have something to donate for us to trade."

"I'll take whatever she's willing to give."

****

Jem crossed the Long Bridge and followed Sid's

directions to the Patent Office between Seventh and Ninth streets on the north side of F Street. Like many of the government buildings, it was impressive in style and architecture with a large Doric portico visible three blocks away from Pennsylvania Avenue. Inside, large columns supported high arched ceilings. She climbed the staircase to the third floor, following a trail of dusty footprints, the remains from the mud clumps soldiers had tracked in after escaping the rain the night after the battle.

Inventions sent with patent requests were displayed in the galleries of glass cases. Bunk beds were stacked between them. A petite woman in her thirties was writing a letter for one of the men.

Jem waited while she finished. A miniature model caught her attention. "A water closet?" Jem read the description. "A toilet inside the house?"

"Beats peeing outside on a cold winter morning." Clara Barton extended her hand and introduced herself. "Are you here to help?"

"I'm Jennifer Collins. I'm helping at a hospital in Arlington Heights and need some supplies."

"We're short medical supplies." She looked around. "I have plenty of jellies and lace edged handkerchiefs."

"I'll be happy with whatever you can spare. I have a horse trading corporal who is searching for crutches and wheelchairs."

"He's good at bartering?"

"Sid is one of the best I've met." She looked at the models on display. "Do you know what the men do here?"

"I worked as a clerk before politicians determined

a woman shouldn't have a government position, especially at the same pay as a man. $1,400 a year," she said. "After three years of being out of work, I was hired as a part time copyist at ten cents per hundred words after President Lincoln was elected."

"Is that what you do now?"

"My boys need me more."

Jem stopped in front of a framed document hanging on the wall, the paper yellow, and ink faded from the sunlight striking it through the glass windows. "Is this the real Declaration of Independence?"

"Daniel Webster sent it here in 1841 when he was secretary of state. That's George Washington's commission as commander in chief next to it."

"Shouldn't it be in a museum?"

She waved her hand at the display cabinets. "The Patent Office is a museum." She led the way downstairs. "Why do you need crutches and wheelchairs?"

"The Wisconsin boys were in the thick of battle, but the wounded are ready to return home. Only they don't have enough wheelchairs and crutches for them. At least not at the hospital on Arlington Heights. I was hoping you could help provide supplies to trade for what we need."

"Wait." Clara studied her. "My boys have been telling me about a woman with red hair who ordered the 69th New York soldiers to carry the men outside so she could scrub out the building and make it fit to live in. You!"

Jem stepped back and raised her hands. "It was a pig sty."

"We need you in Washington."

She shook her head. "I'm looking for my husband, not a job. He was with the First Ohio."

"Taken prisoner?"

"I hope so."

Clara's eyes widened. "You do?"

"It's better than the alternative."

"I see. Well, we need women who can take charge and accomplish tasks. If you ever want to volunteer, ask me, and I'll find plenty of work for you."

"Do you have enough supplies to spare?"

"People from home send boxes for the troops, and I store them in my room until needed. It's not far."

"Any sheets or blankets?"

"No, but I'm planning to take out an advertisement asking for donations of medical supplies," Clara said. "After Sunday's battle, we need them."

She couldn't stay in Washington City, but she could provide support at home. "I know people in Ohio would like to donate items."

"Send them to me."

Jem shook her head. "I've never met anyone like you."

"I like the challenges. I see a problem, and I want to solve it. I tried telling a man how to do something, but he wouldn't listen to a woman. So I did it myself."

She followed Clara to a boarding house near the corner of E and Seventh streets a block away. Clara's rented rooms were on the third floor and divided by a partition. Her bed was on one side with barrels and crates crowded on the other side. Inside were pies, cakes, and homemade jellies. "I feel guilty for asking for donations so I can trade them," Jem said.

"The baked goods won't keep. Do you have a

wagon?"

"I don't even have a buggy."

"I have one."

****

Jem found Sid and Logan with a group of soldiers near the hospital. They surveyed the wagonload of supplies.

Logan whistled. "Where did you find all this?"

She introduced the woman driving the wagon. "We have Clara Barton to thank."

"Miss Barton." Sid removed his cap. "I appreciate your generosity."

"Where do you want the merchandise?"

"Logan said the hospital in Georgetown has plenty of wheelchairs and crutches," Sid said. "They would be happy to trade. It's across the Chain bridge."

"Hop on," Clara said.

Logan paused by the horses. "Would you like me to drive?"

Clara tied off the reins. "You know the way."

Logan helped her disembark and took her spot on the bench next to Jem. "You've had a busy day."

"It's been productive."

"Marked off a lot of items on your list?"

Was he making fun of her? His deep dimples meant he was teasing. "Have you filled your notebook?"

"Nearly. If the officers had listened to the foot soldiers, they would have won the battle."

Sid helped Clara sit on the back edge of the wagon and joined her. "How's the patent business?"

"Always something new."

Sid laughed.

"I like her," Jem confided. "If you want something done, ask Miss Barton."

"I showed the photograph around," Logan said. "A man named Herman in another company said he was near the Cub Run Bridge when someone shouted his name. He saw a man tumble over the side."

"Was it Herman Stratman? Did he see Ben?"

"He was shoved forward by the crowd."

"Neither of them was with the wounded at the other camps?"

"No sign of them in the military camps, but men were taken to private homes, too," Logan said. "He could be convalescing somewhere in town."

Logan had searched for her husband and Herman for hours. What man worked so hard to help someone he had only met a few days ago? "Who would know if they're prisoners?"

"I don't know if any names have been released. My friend, Pete, has been talking to officers and politicians at Willard's about the battle. I was planning to join him tonight. He may know something."

"What is Willard's?"

"It's a hotel where all the officers and politicians meet. If you want to find out anything, make a deal, or spread gossip in Washington, you go to Willard's."

"Do you go there often?"

"Only when necessary," he said.

"Do you think someone will have news about Ben?"

"If the officers and congressmen don't have answers, no one will."

"Would you mind if I joined you at Willard's?"

He studied her work dress. "It's pretty fancy. Do

you have something else to wear?"

She frowned. She wasn't a country bumpkin. "I have a lovely dress made out of flour sacks and trimmed with paper flowers."

He cringed. "Sounds lovely."

"Liar. I packed a party dress. If it isn't fancy enough for you or your friends, I'll pretend I don't know you."

"I'll call at seven."

****

Ellen helped Jem dress in the blue and white plaid evening gown. An elaborate castle pattern in black velvet braiding decorated the wide skirt and bell-shaped sleeves. The bodice was cut off the shoulder and dipped in the front and back. Her grandmother, Caroline Josephine Donovan, had made it for the Independence Day dance last year. Ben had escorted her, and she had been happy and confident of their love.

The festivities had been interrupted by Edward Vandal's chasers, Clyde and Buck. They were brutish men who dragged Noah into the square after grabbing Tess and threatening to kill Adam if he didn't surrender. Jem had helped remove stones and dirt from Noah's wounds.

It was more than a year, yet the memories were raw and fresh. She hadn't worn the gown recently and gasped as the décolletage revealed the fullness of her breasts created by the tightly-drawn corset. She didn't have time to add lace trim, and sticking flowers in her cleavage drew attention to her feminine abundance instead of distracting from the view.

"Do you think it shows too much?"

"I'm nursing," Ellen said. "If you want to see too

much, I should put on the gown."

Jem walked around the room, examining the movement of her skirt beneath the small hoop. For the dance she had borrowed a six-foot wide frame to wear beneath the yards of fabric, and her smaller hoop left the skirt in thick folds. She had considered the gown elegant, but would it resemble a flour sack next to the sophisticated silk gowns worn by the ladies of Washington? She had no illusions of impressing them, but she didn't want Logan to be ashamed of her. She gathered her accessories. She had white gloves, a beaded purse, and a fan, but no hat. Her bonnet didn't match and looked dowdy, but she had nothing else to wear. She put on the bonnet.

"You can't wear that!" Ellen protested. "And you'll mess your beautiful hair."

Jem glanced in the mirror on the wall. She had piled her hair high on top of her head with a thick braid around ringlets flowing down her back. Although her hair was darker than her mother's ginger curls, the mixture of red and brown strands provided a sharp contrast against her pale skin and cool blue eyes.

"Why not add some flowers?" Before she could say most flowers clashed with her hair, Ellen dashed from the room. She returned with a handful of white daisies and helped place them around the braided knot crowning her head.

"They're the perfect choice. Thank you, Ellen."

"You look beautiful," Inga said from the bed where she and Odin studied the preparations.

"Bootful," Odin imitated.

Jem draped a shawl around her bare shoulders. "I don't know how long I'll be."

"Don't be too late."

How much did Ellen and the others suspect? Did they know about Logan's kiss? How could she explain it? If they did know, why weren't they treating her like a pariah? What married woman enjoyed a kiss from another man? "I'll be home early," she promised.

Annabelle greeted her as she entered the dining room. "When is your young man calling?"

"He's not my young man. I'm married," Jem reminded her. "I'm going to Willard's to find out about Ben."

"Willard's? Why would you go near that disreputable place?"

Jem frowned. What sort of place was Willard's?

Chapter Nineteen

Logan had expected a country girl in her best Sunday dress. Jem's gown didn't have the fancy gathers and bows wealthy women added to state their superior status, but it was elegant in its simplicity. The form-fitting gown emphasized her slender figure, and the low cut bodice displayed a wide expanse of creamy skin from bare shoulders to the swell of her breast. She gathered the front of her skirt to descend from the carriage and missed the step.

Logan caught her in his arms, crushing her against his chest. "This is how we met," he whispered in her ear. He released her and fought the urge to tug her dress a little higher. He didn't want to share her, any part of her.

Jem smoothed her skirt. "I was staring at the building. It's impressive."

"You're looking toward the Treasury building where I work." Logan waved toward the building in front of them. "This is Willard's."

Willard's Hotel was strategically located at 1401 Pennsylvania Avenue, a block from the Treasury Department. The Willard Brothers had purchased the hotel in 1859 and expanded it by purchasing the Presbyterian Church on F Street. The combination of the two buildings created a rambling six-story hotel with rooms that varied in size and quality.

213

He escorted her inside. "Anyone who wants something comes to Willard's. Congress may vote at the Capitol, but this is where all the deals are made."

Lincoln had stayed at Willard's upon his arrival in Washington and until his inauguration March 4. The public rooms were lit by gaslight and decorated in polished woods and rich velvet fabrics. The lobby and hallway were crowded with men making deals.

Senators and congressmen conducted business with an official document in one hand and a glass of liquor in the other. Ranking officers in personally-made uniforms strutted around, although several were missing after the recent defeat.

Logan blocked Jem's path as a stream of tobacco juice left one officer's mouth and splattered in a brass spittoon on the floor. The floor was littered with scraps of paper, cigar butts, and a plethora of stains. "How can guests be so disrespectful?"

"The more important a man, the more he thinks others should overlook." Logan waved to Pete. He was talking to a colonel but rolled his eyes after he escaped to join them.

Pete's gaze lingered on the swell of Jem's breast exposed about the décolletage of her gown. "Hello, beautiful lady."

"This is Mrs. Ben Collins." He turned to Jem. "Pete Burdett."

"Mrs. Collins?" Pete winked at Logan. "You're risking being seen with a married woman? Her husband might become jealous and shoot you."

Pete never censored his words. "Her husband is missing."

He raised a bushy black eyebrow. "How

convenient."

"I'm helping her locate him."

"You're not serious." He turned to Jem. "What are you going to do when you find him?"

Jem's blue eyes fluttered wide. "Go home."

Pete put his arm around her waist. "Then let's hope he stays lost."

Pete was attempting to be charming, but he didn't understand love or loyalty. Jem extricated her body from Pete's grasp and stepped beside Logan.

But what was he doing helping Jem find her husband? Did he expect Ben to be grateful? Or was he hoping Jem would reward him? He turned his attention to Pete. "Have you interviewed anyone about the battle?"

"I've talked to majors, colonels, and generals. They all agree McDowell should have been fired."

"So Lincoln blames McDowell for the defeat."

"He's not the only one to take the fall. I talked to John Nicolay earlier. The generals are meeting to discuss promotions and retirements."

"Who is John Nicolay?" Jem whispered to Logan.

"Nicolay is one of Lincoln's secretaries. He knows everything going on at the Executive Mansion and the city." He turned to Pete. "What reason did he give for losing the battle?"

"Besides McDowell's hesitation to commit troops, General Robert Patterson is being retired for failing to contain General Joe Johnston and the Confederate troops in the Shenandoah Valley. The old goat retreated to Harpers Ferry instead of attacking Johnston's army. During the night, the Confederates marched to a train depot and rode the train all the way to Manassas, fresh

and ready to fight."

"The Union troops had been marching since the sixteenth."

"They should have come in coaches and carriages like the citizens of Washington. Some of us had tickets for a grand ball in Richmond."

Pete talked about everything but what was important. "You were there?"

Pete ran his hand along his hair to smooth it in place. "I didn't want to miss it."

"You didn't say anything yesterday about watching the battle."

"You asked if I knew what happened. I was too busy entertaining a raven beauty named Molly to notice the battle," Pete said. "We watched, but it was confusing with all the different uniforms. Sometimes we were cheering for the Confederacy and didn't even know it."

Jem stepped closer. "Did you witness the retreat?"

"I was in the carriage with Molly at that point." He leered at Jem and winked. "She had grown weary of the noise, although we made a bit ourselves."

To her credit, Jem didn't gasp in shock at his confession. Pete bragged about previous lovers to bed a new one. Some women were impressed by his narcissistic boasting.

"It must have been inconvenient to have a battle interrupt your tryst," Jem said.

Logan admired her choice of words, delivered with sweetness to disguise the insult. She'd survive in Washington City.

Pete continued his story. "Suddenly, people were leaving. I didn't want to be left behind and hollered at the driver to head for Washington. The street was so congested and muddy from the rain, we didn't arrive in the city until after dark. Molly was distraught, and as a gentleman, I stayed with her."

Jem's smile was forced. "Did *anyone* watch the battle?"

"Some of the war correspondents claim they witnessed the fighting, but their accounts aren't flattering."

"I read *The Washington Post. The men fled, whipped and repulsed by the South. Dirty faces, fatigued with battle running scared.*" Logan frowned. "I don't need poetic description. I want to know the facts."

"No one censors the press. The correspondents claimed all the telegraph lines after the battle and wrote their version of the war. Mr. Lincoln is talking about putting his own telegraph office in the war department so he doesn't have to read the paper to find out what happened."

"Will that help?"

"He wants to know what's going on at the front lines, but even McDowell couldn't call the correct orders, and he was on the battlefield."

"How is that possible? When his line failed, why didn't he send the reserves to attack?" Logan demanded. "The volunteers realized what needed to be done. Why didn't the generals?"

"Why do you think McClellan is in charge now?"

"Lincoln is going to need more than a different general to win this war."

"Nicolay said Mr. Lincoln is looking for a couple of brigadier generals who aren't afraid to fight."

"The men deserve nothing less," Logan said.

"They ran."

"Not all of them." He'd interviewed many of the men who had fought all day and had survived. They weren't the men described in the papers. "How do you think you and the others escaped back to Washington? A few men, outnumbered and lacking support, stood their ground and fired at the enemy long enough for the rest to retreat safely."

"You've received a heavy dose of idealism, Logan. Do you know any of these brave souls?"

"I met a few." Ben Collins was probably one of them. Whether he was alive, wounded, or dead was the mystery.

Jem relaxed against him. The curves pressed against him elicited a response that wasn't comforting. "Do you know if prisoners will be exchanged?"

Pete snarled. "We didn't take any prisoners."

"We took some in the previous encounters," Logan reminded him.

"We can go inside and ask." Pete nodded toward a closed door. "They've been debating the future of the army for at least an hour."

Jem headed toward the door.

Pete blocked her path. "Sorry, Mrs. Collins, but men only."

A flash of anger marred her pretty face. The generals were lucky they didn't allow women in their sacred halls. Jem would offer truth without regards to rank or consequence. Logan led her to a bench in the hallway. "I won't be long." As soon as he had the information, he'd escape and rescue Jem from the halls of hypocrisy.

****

When Logan opened the door, smoke billowed out. The loud shouting of men interrupted the quiet murmurings in the hallway and caused a few heads to turn. Inside men were deciding the future of the nation. None of the participants was probably considering the impact on the women of the nation.

Jem studied the opulent surroundings. She would never be comfortable in a place like Willard's. She preferred a simple farmhouse, the town square, and the familiar shops of Darrow Falls. But she'd made friends like Sid, Davy, and Clara Barton. They were part of Washington City. But what about Logan Pierce? He appeared uncomfortable at Willard's. But why?

"Hello." A woman wearing a red silk dress with a three tiered skirt edged with several rows of small gathers greeted her. "I'm Lily Divine." She sat on the far side of the bench and spread her skirt to cover most of it. Lily wore a necklace with rubies arranged in gold petals with the largest nestled between breasts barely contained by her low cut bodice. She didn't seem to mind the men ogling her or the women who smiled coldly and hurried their escorts past her.

"I'm Jennifer Collins."

Lily pointed toward the double doors the men had entered. "I couldn't help but notice you were talking with Pete Burdett and that other man. Isn't he Logan Pierce?"

"Yes. Do you know him?"

She waved her hands and several ornate rings sparkled from the glow reflected from the gaslit chandeliers. "Only by name, but the ladies of town are anxious to make his acquaintance. It's good to see him socializing."

"He's been busy working for Mr. Chase."

"His brother worked for Mr. Chase, and he found time to visit Willard's."

Logan had said little about Derek and nothing of his death. "You were acquainted with his brother?"

"Indeed. Derek was handsome and charming. Everyone fought for his attention." She snapped her fan closed. "Who would have believed mousy little Hannah Smith would win his affection and cause his death?"

Jem's hand covered her mouth. "His death?"

Lily grabbed her wrist and examined her wedding ring. "You're married?"

Why was Lily surprised? Pete had alluded to her marital status causing Logan's death. Wasn't he joking? Pete couldn't be taken seriously. "Yes, Logan is helping me find my husband. He's been missing since the battle."

Lily leaned toward her. "I guess he isn't much different from his brother after all."

Lily, like Paula Stone of Darrow Falls, wanted to share gossip, and Jem had fallen into her trap. She had no choice but to listen to whatever tale she wanted to share. She spoke her line. "What do you mean?"

"It's been five years since the incident. Six," Lily corrected. "Derek Pierce was secretary to Senator Salmon Chase."

"Before he was elected governor of Ohio." Jem stated more than asked. Logan had said after finishing his education at Ohio University, he began working for Mr. Chase when he was governor. His brother had died while he was at school.

"Was he governor?" Lily brushed the news aside with her ornately decorated hand. "I don't pay attention to local politics. The only important events occur in Washington City."

Arrogant twit.

"I don't know when the affair began, but it was common knowledge by the fall of 1854. Young gentlemen are expected to be available as escorts to social functions, especially when their husbands can't attend." She lowered her voice. "Usually they're too busy with a mistress or two, but that's no excuse for a woman to flaunt her affairs." She touched the necklace caught in her cleavage. "I never reveal the name of the gentlemen bestowing gifts upon me. I wouldn't want another woman competing for his favors."

Jem withdrew her fan from her purse and waved it in front of her face, which had grown warm. This was not a conversation she had anticipated. The woman was a paramour or courtesan. Back home she'd be called a prostitute or whore. How could a woman brag about her illicit affairs? Where was her shame? "Don't you think about marriage?"

She lifted her left hand. "I am married."

"And your husband doesn't object when you accept gifts from other men?"

She smiled, but it was forced. "He encourages my liaisons."

"Why?" Lily had been forthright about her unusual lifestyle, so Jem dismissed her rude question.

"My husband benefits from the information I gather, and I prosper from their generosity."

No wonder Logan had a low opinion of women. Did it include her? "You don't weary of the lies, deception, and intrigue?"

"I thrive on it. Men with connections and wealth

enjoy bestowing gifts. A smart woman knows how to be the recipient." Lily nodded toward the door. "A woman with your beauty should set her sights higher than a secretary."

Jem couldn't answer. Lily was recruiting her to join the ranks of mistresses. "I don't think my family would approve if I had a lover."

Lily stroked her necklace. "Don't tell them. Discretion is the key. Derek made his mistake by flaunting his affair with Hannah. He was seen entering and leaving her home at all hours, and they didn't behave in public."

"Behave?"

"Instead of acting aloof, they danced, cuddled, and behaved like newlyweds in public."

"They were in love."

"They were reckless," Lily corrected. "Lewis Smith didn't love his wife, but Derek left him no choice. He had to defend his honor."

A married woman killed Derek through her husband's jealousy. "He killed him?"

"They were in the throes of lovemaking when Lewis confronted them with a pistol." Lily had a smug look. "Derek died in the bed where they had been making love."

"That's awful!"

"I think it's romantic," Lily said. "They said he shielded Hannah with his body. I wish a man would die for me."

"Why?"

"Haven't you ever read *Romeo and Juliet*?"

"Yes." She doubted Lily had read every page. "Did you miss the part where Romeo dies?"

"But to have a man prove his love so completely would make the old biddies green with envy," Lily said.

She did value others' opinions. "I'd rather have a husband who is alive than the memories of a dead one."

"Is your husband a jealous man?"

Jem had never given Ben any reason to be jealous. She had never been interested in any other man until Logan. How would Ben react if he met Logan and learned of the kiss they had shared? She waved her fan. "If Hannah's husband was jealous, why didn't he spend more time with his wife?"

"He wasn't jealous. He was proud. Besides, he was too busy with his mistresses to bed his wife."

Mistresses. "More than one?"

Lily smiled. "Wives who are prudes keep the rest of us in jewels."

Did men want something more in the bedroom? Ben had never asked for anything more than a traditional sex life. She would never share Ben with another woman, but would Ben share her with another man? She had to clear her head of the dark images. She took her vows of marriage seriously. Logan did not belong in her marriage bed. She needed to focus on Ben. "I think I need some fresh air."

Lily pointed to the end of the hallway. "Those doors lead to a balcony."

The balcony overlooking the town was small but empty. Lights twinkled along the avenue, and camp fires decorated the surrounding defenses.

She wanted Ben to be alive.

She loved him.

His faults were small, and her anger with him spent. She wanted to build a life with him.

So why did Logan's image fill her thoughts? Why did she compare one with the other?

Chapter Twenty

Logan leaned against the wall. The generals were dividing the spoils of war. Irvin McDowell and Robert Patterson were out. George McClellan was the army's new leader, and William Sherman was being promoted. Other names were being proposed for promotion for the larger army. The talk of a prisoner exchange was too far down the list for discussion. No one talked of recovering the dead since they had been buried hastily in mass graves and would be in various stages of decay and difficult to identify.

Logan exited the meeting in time to see Jem talking with the woman in the red dress. She escaped to the balcony, and he followed. He had kept a respectful distance all day, but his eyes had lingered on her figure, studying every detail. The sunlight set her hair ablaze while working outdoors. Her smile calmed the fears of the wounded in the hospital. Her eyes twinkled when she talked with the men as if they were old friends.

Only he wanted to be more than a friend. Her kiss was unforgettable and haunted him. He had to know if she had experienced the same passion. When he opened the door to the balcony, she turned.

"It's you." She seemed relieved. "I worried it might be that horrible woman."

"The woman in red?"

"Lily Divine." Jem shook her head. "She's an

225

awful gossip."

"It's the national pastime for socialites."

"Is that the name for a woman who hops from bed to bed for financial gain? We have another term for it in Darrow Falls. I might be sympathetic if I believed she had no choice, but she enjoys others' misfortunes. She couldn't wait to talk about your brother, Derek, and Hannah." She placed her hand on his arm. "I'm sorry. His death was such a tragedy."

Logan stared at the city's skyline. "He was a fool."

Jem pushed against his chest, forcing him to face her. "How can you say that?"

"He had an affair with a married woman." Logan shook his head. For a moment he had desired the same. "What future was there for them? He never should have allowed her to seduce him."

"What makes you think *she* seduced him?"

"She was married. She shouldn't have encouraged him."

"Why do men blame women for their lack of control? Is it a crime to look pretty or should women dress in sackcloth?"

His fingertips hovered above her bare shoulder, knowing his body would react to the touch of her bare flesh. She was a natural beauty, yet she hadn't used her femininity to win favors from him. He had chosen to help her. "Women like Lily Divine use their beauty to take advantage of naïve men."

"Are you comparing me to Lily Divine?"

"No. You're too innocent to compete with her."

Jem stabbed his chest. "You don't think I could compete?"

He was confused. "Do you want to compete?"

"Lily Divine is not my future. I have a family in Ohio. Once you choose a life of promiscuity, it's difficult to regain respectability. I won't dishonor them with an affair that can only result in heartache."

"Even if you were in love with the man?"

She turned away. "Love can be fleeting. That's why a man and woman make vows of marriage."

He rested his hand on her shoulder. "Didn't Ben break his vows when he joined the army?"

"It doesn't matter. Whatever reason Ben had for joining, it doesn't give me license to abandon my promises. I forgot that for a little while."

His lips lingered near her ear. "When you kissed me?"

"No."

He pulled away.

"Remember the letter Captain Mercer gave me?"

She had his interest. "The last one you wrote to Ben."

"I gave him an ultimatum. I wanted him to choose me over the army. I said if he re-enlisted, I would divorce him on grounds of abandonment."

Divorce? "But he didn't read the letter."

"I'm glad." She wiped at a stray tear. "I was wrong."

Logan embraced her, offering comfort. "You don't love him."

"I do," Jem said. "I promised to love him when we were married, and I was wrong to think I could break my vow so easily. Not receiving my letter is a sign. It gives me a second chance for our marriage."

"Then you felt nothing when I kissed you?"

"It was a moment of weakness. I won't allow it to

happen again." Jem met his gaze. "I can't deny I care for you, Logan, but we have no future beyond friendship."

He couldn't settle for friendship. "Are you afraid your husband will shoot me?"

"Don't joke about death." She placed her hand on his chest. "Lily said Derek blocked the shot to protect Hannah. He must have loved her to protect her."

"It doesn't matter. The Pierce name was ruined. The gossips have been waiting to see what scandal I will initiate. That's why I didn't want you to come to Washington with me. A married woman's name is automatically tarnished by association with a Pierce."

"Your brother paid for his mistake with his life, but if people in Washington think that you will commit the same error in judgment, they're ludicrous. You are my friend, Logan Pierce. I will not desert you."

He laughed. "I've never had a woman champion."

"I hate lies and the people who spread them," Jem said. "Men can clobber the liar, but women have to endure the slander. My sisters and I have had to tolerate our share of malicious gossip. That's why we guard our reputations so vigilantly."

"Then don't risk it on my account."

"I can't deny the pleasure I have in your company, Logan. But I would rather be a long-term friend than share a brief affair."

He reluctantly released her. "I wonder if Hannah regrets her brief affair. She wrote me."

Jem gasped. "She did?"

"She's in Washington City. I had a letter waiting for me when I returned. She wants to meet at an inn called the Mermaid's Mirth."

"You should meet her. You need answers about your brother only she can give."

"And give the gossips what they've been waiting for? I can't meet Hannah alone."

She touched his arm. "What if I accompanied you?"

It would give him another evening with her to test her resolve. But he couldn't let her know his intentions. "You'd protect me from Hannah's powers of seduction?"

She headed for the door. "I promise to rescue you from danger."

They laughed as they entered the crowded hallway. Some of the officers and politicians had joined the ladies. Lily was talking to a colonel, who was ogling her breasts. She waved. Pete collided with her on route to intercept them.

"We better escape while we can." Logan took her arm and steered her toward the exit.

"What did you find out from the meeting?"

"Nothing useful." As they hurried outside, her low cut gown presented him with a splendid view that would keep him awake tonight. "The men are more concerned about who is going to make general than the prisoners or dead."

"What can I do?"

"John is returning home Monday. You should go with him." He didn't want to break all ties. "I'll send word if I have news."

He helped Jem board a hired coach. "Tomorrow could be my last night in Washington City." Her voice was sad.

"Besides joining me for dinner with Hannah Smith,

what would you like to do?"

"I'm attending church in the morning. I'm hoping some of the soldiers will recognize Ben or Herman in the photograph and remember something to help find them." Her tone was deadpan. "I'll pray for our souls."

"Are our souls in jeopardy?"

"I'm a married woman, but I don't feel married. Am I a widow or a wife with an absent husband?"

"It may be a long time before you know."

"How can I go forward with my life until I know the truth?"

"How are you going to feel if you receive bad news about your husband?"

"I'll cry." Tears beaded on her lower eyelashes. "I'll grieve for my husband and all our dreams of a future together. But until then, I'll hope and pray he's all right."

The carriage stopped. They had reached the boardinghouse. Logan escorted Jem to the door and said goodnight. He told the driver to return to Willard's. Would the raucous companionship of Pete and the other men make him forget Jem? Would drink dull his heartache? He was in love with her. What other explanation was there for turning his world upside down. He was interviewing soldiers and asking them about a battle because he wanted to be near her. He was searching for her husband even though he could lose her if he found him. What other noble deeds would she inspire? He ordered the driver to take him home.

****

Jem debated whether to change her hair again. She wanted to make a good impression on Hannah. She had braided her hair in several small strands and pinned them in cascading loops on the side and back. A large braid was knotted into a chignon at the back of her neck and covered with a beaded snood. She separated a yellow ribbon from one strand.

"Can I have a ribbon?" Inga played with the cornhusk dolls Thornton had made the previous night.

Life was simpler as a girl. Ribbons and dolls. Now she was dealing with a missing husband, a man who longed to be more than a friend, and a woman who had caused the death of Derek Pierce. She wanted to hate Hannah. Derek's death had left an emptiness in Logan's life, and his parents' death in 1858 left him with no family.

His loneliness elicited her sympathy. She had made it clear they could be nothing more than friends, but the words hadn't erased her desire to feel Logan's arms around her and his lips upon hers.

Inga attempted to tie the long ribbon around the small doll's neck.

"Let me cut it." Jem helped Inga tie a ribbon around each of the dolls.

Inga showed her the remaining ribbon. "What do I do with this?"

After braiding Inga's hair into a single strand, she tied the ribbon on the end. "You look pretty."

Ellen looked through the half-opened door. "What are you doing in here, Inga?"

"I'm helping Miss Jenny."

"Mrs. Collins to you." She looked at Jem. "Logan is here."

Inga showed her mother the two dolls. "Look at the ribbon Mrs. Collins gave me."

"Did you give her anything?"

"It's an old ribbon," Jem excused.

Inga stuck one of the dolls in her hand. "You can have one."

Inga's face glowed, making it impossible for Jem to refuse. "Thank you. It's a beautiful gift."

"You can give it to Cassie."

She had remembered her story. She didn't have the heart to tell her Cass was too old for dolls. She put the figure in her handbag after Ellen led Inga from the room.

Jem's gown was the one she had worn the day she met Logan. After church she had borrowed Annabelle's iron to smooth the wrinkles from the pale yellow fabric embroidered with tiny forget-me-knots. The wide sleeves were edged with blue silk to match the large bow at the back of her waist. She gathered her gloves and the wide-brimmed straw bonnet she had packed. It was trimmed with matching blue ribbons.

Logan was arguing with Annabelle when she joined them. He offered his arm and escorted her outside where the hired carriage was waiting.

"I don't know why you don't like Mrs. Sharpton."

"She said Abraham Lincoln was proof man descended from monkeys."

Jem looked back at the Southern Belle. "How can she say something so awful?"

"Insult her precious Lee family, and she's in an uproar, but she thinks it's acceptable to insult the President of the United States."

"President Lincoln could grow on her. I didn't like his beard at first, but it makes him look distinguished now."

"Should I grow a beard?"

"Don't you dare," she said. "A beard would hide your dimples."

He offered his hand to aid her into the carriage. "You like my dimples?"

"They deepen when you're teasing."

"And when I'm serious?"

"They disappear. You could never tell a lie."

"That's discouraging. Deceit is a necessity for a politician."

"Do you have ambitions in government, Logan?"

"I think with my experience in Washington City, I could run a small town."

"Mayor Logan Pierce." She smiled. "I like it."

****

The Mermaid's Mirth had been recently purchased by Blake Ellsworth. He had black hair and a trimmed mustache above a wide smile and square jaw. He was a competent innkeeper, although more work was needed to repair years of neglect by the previous owner and the recent occupation of soldiers. Fresh paint coated the interior walls, and clean linens covered the tables in the dining hall.

Instead of an exotic seducer like Lily Divine, Hannah was dressed tastefully, her hair pulled across her ears and secured in a bun. She introduced a young girl with her as Deidre, who wore a dark blue dress with a lace trimmed white collar.

The child had nearly white hair in a single braid and warm brown eyes. A fleeting smile revealed a dimple in her cheek. The resemblance to Logan was unmistakable. This was Derek's child. Deidre, like Inga, had to be nearly six by the gap in her teeth.

Blake served slices of ham, peas, and yams in a

sweet syrup. Jem took a bite. "The food is delicious."

Hannah sliced Deidre's ham. "Make sure you chew it well."

"I wondered why you wanted to meet, but Deidre makes it obvious." Logan's gaze met Hannah's. "Did Derek know about her?"

"I was expecting his child. We wanted to be married," Hannah said. "Derek was helping me file the paperwork for a divorce. That's what angered my husband. He didn't care if I had a lover, but to file for divorce was unforgiveable. We dared to believe we could be free of him, but he destroyed any chance of happiness when he killed Derek."

Hannah wiped her tears with a lace-trimmed handkerchief. She looked at her daughter. "But I have Deidre. That's the gift of our love."

"Why didn't you write me about the news?"

"You were in college. I wrote your parents," Hannah said. "Didn't they tell you?"

Correspondence had been sparse the years between the deaths of Derek and his parents. "No."

"When you joined Mr. Chase in Washington, I wanted you to see her. She's part of your family, too."

"She looks like Derek."

"Then you don't deny she's a Pierce?"

Her demand made him suspicious. "No, do you need money?"

Hannah shook her head. "My family provides for us."

Was everything he believed about Hannah a lie? "You don't want anything from me?"

"I want you to take Deidre."

Chapter Twenty-One

Jem looked at Logan. His look of shock reflected her feelings.

He choked on his food. "Now?"

"No." She lowered her voice. "I'm ill. The doctor said a year, but I think he was optimistic."

She had barely touched her meal. Hannah wore a heavy brocade dress to add weight to her slim build, but her exposed lower arms were bones covered with flesh. The dark circles beneath deep set eyes and gray pallor indicated impending death.

Logan lowered his fork. "What does your husband say about this?"

"I'm done eating. Can I play?" Deidre interrupted.

"Please sit quietly, dear."

Jem withdrew the cornhusk doll Inga had given her from her handbag and showed it to Deidre. "Would you like to play with this?"

"What's her name?"

"Her name is Inga."

She examined the doll. "Thank you."

Hannah stroked her daughter's head. "Lewis would raise her only to defile her in the ugliest way possible."

Jem's father had protected her from some of the sordid lifestyles uncovered in his medical practice but not all. She needed to be sure what Hannah meant. "What perversion does he promote?"

Hannah's face was cold. "Some men prefer children for their pleasures. They'll pay a fortune to send an angel to hell."

Jem had treated a young girl who had been raped by her drunken father. He'd apologized and asked for forgiveness but repeated the crime when he had become drunk again. This was a deliberate act by a man sober and without financial need who wanted to sell a child into sexual enslavement. It required a lack of any empathy; a monster.

"Is there anyone in your family who could help?"

"My father arranged my marriage to Lewis to expand his business. Money is his god. Lewis bought his loyalty, and he believes he has a responsibility to ensure I don't disgrace either one of them again. A pretty girl grows into a beautiful woman, a bartering chip for an ambitious man like my father. I don't trust her future in his hands, either. I trust you."

Logan had hundreds of reasons to say no. He was a single man, and she was a little girl. He had a demanding job requiring frequent trips. He had no experience being a father.

"You're her uncle. The closest kin she has. I think Derek would have…"

"I'll do it."

Logan was sincere. He was taking a leap of faith accepting this responsibility. She believed he could do it. Jem grabbed his hand and squeezed.

Hannah took her daughter's hand. "Deidre, this is your Uncle Logan."

She stared at Logan with the same eyes. He smiled, displaying his deep dimples. She smiled back, a reflection of family traits. "How do you do, Uncle

Logan."

"Fine, thank you. Would you like some dessert?"

Deidre, who had been rolling the peas around on her plate, turned to her mother. "Do I have to finish my food first?"

"Not this time."

Blake served ice cream with strawberries. "I hope you enjoyed the meal. Tell your friends to visit."

"I will." Logan paid him for the meals. Hannah removed an envelope from her handbag. "I have a lawyer who is writing the guardianship papers for when I can no longer care for Deidre. His information is in this envelope. I'll have him contact you and keep you informed of my progress." She forced a small laugh. "My progress toward death."

Jem reached across the table and grabbed her cold shaking hand. "Can the doctors do anything?"

"No. I've stayed alive this long because of Deidre. I can go in peace knowing you'll take care of her." She stood, wavered, and grabbed the chair.

Logan put his arm around her to assist. "I wish I could help more."

"You've proven I made the right choice. I think Derek and I would have been happy if given the chance."

"I was angry with both of you."

"I understand. I will never forgive Lewis for what he did. He keeps his distance, but his fist maintains control on my life. He may fight you for Deidre, but the doctor who registered Deidre's birth, recorded Derek Pierce as her father. I've kept the certificate safe along with other papers I've entrusted to my lawyer. I will surrender Deidre to you before I die to make sure no one else claims guardianship."

"But don't you want to spend every moment with her?"

"I don't want her to remember me bedridden and wasted away. Once the paperwork is complete, I'll return with her."

"I share an apartment. I'll need time to find a home, nurse, and cook. And a school." He ran his fingers through his hair. "Are you sure I can handle this?"

"Yes," Jem and Hannah said in unison. They looked at each other and laughed.

"We believe in him even if he has doubts," Jem said.

"I'll give you until Christmas," Hannah said. "I don't dare wait any longer."

"I'll try to be ready."

"Thank you, Logan." She touched his cheek. "When you entered, I almost swore it was Derek. He was such a gentle, loving man. He didn't belong among politicians, but that is why he needed to be here."

"He told me he was a compass for morality. I judged him a hypocrite when I learned of your affair."

"It was a love affair for us." She looked at Jem. "Love can't be arranged, bought, or forced. It begins as a spark between two people and grows." She paused. "At some point it binds you to one another, and life is defined by the other person."

"I'm glad we met," Logan said. "I understand my brother better now."

"He spoke often of you." Hannah smiled. "That's why I decided I could trust you with Deidre."

He kissed Hannah's cheek. "I promise I'll take care

of her."

They had rooms at the inn. Deidre turned on the staircase and waved. "Thank you for the doll."

Logan waved. "It was a pleasure meeting you."

****

Jem and Logan walked from the inn to the boardinghouse. The streets were quietly deserted. Sunday meant the bars, whorehouses, and seedier activities were closed for the Sabbath.

Logan took Jem's hand. "Are you leaving tomorrow?"

"Yes." Jem dared not say another word. She had lied to Logan. She planned to say goodbye to John Herbruck and the Strasburg family at the train depot, but she wasn't going home. A man at church had recognized Herman's photograph. He had hidden in the woods while the Confederates gathered the wounded and prisoners. Herman's head was wrapped in a bloody scarf. He remembered him because he kept shouting "Ben" until one of the guards knocked him to the ground.

He hadn't seen Ben. That didn't mean he wasn't alive. Captain Mercer had said the wounded were locked in the newly built Alms House. She hoped to find Ben and Herman there.

While Logan talked about Hannah and Deidre and what he would do as a guardian, Jem plotted her trip to Richmond.

He stopped walking. Night had fallen, and stars filled the sky. They had reached the Southern Belle. "This is goodbye."

Jem didn't resist when his arms encircled her. "I want you to stay, but there's no future for us," Logan

239

said. "Someone will hear news of Ben eventually, but until then, you're his wife. I have no claim on you. If you did stay, I'd ruin you." He murmured in her ear, "I'd make love to you every chance and parade you around in public for all to see. Curse the name of Pierce. I'd want everyone to know I love you."

His declaration frightened her because she shared his feelings. Women like Lily were ridiculous to trivialize marriage and respectability for a few pretty gifts and gilded excitement. But love could blur the lines between right and wrong. She wanted more than a brief affair. She wanted a future. Whether it was with Ben or Logan, fate would decide.

"What time does your train leave?"

"Oh, please don't come to the station," she begged. "So many people will be there, and I'll start to cry if I see you. Let's say our farewells tonight."

"I can't kiss you." He nodded toward the window where Annabelle was staring.

She kissed him on the lips, a chaste expression, a farewell, but Logan wasn't satiated and deepened the kiss, demanding more.

It was the last time she would see him, the last time she would feel his arms around her, his lips upon hers. She surrendered to his passion, burning the memory of his love on her heart.

****

When Monday morning dawned, Jem was still debating whether to proceed with her perilous plan. She could return home with John and wait for news about Ben and Herman, or she could risk traveling to Richmond and find out what had befallen them.

If she traveled to Richmond, she would go alone.

Logan couldn't find out about her plans. He would insist upon traveling with her, which could result in his arrest and hanging for spying. She couldn't risk that. She hoped he didn't surprise her by visiting the depot to wish her a safe trip.

She knocked on Ellen's door. She was packing her bag. Inga and Odin were restless, bouncing on the bed. They woke the baby.

"Stop that." Ellen cradled the baby. "I hope I can put him to sleep."

"Why don't I take them downstairs for breakfast? You take your time."

"Behave for Mrs. Collins," she warned.

Jem seated the children. Inga played with her cornhusk doll. "My doll is lonely. Where is the doll I gave you?"

Jem knelt beside her chair. "I met a little girl last night named Deidre. She was lonely, and I gave her my doll."

Inga pouted. "But that was my doll."

"I told her the doll was named Inga after another little girl. She'll think of you whenever she plays with it."

Inga raised her doll. "Do you think I should call my doll Deidre?"

She patted Inga on the head. "That's a good idea."

Jem joined Annabelle in the kitchen. "Would you like some help?"

"In a hurry to leave?"

"Ellen doesn't want to miss her train, but I'm not leaving," Jem said. "I plan to stay for a few more days."

She placed hot biscuits in a bowl. "Still hoping for news of your husband?"

"I think he may be in the prison in Richmond."

"You think your pretty friend Logan Pierce can use his influence to have him released?"

"No, but I want to see my husband. I want to know he's safe."

"You didn't look too concerned about his welfare last night."

"I was kissing Mr. Pierce goodbye. I'll never see him again."

"What if your husband is dead?"

Annabelle could be brutally honest. "Then I'll put flowers on his grave at Manassas." She took the bowl of fried potatoes and plate of scrambled eggs to the children.

"Are you crying?" Inga asked.

Jem shook her head as she wiped her tears and placed her napkin in her lap. "You better eat. It's a long trip to Wisconsin."

"Are we riding the train?"

"Yes."

"Train!" Odin attempted a whistle.

****

Sid directed the men to load the wheelchair-bound men into the baggage car. The passenger car couldn't accommodate them. Thornton struggled on crutches so he could sit with his wife and children in coach. He had to hop on the steps, but once inside, he found a seat, and the children joined him.

Ellen handed Thornton the baby and turned to Jem. "Are you sure you don't want to travel home with us?"

"I planned to stay a week," Jem said. "It's only Monday. I may uncover news by Thursday."

"I hope you do." She hugged her. "Thank you for

all your help." She glanced at her husband. "Thornton is making so many plans."

"He'll have some bad days. You may, too," Jem warned. "But good days will follow."

"I won't baby him. I wanted to help him climb the steps, but I didn't. And he did it alone."

"Someday he won't realize his leg is missing." She gave her a letter. "Write me. I want to hear about you and the children."

Ellen swiped at a tear and hugged her again. She put the children in an empty seat and sat next to Thornton, who was playing with Thor.

Jem turned to leave and met John leaning on his crutch in the aisle. He had shaved and someone had cut his hair. "You haven't changed your mind?"

"No, I'm staying."

"I don't like leaving you to face this unfinished business alone," John said. Although they had lived in the same town, their relationship had been defined by Ben. Now it was defined by a few days in July when they had shared a bit of the war's horrors and pains. "I should stay and take care of you."

She nodded at Sid who was outside ordering his subordinates. "I have Sid if I need any help."

"And Logan Pierce." John looked out the window. "Where is he?"

"He has a job, John. Mr. Chase is an important man."

"We told him our story, and he's done with us."

"That's not true. He's working to find out about Ben and Herman."

John studied her. "Don't do something foolish, Miss Jenny."

243

Did he suspect something? "When have I done anything foolish?"

"Backing into a fireplace and catching your dress on fire, jumping into the river to rescue a sack of pups, racing your buggy through town to deliver Mrs. Wade's baby…"

"That's enough." Jem laughed. "I didn't realize you were keeping track."

John patted the cover of his Bible. "I'll pray for you."

She handed him a letter. "I sent a telegram, but this letter has more details. Can you deliver it to my father?"

He nodded as he opened his Bible. Inside were the photographs she had given him. Would she learn the fate of Ben and Herman? He tucked the letter behind the photographs.

"When will you return home?" John asked.

"By Friday or Saturday, depending on the train schedule." Depending on when she returned from Richmond.

The whistle blew, and Jem hurried to the steps. She waved from the platform.

Sid joined her. "Are you sure you don't want to go with them?"

Everyone was trying to send her home. "I'm here to find my husband. My task isn't done."

"We talked to hundreds of soldiers yesterday. We searched hospital tents and homes. He's not in Washington City."

Jem agreed but said nothing.

"What do you plan to do, Miss Jenny?"

"I promised Clara Barton I would help her

rearrange supplies at her apartment." A plausible lie since she was wearing her work dress. "I owe her for helping us."

"You say hello from me," Sid said.

She'd lied to every friend she'd made in Washington. Would they forgive her?

Chapter Twenty-Two

Jem stopped at the Southern Belle and changed into her traveling clothes. She hoped the neutral skirt and short cape would make her look plain and prevent any unwelcomed attention. She covered her red hair with a white scarf and pinned the wide straw hat on top.

She hoped none of the soldiers she had talked to in the last few days recognized her. She didn't want any of them mentioning seeing her to Sid or Logan. Had she forgotten anything? Jem's medical bag was packed with supplies in case Herman or Ben needed care.

She tucked the photographs of Ben, Herman, and John into a side flap of her medical bag along with the letter from Herman's mother. She included the photographs Davy had taken of her. She would give one to Ben. Logan had claimed one, exchanging his photograph for hers when they returned to Brady's shop. She studied the two men side by side captured by a camera's lens. Two handsome men who plunged her heart in emotional turmoil. Ben was her husband. Logan was forbidden. Was that why her dreams had been filled with a blonde-haired hero?

Annabelle was in the kitchen. Jem inspected the basket she had packed for her trip. She had wedged a nightgown and undergarments on one end so she wouldn't have to carry another bag for her clothes. She wanted to travel light. "I may not be back for several days."

"Do you want me to wash your clothes?"

"Do you mind?"

"It's Monday. Wash day."

"My clothes are in my trunk. It's unlocked." She put her arm through the basket handles. "Thank you for the food."

Annabelle studied her appearance. "Are you going to Manassas?"

She didn't want Annabelle to know her plans. "I'm going to follow the path of the soldiers." Another lie.

Instead of marching the direct route to Richmond, the Union army had first marched west to Manassas to cut off supplies transported by the Orange and Alexandria Railroad. If they had beat the Confederate Army, they would have marched on to Richmond, but defeat vetoed those plans. She could rent a hack to take her the eight miles to Alexandria where she could board a stagecoach to Fredericksburg and the train to Richmond.

Union forces had occupied the Southern town of Alexandria since the people of Virginia approved secession in May. Alexandria formed a line of defense for Washington City and was a hub for the Potomac River and railroad system. The Southern town had been the scene of the first fatalities of the war when Colonel Elmer Ellsworth, who led the 11th New York Zouave Regiment was fatally shot after removing a Confederate flag from the Marshall House, an inn at King and South Pitt streets. A corporal in the Zouave Regiment killed the innkeeper, James Jackson, who had shot Ellsworth. Each man was elected as martyrs for the two sides.

After the Battle of Bull Run many of the soldiers,

who had been separated from their commanding officers or companies, had escaped to Alexandria, confused and exhausted. Only a few of the more seriously wounded remained. Jem visited the hospital facility and showed the doctor the photograph of the three men. He confirmed they were not among the patients.

The sentries stood guard but weren't concerned with people coming and going during the day. After dark, the sentry would challenge anyone trying to cross the picket line and demand a countersign or pass. Anyone without one could be shot.

She arrived at the stagecoach stop, where she washed and ate her dinner of a sandwich, carrot slices, and a small fruit pie. The stagecoach, drawn by a team of six horses, arrived fifteen minutes behind schedule. The driver put her medical bag on top with the luggage of the other passengers. Jem kept her basket. The coach door was small, and she struggled with her hoop skirt. She sat on the leather bench seat facing forward next to the window. A leather flap had been rolled to the top and tied to allow air to circulate through the opening. Jem was crowded against the side wall next to a large woman who talked continuously to the two men seated facing them. She ignored the conversation and stared out the window.

The countryside passed. They left the Union pickets and passed abandoned homes along the road between North and South. Well into Southern territory, the Confederate pickets stopped the stagecoach. A soldier opened the door and ordered everyone out.

"Where are you going, miss?" the Southern guard asked.

"Mrs. Collins," she corrected automatically. "Mrs. Ben Collins."

"Where are you traveling?" he repeated.

Half-truths were more convincing than whopper lies. "Richmond. I'm meeting my husband."

"Is he a soldier?"

"Yes."

"Who does he serve under?"

Jem wasn't familiar with Southern generals. Why hadn't she paid more attention to the names when the men talked about the battles? She recalled a simple one. "Joe Johnston."

"But he's near Centreville since President Davis put him in charge of the army."

Now she remembered. Joe Johnston had transported his troops to Manassas by train from the Shenandoah Valley and must have earned a promotion. His men weren't in Richmond. Half-truth again. "My husband was wounded. He's in a hospital in Richmond."

When he began questioning the other passengers, she grabbed the wheel of the stage to steady herself. Her clothes were damp and her heart hammering. She had resumed some sense of calm by the time the soldiers finished their interrogations.

"Let's board," the driver ordered. "We're half an hour behind schedule."

More Southern soldiers were evident as the coach neared Fredericksburg. The inn served supper and provided rooms for the travelers. The train wouldn't depart for the capital of the South until morning. She welcomed a good night sleep. She'd need her wits to locate the prison and face the challenges of meeting with Ben and Herman. The innkeeper accepted her coins even though they were minted in the Union. The single room was small with a washstand and chamber pot. The door had no lock, and she placed the chamber pot in front of the door, hoping the noise of the door hitting the porcelain pot would wake her. After hanging her cape and blouse on pegs near the bed, she untied her skirt, removed her corset cover, and loosened the strings on the back of her corset before unhooking it. She removed her bodice and drawers, washed, and slipped on her nightgown. Climbing into bed, she tucked the knife her father had given her beneath the pillow.

In the morning she ate a biscuit and slice of ham before boarding the train. As she neared Richmond, encampments were arranged in neat rows to her left. Farther in town she could see a group of church spires in the distance. Two story homes were arranged in neat rows on a grid. She was in enemy territory.

She gripped her medical bag in one hand and her basket in the other as she headed for the prison for the wounded. The Alms House was a four-story building in the northeastern portion of the city built to care for the elderly, poor, and destitute but repurposed as a hospital after the battle.

Richmond was bustling with activity. Well-dressed women and men rode in ornate carriages or strolled along the wooden sidewalks in front of the stores and shops. Soldiers walked the cobblestone streets, bantering in cheerful comradery. A few tipped their hats as she passed. She hurried her pace. These men were designated as the enemy. They were Confederates, rebels against the government of the United States. She had expected the enemy to be evil in appearance, but most of the soldiers didn't look any different from the Union men she had left playing cards, tossing horseshoes, and telling tall tales.

One difference did stand out. Slaves accompanied the wealthier citizens, and officers were followed by black men at a discreet distance.

She found the Alms House, but what did she do next? It should be easy entering a prison. The hard part was escaping. She approached the military guard standing by the door.

"Do you have a pass?"

She didn't answer.

"What's in the basket?"

She offered him a peach.

"Go on in." He took a bite. "You women treat the prisoners better than us."

Other women had visited the prisoners. That would make it easier. He opened the door, and she entered the dark interior.

A few soldiers were gathered in a large dining hall to the right to escape the morning sun. A kitchen was in the back and an office to the left. Straight ahead were steps, which were guarded by two armed soldiers.

A sergeant approached her from the office. He looked in her basket and removed a sandwich. Bribery was the order of the day. "What can I do for you?"

Footsteps paced overhead. She glanced at the roof. "I'm looking for a prisoner. I was hoping you could tell me if he was here." She clutched the basket against her chest to keep her hands from shaking.

"What's his name?"

"Ben Collins."

"What's your name?"

"Mrs. Ben Collins."

He turned to a private sitting in the dining room cleaning his gun. "Go ask the prisoners if a Ben Collins is here."

The private studied Jem before passing the guards to go upstairs.

The sergeant returned to the office while Jem waited in the foyer. She stood near the entrance out of view of either doorway, ready to run if anyone attempted to arrest her.

The private returned and paused on the steps. "I found him."

The sergeant appeared in the foyer. "Do you have a pass?"

"I didn't know I needed one."

"I'll let you see him today, but General Winder will have to approve a pass if you want to come back." He turned to the private. "Doctor Gibson is out of town. You can put Ben Collins in the surgery room."

Ben was alive. She was going to see him. She would know when they were reunited whether she still loved him. No. Her feelings had been in turmoil since his departure, relief with each letter and despair as the days turned to weeks and the weeks turned to months. Logan had reminded her about the euphoria resulting from being in love. Happiness would return with her reunion with Ben.

She would never tell him about Logan while he was a captive. She couldn't torture him with fears he had lost her to another man. She would stand by him as a wife should. She'd forget Logan in time. And someday Ben would return home.

The sergeant pointed to her bag. "What do you have?"

The metal hinges opened wide for his examination.

"Medical supplies. Are you a doctor?"

"I'm a midwife and nurse. Do you know how badly my husband is wounded?"

He looked at the soldier who had returned. "What floor was he on?"

"Second."

"We put the worst cases on the third floor."

Jem passed the guards and followed the soldier. She could smell the men even though she didn't see them. The body odor, sweat, and waste were similar to the smells of the hospital she and the others had cleaned in Arlington Heights. She saw the men in beds, some sitting on benches. They silently stared.

"He's in here." The private opened a door to a small windowless room. A lantern hung from the ceiling, casting harsh shadows on a narrow wooden table in the center. A cabinet was to the side, but a padlock prevented access. A few mismatched chairs finished the décor. "I'll be outside if you need anything."

Jem panicked when the door closed and locked. She put her hand on the knob.

"Miss Jenny."

She spun around and stared at the man in the room. He bumped his head on the lantern, and it swung back and forth, distorting his image. He wasn't wearing Ben's coat. He wore a short shell jacket and clutched a rolled blanket in his hands. A dirty bandage was wrapped around his head.

Jem barely recognized the man with a full beard

and long, dirty brown hair. "Herman," Jem called his name. "Where's Ben?"

"Miss Jenny."

He looked as if he would faint. "Sit." Herman sat in the nearest chair.

She sat opposite him. "Isn't Ben here?"

"I'm sorry. When they asked for Ben Collins, I hoped someone had news about him and said I was him."

"Do you know where he is?"

"No. I looked for him when they loaded us on the boxcars to Richmond, but I didn't see him, Miss Jenny. And he's not here."

She shoved the basket across the table. "Eat."

He grabbed a sandwich and bit into it. "Do you want any?"

She shook her head, afraid words would reveal the tears she was choking back. She had come all this way, and Ben wasn't here. "What do you remember about Sunday? About the battle?"

Herman struggled to swallow. Jem placed a jar of tea in front of him and removed the lid. He took a long sip. "We were by Stone Bridge most of the day. John was hit with some shrapnel from a cannon shell. His leg was split open. Ben wrapped it, but it kept bleeding so we put him in a medical wagon." He stared. "Is John alive?"

"He's on a train home." She nodded toward her medical bag on the table. "I had to stitch his leg wound, but he'll be fine. How are you doing?"

"I have a fierce headache I can't shake, but I'm alive."

"Do you want me to take a look at your wound?"

He touched the bandage. "Maybe you should."

"You were telling me about the battle." She wanted him to talk while she arranged items on a towel on the table.

"The battle was going our way, and suddenly men were running straight at us trying to cross the bridge. The Rebels sounded like the hounds of hell chasing them." He grabbed a peach. "Pardon my language, Miss Jenny."

She glanced at the remaining contents in the basket. "Don't you want to save any food?"

"The other prisoners or guards will take it." He bit into the peach.

"The men were at the bridge," she reminded him.

"They were pushing and screaming. I couldn't believe they were our boys." Herman took a drink. "We were given the order to cover the rear during the retreat. It's one thing to march at the front of the line going into a battle. You have the rest of the army behind you. It's frightening to be at the end of the line when everyone is leaving. We kept moving north along the road, fighting the urge to run, hoping the Rebels didn't attack."

"When was the last time you saw Ben?"

"We were on the bridge. The one over Cub Run," he added. "A wagon was overturned, and we were shoving it over the side. A bullet struck me." His hand touched the bandage on his head. "I don't remember anything after that."

"Sit still."

Herman grabbed the scissors in her hand. "Don't cut it. I want you to put the dirty bandage back around my head."

Had the wound affected his sensibilities? "Why?"

"I don't want them to know I'm getting better. They might send me to the other prison or ship me farther south."

Jem managed to slip the dirty bandage off his head and worked the knot free so she could retie it. The fleas jumped from John's clothing onto hers. They'd jump free outside in the sunlight. "How can I learn if Ben is in one of the other prisons?"

"Somebody has to have a list. Do you know anybody important?"

If a list of prisoners existed, Logan would have shared it. "I don't know anybody in Richmond."

Herman searched the basket and took a small pie. "What is today?"

"Tuesday, July 30."

"Nine days as a prisoner seems like an eternity."

"How are they treating you?"

"Nuns cook food for us. I had my jacket and belongings when captured. I'm better off than those who threw everything on the ground and ran." He unfolded his blanket. Hidden inside was his haversack. "I don't dare let go of it, or someone will steal it."

Chapter Twenty-Three

Jem cleaned his matted hair of dried blood and examined the wound. A lead ball had creased his skull leaving a gash several inches long. "Did a doctor look at this?"

"The doctor was busy with the other wounded men. I haven't seen him for a couple of days. How bad is it?"

The swelling was reduced. The thin scalp had pulled away from the wound and wouldn't heal properly without a few stitches. "I need to clean and close the hole in your head. It's going to hurt."

"Don't make me look too good. I figure I'm better off at this prison than one of the others."

"I'll put your dirty bandage over a clean one once I'm done."

"Do you know if they're negotiating our release?"

Jem told another lie to a friend. "They're working on it."

"Do you know how long they'll let you visit?"

"No. I better work quickly." Jem threaded her bent needle. Herman drained what was left in the whiskey bottle she had stored in the medical bag. "Bite on the beef jerky," she instructed after applying morphine to the wound. She pinched both sides of the hole together, stabbed the needle through the matched sides, and tied off the threads.

Once the gash was closed, Jem cleaned her needle

and stuck it through a cloth with the others. "Are you done eating?"

Herman took the remaining items and hid them in his haversack. "I'll eat them after dark so no one will see them. Those biscuits remind me of Ma."

She had made a promise to Juanita McFarland. "Why haven't you written your mother?"

Herman didn't answer, but his shoulders sagged, and he swiped at his eyes.

"She's worried. She talked to me at the train station when I left Darrow Falls. She wrote you." Jem searched her bag and handed him the letter.

He tore open the missive and read the penned words. Tears welled in his eyes. "I should have wrote her."

"Why didn't you?"

"I was mad because she married Randall."

She folded a bandage for his head. "But he's a good man."

"It didn't matter. She betrayed Pa by marrying him."

Jem placed the clean bandage against the freshly stitched wound. "She took care of your father for two years after his stroke. That's a hardship for anyone."

"I should have helped her more." Herman wiped his runny nose on his sleeve. "I didn't know about the debts. She had to marry Randall." He sniveled. "I failed her."

"She married him because she cares for him." She patted his hand. "Not as much as your father, but he's kind."

"You're not just saying that?"

"I saw them together. They were happy."

"I'm glad she has someone while I'm in prison."

She reached into her bag. "I have some paper if you'd like to write." She handed him a pencil.

He wrote the salutation and paused. "What should I write?"

Sorry for being a stupid, ungrateful son. "Write from your heart. When I return to Darrow Falls, I'll call on your mother and let her know you're doing well."

He swiped at a tear. "Tell her I love her."

Jem pointed at the paper. "You tell her. She'll recognize your handwriting." She removed the purse his mother had given her at the train station and placed it in front of him. "That's from your mother."

Without counting it, he shoved it into his boot. His hand shook, but he wrote the letter.

Herman's hair was matted from dried blood. He needed a shave and bath, but she ignored his disheveled appearance and tied the dirty bandage over the clean one. He looked like a dirty, battered prisoner of war. Would she recognize Ben if she saw him? "Do you know where they're keeping the other prisoners?"

"In a warehouse near the James River," he said. "I'm sorry, Miss Jenny."

"For what?"

"I was the one who talked Ben into joining."

She wiped her hands on her skirt. "Why?"

"After mother married Randall, I wanted to leave town. When President Lincoln asked for volunteers, I wanted to go but not alone. I talked John into joining. He does about anything I say, but Ben needed some convincing. I made him think he was henpecked. You wouldn't give him permission to go, or you'd talk him out of it," Herman said.

"It was a bunch of lies." He met her gaze. "Ben always said he was the luckiest man in the world to be your husband." He looked at the paper. "He talked about you to anyone who would listen. He wore the coat you made him all the time."

Jem removed the photograph from her bag and showed him. "I was planning to give this to your mother."

"I hardly recognize myself." He stared. "We didn't have any idea what a battle meant. We were stupid."

She returned the photograph to the bag. He had filled a page and continued to write.

Footsteps grew louder outside the door. "Someone is coming."

Herman signed his letter, and she shoved it into her bag. Herman hid his mother's letter in his coat pocket.

"Have someone remove those stitches in a week," she whispered.

The door opened. "Your visit is over."

Even though Herman had said Ben wasn't at the Alms House, Jem showed the guard the photograph of Ben. "Is this man one of your prisoners?"

He shook his head. "Come with me."

Jem gave Herman a quick hug. "Take care."

"I'm sorry I couldn't help about Ben."

Jem didn't cry in front of Herman, and she kept her tears in check in front of the soldiers. She showed the photograph to the sergeant, but he didn't recognize Ben either. She expected him to search her empty basket and medical bag, but he opened the door. "You can go."

She wasn't ready to suffer the same ordeal at the other prison. She collapsed on a bench beneath a tree and gave into her grief. All this way and no news of

Ben. She still didn't know if he was alive.

What if Ben wasn't at the other prison in Richmond? What if he had been shipped to a prison farther south? Would she have to search each one to find him? She may never know her husband's fate.

Her tears were spent, and she searched her pocket for a handkerchief. After wiping her face, she looked around. A commotion outside the door to the Alms House attracted her attention. The soldiers pointed in her direction.

The sergeant and others headed toward her. Were they going to arrest her? Should she run?

"This is the woman," the sergeant said. "She said she was a midwife and nurse."

"Ma'am," someone remarked.

Even after a year, she recognized the cultured syllables drawn out in a lazy southern drawl. His face had been in shadow, but when he moved to the side, she recognized Edward Vandal. His dirty blonde hair was shorter, and his mustache drooped around crooked teeth. His nose was long, narrow, and sported a bump on the bridge between dark brown eyes. He wore camel-colored trousers and a black frock coat trimmed in velvet. His vest was intricately embroidered, a skill of his wife.

The bump was from a broken nose. Tyler Montgomery had broken it twice. She had witnessed the second assault when Tyler had hit Edward Vandal in the town square of Darrow Falls the night of the Independence Day dance. Edward's hired chasers had beaten and dragged Noah through the street and Tyler had retaliated. He and Edward were long-term enemies, and by marriage, Jem was an enemy.

Edward had won a seat in the state House of Representatives for the Commonwealth of Virginia last fall. How much power could he exercise in Richmond? Could he have her thrown in jail? She clasped her medical bag. "How do you do, Mr. Vandal."

His eyes widened. "Miss Beecher."

Jem looked around. The Beecher name might draw attention in Richmond. "It's Mrs. Ben Collins."

"The sergeant said you asked for Ben Collins. Is he well?"

"I don't know. He wasn't there." She waved a hand toward the prison. "His friend, Herman, is a prisoner. He doesn't know what happened to my husband." Fresh tears flowed in trails on her cheeks, and she dabbed them dry.

His gaze rested on her bag. "The sergeant said you're a midwife."

"I don't have much call for midwife duties, but I have some nursing skills if you need help with a soldier."

"I need you to come with me."

The soldiers who had accompanied him, watched from a distance. The sergeant stepped forward. "Is she the person you wanted, Mr. Vandal?"

"Yes. Thank you, sergeant."

She was caught. Edward offered his arm, more securing than manacles. She accompanied him to an ornate carriage with a gold "V" on the door created with contrasting woods. A stocky man with a gun in his belt and a knife protruding from his boot stood by the carriage. It was Buck, one of the slave chasers Edward had hired to capture Tess and Adam. When he opened the carriage door, she stared at the large, hairy hands capable of violence, especially against women. Had he recognized her? Did he hold a grudge because her cousin Jake Donovan had knocked him out and tied him up?

"You're a Beecher bitch," he growled.

She was going to die.

Edward stood behind her. She had no choice but to board. He sat opposite her. "What are you doing in Richmond?"

Jem had lost the desire to lie. Edward was already suspicious. "My husband fought in the battle of Bull Run."

"You mean Manassas," he corrected. "The battle we won. The way this war is going, all those ex-slaves will be wearing shackles again."

Jem took his words as arrogant boasting, but if the South was confident it could invade the North, it could capture free blacks and enslave them like they did under the Fugitive Slave Law. Noah St. Paul had lived in fear of being sold into slavery. He'd even been put on trial for helping Tess and Adam escape, but Tyler had kept him from going to prison for six months or paying the thousand dollar fine commonly imposed on anyone helping runaways. Had Noah and his family returned to Ohio prematurely? They were safer in Canada.

"My husband is missing. He wasn't among the wounded in Washington or here." She removed the photograph of Ben, Herman, and John from her bag. "Do you remember him? He was my escort to the Independence Day dance."

Edward pointed to Ben. "Tall man with a scar over his eyebrow?"

Laura Freeman

"Yes. He received the scar when he was a boy and fell against a stone hearth." Fresh tears fell. "I don't know where he is or what has happened."

Edward studied the photograph. "Is he an officer?"

"No, why do you ask?"

"The coat looks like an officer's jacket."

"I made it as a wedding gift. The cuffs are velvet from a dress I wore, and I added some braiding along the lapel. He gave away his short jacket."

"He was wearing this in the battle?"

Jem nodded.

"Can I borrow this?"

"Why?"

"You said you were looking for your husband. What prisons have you checked?"

"The Alms House where you found me. I thought Ben was wounded, but he wasn't there. I was heading to the other prison when you found me. Perhaps you wouldn't mind letting me out there?"

"I have other plans for you."

She closed her eyes and silently prayed.

The carriage stopped. Edward gave Buck the photograph, and he hopped to the ground. "Show this at the other prison and to the soldiers who fought at Manassas. Someone might remember the coat. If you have any news, we'll be at my house."

****

Logan reviewed his report with Salmon Chase, who would meet with President Lincoln and his cabinet later in the day. Pete had presented his findings and excuses of the generals who had commanded the five divisions. They faulted McDowell's plan and the inexperience of the soldiers.

264

Logan focused on what the fighting men had shared. "The mistakes I discovered can be fixed, but errors were made from the beginning. The army needs to learn how to mobilize faster. We need better maps, reliable guides who don't sympathize with the South, and a cavalry that can find the enemy and avoid unexpected encounters like the one at Blackburn's Ford."

He turned to a copy of Thornton's testimony. "We need to adopt a uniform for all the men. The Wisconsin boys were wearing gray. Our own men fired on them."

Logan presented another page in his report. "Those were problems before the battle began. Once engaged, the soldiers were abandoned. The same men fought hour after hour trying to take a hill or defeat the enemy but instead lost manpower and ran out of ammunition. The generals need to know when to reinforce troops or replace them. Half the men at Bull Run never fought in it."

"McDowell said he kept men in reserve because the Confederacy had troops in reserve," Salmon said.

"The battle was lost on the hills because of his cautious strategy."

Logan paced in front of the desk where Salmon reviewed a copy of his report. "We had problems after the battle. We left the dead on the field and wounded undefended. Some claim the Rebels bayonetted the wounded. They captured the medical staff at the field hospitals. Those who escaped had to fight for a space in the wagons or walk back."

He took a breath. "We didn't expect a defeat, but we should have been prepared for one. We need hospitals and staff. If not for the efforts of one woman, wounded men would be lying in their own filth in a makeshift hospital in Arlington Heights."

Salmon nodded. "This is a thorough report, Logan." Pete coughed. "And your contributions are appreciated, Pete. I'll share this with the president and cabinet members. Although it doesn't exonerate McDowell, it clarifies the problems."

After finishing his presentation, Logan focused on his other duties. The day dragged on. He removed a photograph of Jem from his breast pocket and studied it. She was on a train heading home to Ohio. He missed her and wondered if he would forget her in time. He could write. He could inquire if she had any news about Ben. She'd see through any ruse. He was in love with her but was it one sided?

She said she loved Ben. Why couldn't he accept that? Why couldn't he find someone else? He'd courted women while attending college and working in Columbus, but none had made him feel like every day was a gift to be savored. He didn't need the sunlight when Jem was around. Her hair rivaled the sun. She was equally clumsy when exiting a carriage and graceful as she stitched a wound. She could laugh and cry in the same moment. She could love two men but remain loyal to one. He put the photograph in his pocket and returned to work.

Chapter Twenty-Four

Logan was free from his duties by late Tuesday afternoon but captive of his memories of Jem. Would it be too early to pen a letter? Was she even home yet? He was blind to his path as his feet followed familiar steps across Long Bridge into Arlington Heights and his favorite memories of Jem among the soldiers. Sid was making a cup of coffee.

He sat on a crate opposite him. *A Tale of Two Cities* was on a barrel. Logan grabbed the book and opened the cover. *Sterling Beecher* was printed on the first page. "Mrs. Collins didn't take this with her?"

"She loaned it to me."

Logan puzzled over his answer. "How are you going to return it?"

"I'll finish it before she leaves."

Logan grabbed Sid's arm. "She didn't leave Monday with John and the others?"

Sid shook his head. "No, she said she was going to help Clara Barton organize her supplies."

Jem was still in the city. But why had she lied about leaving? "I was under the impression she returned home."

Sid looked at the signature. "This book belongs to her father?"

"She wouldn't have left it behind." Logan reviewed a list of possibilities. She had initially planned to return home on Monday and had changed her mind. She'd been too busy helping Miss Barton to contact him. He had been too busy. She was searching for news of Ben. But she had searched the hospitals in Washington City. "Where would she have gone?"

"I haven't seen her since Monday at the depot." Sid dropped his cup of coffee. "You don't think she traveled to Richmond?"

"Did someone see Ben taken prisoner?"

"A couple of men noticed Herman among the prisoners," Sid said. "But Miss Jenny wouldn't go alone."

She'd kissed him goodbye while plotting to head south. But why?

Sid put his hand on Logan's shoulder. "Don't do anything foolish, young man. If she did go to Richmond, she'll be safer than you would be if you follow her."

She'd lied to protect him, but he didn't hide behind a woman's skirt. Logan stopped at the Southern Belle and yanked on the bell chain until Annabelle answered. "I'm here to see Mrs. Collins."

"She's not here."

Logan forced his way into the boardinghouse. "Where is she?"

"Get out, you no good Lincoln lover. She's gone. If he isn't in prison, she'll put flowers on his grave at Manassas."

Richmond or Manassas. Logan had two choices. She would have gone to Richmond first. He would go to Manassas. Then take the rail to Richmond if necessary. With luck their paths would cross.

****

Jem glanced at the door of the carriage. Could she jump from the moving vehicle safely? If history were any indication, she would probably catch her hoop skirt on the carriage step, and the team of horses would drag her under the moving wheels. She settled back in the seat. When they arrived at Edward's home, she'd make her escape.

"Where's that guttersnipe, Tyler?"

He still hated him. "He's not here," she answered. "He's in Ohio."

"I don't believe you, Miss Beecher."

Jem didn't bother to correct him. "My sister is expecting a baby," she explained. "Tyler's responsibilities are at home."

Edward studied her. "He didn't enlist?"

"No, but my husband did with his two friends."

"You said one of the men was in the prison. What happened to the third?"

"He was wounded but made it back to Washington City. He's on a train to Ohio. Their enlistment expired."

"Did you think we would release the prisoners because their service is over?"

"No. The generals are more interested in promotions than prisoners of war. I didn't come to barter for my husband's freedom. I wanted to know Ben's fate."

"Where is your family?"

"I traveled alone."

"Your father remained in Ohio?"

"He has patients."

"My wife needs a doctor, but none is available."

Cory had told her about Edward's wife. "Reggie?"

"Regina. She had a baby early this morning."

269

"She's here in Richmond?"

"Where else would she be but with her husband?"

Reggie had helped with Tess and Adam's escape from Vandalia. Cory had worried Edward would punish her, but his political career had distracted him from punishing his errant wife. A baby may have mended fences, too, especially since the loss of their son had precipitated Reggie urging Tess to leave Vandalia. "Is something wrong with the baby?"

"No, he appears to be well, but Regina is not recovering from giving birth. The midwife is incompetent, and I can't find a doctor. The sergeant said you were a midwife and nurse. I didn't know you were a Beecher until I saw you."

He had come to the prison looking for a doctor and had found her. "You want me to help?"

"I know you think I'm an animal because of Tess, but Regina never harmed a soul. If you won't do it for me, do it for my wife. Do it so our son will have a mother."

She hadn't meant to refuse him. She was surprised he was seeking her help. She was an abolitionist, and he was a slave owner. "Of course I'll help. What are the symptoms?"

"She won't stop bleeding."

Some bleeding was normal, but it should have slowed after the delivery. "What time did she give birth?"

"About two-thirty. I had retired for the night and didn't know she was in trouble until this morning. The servants should have awakened me."

The slaves were probably afraid to disturb him. She should be on a train to Alexandria and back to

Washington City. Logan might miss her. No, he believed she had returned to Ohio. "How long before we arrive at your home?"

"It's ahead." He relaxed against the seat. "Then you'll help."

"I'm not a doctor," she reminded him. "But I'll do what I can."

The Vandals lived in a wealthy part of town known as Church Hill, in a three-story house on a cobblestone street. Jem would have expected nothing less for someone like Edward. He valued the respect of others. He would want to impress the people of Richmond by his dwelling. A black man opened the door before Edward touched the knob. Like the coach driver, he was a slave. He was dressed in the finery of a house servant. He took Edward's hat.

"She's upstairs."

Most sick rooms were on the first floor to make it easier to care for the patient, but in a wealthy home, Reggie had remained in her bedroom for childbirth.

Jem removed her bonnet and gloves before she entered the dark room. She opened the draperies.

Reggie moaned. "Edward."

"I'm here, Regina." He sat beside her bed and took her hand.

She was pale and in pain. Jem lifted the embroidered blanket. Her nightgown was rolled to her waist. Her belly was rounded from her pregnancy, which was normal. The towel beneath her was soaked with blood and had seeped to the sheet beneath. "How many times have you changed the bedding?"

Edward looked at the black woman standing at the foot of the bed. "How many times have you changed the sheets, Esther?"

She jumped when he spoke. "After the baby was born, this morning, and again after you left for the doctor."

Jem turned to Edward. "When was that?"

"I left the house around ten to find a doctor."

Reggie's forehead was warm and her pulse fast. "I'm Jennifer Beecher. I mean Mrs. Collins," she corrected.

Reggie's eyes flickered, but she was too exhausted to respond.

"I need to examine you." Jem didn't wait for permission. She moved her hands across Reggie's abdomen under the covers. She cried out when Jem applied pressure on the womb. Blood gushed onto the soaked towel.

Jem turned to Esther. "Fetch some clean towels and sheets."

Esther didn't budge.

Jem stared at the stone-faced woman. "What's wrong?"

"I don't take orders from anyone but Mr. Vandal."

Edward jumped toward her, his arm raised. "You'll do whatever she says. You said you were a midwife. If my wife dies, you'll die."

Jem jumped back as Esther evaded Edward's hand and escaped untouched to fetch the linens.

Edward's anger ebbed as quickly as it had flashed. His voice shook but was polite. "Can you help her?"

Jem had seen this problem before and many new mothers bled to death. Jem unbuttoned her sleeves and pushed them to her elbows.

"Do you know what's wrong?"

"Did the midwife save the afterbirth?"

"What?"

Jem waited until Esther returned. "These are the last of the clean sheets."

"Did you save the afterbirth?"

"It's in the bedding." Esther glanced at Edward. "I was going to soak them, but I haven't had time."

"Where are they?"

"In the kitchen."

"Show me." Jem found three piles of laundry and tore them open where they had been knotted. The last one contained the remains of the umbilical cord and placenta. She put it in a pan.

"What are you going to do with that?"

Jem pointed to the placenta. "See where the afterbirth is torn."

Esther studied the mass of bloody flesh. "What's that mean?"

"It means part of it is still attached to the womb. That's why she's bleeding so heavily." A kettle rested on the stove. She carefully touched the side. "I need hot water." She opened the door to the stove. Wood was inside and some cotton to start a fire.

"I was ready to heat it for laundry, but Mr. Vandal said I needed to sit with Miss Regina while he fetched a doctor."

"Laundry can wait." Jem struck a match and started the fire. A pump was outside near the door of the kitchen. She added water to a large pot and placed it next to the kettle. She gathered a few empty pans and the pan with the afterbirth.

"What should I do?"

"After the water boils, carry it upstairs. Then you

can start washing the bedding."

Esther dropped the bundle of laundry she was retying. "Are you a Yankee, ma'am?"

"Yes. I'm from Ohio."

"Master Edward says you lost the battle. Now I'm going to be a slave until I die."

"President Lincoln hasn't surrendered. He's asked for more soldiers." The young men of Ben's generation would be called to fight. "The war isn't over; it's only begun."

Jem returned to Reggie's room and placed the pan on a small table at the end of the bed.

Edward stared at the bloody tissue floating in the pan and cringed. "What's that?"

"The afterbirth. A part is attached to Reggie's womb. I have to remove it, or she'll continue to bleed."

"Have you done this before?"

"Yes."

"Are you going to cut her open?"

Jem shook her head. "She's dilated enough for me to scrape the womb internally."

Edward's eyes widened. "Won't it hurt?"

"I have some ether, but I'll need your help administering it."

"I don't know how."

She arranged her supplies. "I'll talk you through it."

"I sent Buck to find your husband so I could gloat over his fate, but if you save Regina, I'll help reunite you."

That was an unusual offer from Edward. "And if she dies?"

"I'm not a forgiving man."

His threat was clear. One word from Edward, and she could be imprisoned.

Reggie moaned. Her eyelids fluttered. "Edward."

He took her hand. "I'm here."

Reggie looked around. "My baby!" Her hysteria grew. "Did she cut him up?"

Some midwives and older doctors practiced sectioning a baby in the womb to remove the pieces when a normal delivery wasn't possible in order to save the mother's life. Her father used a cesarean delivery to save the mother and child's lives, but it was a difficult operation and required skill.

Where was the baby? Jem turned to Edward. "What happened to the baby?"

He nodded to the adjoining room. "He's in his crib."

"Bring him."

Edward didn't move. "I might drop him."

Jem took Reggie's outstretched hand. "We're concerned about you. Do you have any cramping?"

She tightened her jaw. "Yes."

"Where is the pain? One side or both?"

She grimaced. "I'm not sure."

"I'm going to examine you." She moved the covers aside. The towel was stained with fresh blood. "Tell me when it hurts." Jem pressed several locations on her abdomen, watching Reggie's reaction.

"Ouch!" Reggie gasped.

Jem noted the location of the pain and intensity.

Edward had gone to the doorway. "Where's Esther? She can fetch the baby."

Jem didn't wait for Esther. She found the crib and returned with the baby swaddled in a blanket and showed him to Reggie.

"I want to see him," Reggie begged.

Nearly all mothers wanted to examine their babies upon birth. Jem unwrapped the blanket. "He has ten fingers and ten toes. Look at his fingernails." The baby wasn't used to moving freely and flayed his arms, screaming in protest. "He has a good set of lungs, too."

"I wanted to see him before I die."

"You're not going to die." Jem wrapped the baby securely in the blanket.

"I should name him." Reggie's breath was ragged.

"You think of a name while I take care of you."

"I know I'm dying," Reggie moaned. "I can feel life pouring out of me."

"You're bleeding," Jem agreed. "I have to remove some tissue left inside."

"Will I live?"

Reggie drifted off to sleep before Jem could answer. She returned the baby to the nursery. "We need to start."

Reggie was wasting away. Slowly dying. She opened all the draperies to flood the room with light. She gathered a few lanterns in case she would need them later when dusk darkened the room.

Esther arrived with the kettle. Jem poured hot water over her medical supplies to soak in the long shallow pan.

"Are you going to save Miss Regina?"

"We're going to save her." Jem washed her hands and arranged the tools she might need.

"What's that thing?" Esther pointed at a square shaped piece of flint with a sharpened edge.

"Flint." Trappers used the flint to scrape fat off

animal hides. She would use it to free the placenta, but the scraper could tear the uterus and cause more bleeding.

Jem placed a cupped screen over Regina's mouth and nose. She covered it with a small, thin cloth.

"Can she breathe?" Edward asked.

"Yes, but I don't want her to feel any pain." Jem removed a tin canister of ether from her bag. She placed a few drops on the cloth and handed the container to Edward. "If she stirs, place a few drops on the cloth. Do you understand?"

He nodded.

"Keep the cork in it until you need it." She reached beneath the blanket and felt her way through the birth canal into the womb.

Jem gripped the flint between her fingers, working on Reggie's right side where she had complained about pain, scraping in short strokes, overlapping slightly to cover the area.

Regina groaned, but she continued. "Add some ether," Jem told Edward.

The blood flow increased, but she felt tissue on her hand. She continued to scrape the area until she was satisfied she had covered as much as possible.

She looked at Edward. "No more ether but leave the mask on."

The towel was soiled with several torn pieces of tissue. She added them to the afterbirth in the pan, hoping she had removed all of it. She used the hot water to clean Reggie and put a clean towel beneath her. Her pulse was stronger.

"Will Regina be all right?"

Jem removed the ether mask and listened to her

breathing. "I think I removed enough to stop the bleeding. We'll know by morning."

By the time she had cleaned and repacked her supplies, the room had darkened from the sun setting. "Do you have a room where I can wash and close my eyes?"

Chapter Twenty-Five

Insanity had claimed him. What other reason would Logan possess for riding into enemy territory?

He had spent a restless night, worrying about the fate of Jem, hoping she would return by Wednesday morning. When she didn't, Logan convinced Pete he was ill from exposure to the soldiers and would spend time in the country to recover. He should have told him he might have something fatal. If he didn't return in a couple of days, he probably wouldn't return for the rest of his life. He had written a note to Salmon with the same excuse, asking Pete to deliver it.

Logan had exchanged his tailored suit for broadcloth trousers, a linen shirt, and a wool coat. He'd emptied his pockets of anything that might identify him as a government employee except for a few silver dollars. His hat was wide brimmed to shade his face from the sun and too much scrutiny.

He rented a horse from the stables in Alexandria and rode past the sentries. With luck he would make Manassas before noon. The country road was scarred with the ruts from carts and carriage wheels that had hastily hurried through ten days ago.

Rows of tents were arranged for several miles, and freshly dug ditches marked the perimeter of Union occupied land in Virginia. A wooded countryside replaced any signs of the military. Farmhouses looked deserted, fled by their Southern loyalist owners.

He entered Fairfax Courthouse village where about forty houses and brick buildings lined Main Street. He watered his horse and purchased some food at the tavern.

"You staying the night?" the owner inquired.

"No. Plenty of daylight."

The Warrenton Turnpike to Centreville was easier traveling. Confederate soldiers were busy fortifying the city. He lowered the brim of his hat to hide his youthful face and maintained his horse at a steady pace. He searched for Jem, but few women were in the streets.

He noted an inn but continued out of town and entered a wooded area. Bull Run was ahead.

The scenery changed abruptly as if he had arrived after a horrible catastrophe. The trees were shattered and broken, the leaves ripped from the branches. The grass was dead from the trampling of hundreds of feet. In other areas, it was bare, torn apart by heavy machinery or wagons. The destructive scars of the battle marred the countryside.

He had to find Jem, know she was safe. He paused at the broken Cub Run Bridge. Scrap boards had been hastily added to repair the damage. Logan looked around. This is where Ben had last been seen. Was he in a prison in Richmond? Was Jem with him?

She had rejected his advances because of her loyalty, but did she love Ben enough to wait months or years for his release? The hero in *A Tale of Two Cities* had taken the place of the heroine's husband in prison and faced the guillotine in a noble act of love. He was more selfish. He didn't want to die for Jem. He wanted to live and spend the rest of his life with her.

Logan allowed his horse to drink. An object reflected the light beneath the surface of the water. He plucked a buckle scavengers must have deemed worthless. The land had been picked over by those hoping to make money from death.

A train whistle echoed from Manassas Junction. If Jem wasn't at the depot, should he travel to Richmond?

"What's your name?"

Two Confederate soldiers blocked the bridge. They had their guns aimed in his direction. He turned, but two more men stood behind him, guns pointed. Where had they come from?

"Logan Pierce."

"What are you doing here?"

"I'm on my way to Manassas Junction."

"Not anymore."

A stocky man with a long scar creasing the side of his face and scraggly beard, spat tobacco juice on Logan's boot.

"You shouldn't have spit on his clean boots, Clyde."

"Are you a spy, Logan Pierce?"

How was he going to explain his reason for riding into enemy land? Would they believe a story about his search for a lost woman? What if he endangered Jem by asking about her whereabouts? Logan raised his hands in surrender. "Take me to your commanding officer."

****

Jem didn't know how long she had slept, but light filtered through the curtains. She was in the nursery with the baby, and his fussing had awakened her. The diaper was wet. She removed his wet gown and washed him, keeping his umbilical cord stump dry. She removed a bottle of alcohol from her medical bag and applied it to a clump of cotton. After doctoring the cord, she dressed the baby. He tried suckling at her breast. "No milk there, young man."

She quickly dressed and carried the baby into Reggie's bedroom. Edward had retired to his own room. She couldn't wait to share intimacies with Ben. It was baffling why some married couples had separate bedrooms. The baby proved they had spent at least one night in the same bed.

Reggie's forehead was cool. She opened her eyes. The baby was fussing, sucking on his fist. "My baby."

Jem unfolded the blanket around the baby.

She extended her arms. "Let me hold him."

Jem put the baby on the end of the bed and placed pillows behind Reggie to support her. The baby fussed even in his mother's arms.

"He's hungry."

Reggie untied her gown, exposing a breast. "I want to feed him. Can I?"

"Your color is good. Do you feel strong enough?"

Reggie stroked the whisper of hair on her son's head. "I can do it." For a woman who had been on death's doorway, Reggie's voice was filled with conviction. "I'm his mother. I'm taking care of him."

Jem placed a pillow beneath Reggie's arm to support the baby's weight and placed him in the crook of her arm. He thrashed his head back and forth, seeking a nipple. "Brush his cheek." He turned his head to the touch and latched on.

"He is hungry." Reggie had a look of surprise on her face as her son suckled. "How do I know if he's getting enough?"

"Usually ten minutes on each breast is enough. I have some ointment if your nipples become sore or cracked."

Reggie examined her son. "He's so beautiful."

"What are you doing?" Edward demanded from the doorway. He was dressed in a crisp gray suit and finely embroidered crème vest. "I sent for a wet nurse."

"He's my son. I want to feed him."

Edward strode into the room. "A lady does not debase herself in this primitive manner. Why do you think we have servants?"

"The wet nurse isn't here." Reggie choked back tears. "Do you want your son to starve?"

Edward changed the subject. "I can't believe the difference. You had no strength yesterday."

"I felt I was going to die."

"I wasn't going to let that happen." He looked around the room. "Now that you've had the baby, we can return to Vandalia."

"You can't travel for at least four weeks," Jem warned.

Reggie looked at Edward. "Will it be safe to return to Vandalia? Didn't you say there was trouble with some of the other politicians?"

"If those traitors Carlile and Willey think they can keep me away from my home, they don't know who they're dealing with," Edward said. "The South will win this war, and Virginia won't be split."

Edward and Tyler were still on opposite sides. Vandalia was in the western portion of Virginia. John Carlile and Waitman Willey were the two senators trying to create a new state. Edward wouldn't have a district to represent if they succeeded. He'd be a politician without constituents.

"I'm sure our guest doesn't want to hear about politics." Reggie turned to Jem. "I'm sorry, I don't remember an introduction."

"I'm Tyler Montgomery's sister-in-law, Jennifer Collins."

"What are you doing in Richmond?"

"I'm looking for my husband. He was at Bull Run but wasn't among the wounded in Washington or in Richmond."

"Oh, Edward. You have to help her find him."

"I sent Buck to inquire for any news. He hasn't reported."

"I need to return to Washington before people start to worry about me," Jem said. "I've been gone longer than I anticipated."

"It was providence you were here when I needed you." Reggie studied her son nestled against her breast. "What is your husband's name?"

"Ben Collins." Jem searched her medical bag. "I have a photograph of him." She shared the photograph of Ben and his friends.

"Which one is Ben?"

"In the middle. John Herbruck is on the left. He was wounded in the leg and returned to Ohio. Herman Stratman is a prisoner at the Alms House." She turned to Edward. "Do you know how long he'll be a prisoner?"

Edward shook his head.

"Try to find out, Edward," Reggie urged. "Benjamin. I like that." She traced the soft fold of her baby's ear and studied his face. "Benjamin Edward Vandal." She looked at Edward. "Do you approve?"

He grunted. "I've decided to name him after the president."

"Abraham Lincoln?" Jem realized her mistake when Edward turned red.

"Jefferson Davis is our president," he corrected. "My son will be Jefferson Edward Vandal."

Reggie attempted to remove Jefferson from her breast. "He won't let go."

"Press your little finger on your breast next to his mouth to break the suction."

Jem moved the pillow to the other side, and Reggie moved her baby to the other breast. When she finished nursing, she burped the baby and handed him to Jem, who returned him to the nursery.

Esther arrived with a tray of food. Reggie was hungry and finished everything on her plate. Jem finished her breakfast and washed her hands. She lifted the blankets. "I need to examine you."

"I can feel some bleeding."

The blood on the towel was much less. She pressed on Reggie's abdomen. "Does that hurt?"

She shook her head.

"Are you sure?"

"It doesn't hurt."

"Good. The bleeding has slowed, and you're looking much better."

Reggie struggled to sit. "I could use a bath."

"Not yet." Esther had returned and took the tray of dirty dishes. "I need hot water." Jem turned to Reggie. "You can have a sponge bath."

Reggie looked around. "Where's Edward?"

"He's downstairs having breakfast, Miss Regina."

Esther returned with the hot water and helped bathe

Reggie. Jem combed and braided her hair. "You have beautiful hair."

"It was stringy and dirty when I was a little girl. Did you know I worked in the coal mines?"

"Tyler told us you were lost in the mines when you were about six."

"It was awful. I had nightmares for years," Reggie said. "I had forgotten, but yesterday when I was close to death, I remembered everything. No matter how hard I worked, I couldn't fill my bucket. My pa whipped me when I didn't have a full bucket. So I climbed deeper into a narrow opening to chip away at those layers of coal."

Edward stood in the doorway, listening to Reggie's tale.

"I don't know how long I worked, but when I crawled out, there was no one around. I rushed to find the other miners, and my candle blew out. I didn't know how to light it. I searched, but it was so dark." Reggie lifted her hand. "I could feel the darkness, like a cold mist suffocating me." She shivered.

Jem draped a bed jacket around Reggie's shoulders.

"I listened for voices and called out, but no one answered. I screamed and kept screaming, but nobody came."

"Who found you?"

"I don't remember. One minute I was curled in a ball shivering in the cold and dark. The next I was in a warm bed. I didn't know it at the time, but being lost in the mine was the best thing that could have happened to me."

"What do you mean?" Jem saw Edward enter the

room

"I couldn't go back," Reggie said. "I'd scream if the light blew out at night. I was a horrible coward. I'm still afraid of the dark."

Jem recalled a part of the story. "Tyler said he'd give you candles."

"He was always looking out for me." She looked at Edward. "Like a big brother."

Edward snorted. "I warned your sister not to marry him."

"She didn't listen. They're expecting a baby in two months."

"Write me and let me know what she has." Reggie turned to Edward. "Wouldn't it be sweet if the children could be friends?"

"A Vandal and a Montgomery? That's about as likely as the South rejoining the Union," Edward said.

"More likely the North will beg to join the Confederacy." Buck stood in the doorway.

Reggie paled, and Jem grabbed her wrist to feel her pounding pulse. "What's wrong?"

Reggie didn't answer, her eyes fixed on Buck.

"You're lookin' pretty this mornin', Miss Regina." Buck removed his hat.

"You shouldn't be in my wife's bedroom," Edward said. "Wait downstairs."

"I have news of Mr. Collins."

Jem gasped. "What is it?"

"A man may know what happened, but he leaves on the train to Manassas in fifteen minutes."

Jem looked around for her basket and medical bag.

"You're going with her," Reggie ordered Edward.

"Buck can take her."

"No," she gasped. "You can't leave her alone with strangers." Her eyes rested on Buck before glancing away.

"She reached Richmond alone," Edward said. "I shouldn't leave you."

"Edward, Mrs. Collins saved my life. Promise you'll protect her."

Edward's stony features made no promise.

"Please," she begged. "Don't leave her until she's safe."

Chapter Twenty-Six

Reggie's words were disturbing, especially with Buck leaning against the door frame, staring at them. As a chaser, Buck was willing to do anything for a price, but he had claimed Tess as payment on the trip back to Vandalia. If her cousin hadn't rescued her... Jem shuddered.

Edward ordered his valet to fetch his hat. "Are you ready to leave?"

Jem couldn't find her empty basket to take home.

Reggie reached her hand to Jem. "I'm glad I met you, Mrs. Collins."

Jem hugged her. "I've heard so much about you, I feel like we're old friends. Call me Jenny." She tied her bonnet and gathered her medical bag.

Esther entered with the basket. "I filled it for your trip."

"Thank you." She turned to Reggie. "I'll write. So will Cory."

"The North stopped mail service to the South." Edward kissed Reggie on the forehead.

"But somehow it gets through," Reggie said.

Edward turned to Jem. "Tell Tyler I plan to read those letters."

"Take care of Jefferson," Jem added.

Buck was outside waiting by the carriage. Was it good news or bad news? His expression revealed nothing. Edward opened the door, and she boarded. He sat beside her. Buck sat next to the driver. He kept his back to her.

No one talked until they reached the depot. Jem looked around. "You said a man knows something about Ben, but where is he?"

Buck searched the train and poked his head out a window. "He's on board."

"What does he know?"

"Best you talk to him in person," he said.

Reggie didn't like Buck. Jem agreed with her opinion.

Edward purchased three tickets and followed Jem into the passenger car. Buck pointed to a man seated near the back. The young clean-shaven man had straight brown hair cut in a bowl shape. When he saw them, he stood.

Jem froze. She recognized the coat he wore as her handiwork. It was too big on the man's slender frame. "That's my husband's coat." Tears burned her eyes and choked her throat. Jem had spent months making it. It had to be perfect for Ben.

"This is Private Theo Jameson." Buck returned the photograph of Ben, Herman, and John. "Nobody at the prisons had any news of your husband, but the quartermaster recognized his coat. Theo wore it while he loaded supplies in the stock cars this morning. Looked like a match."

Jem put her belongings on the seat beside Theo and touched the familiar fabric. Theo didn't move. She stroked the velvet lapel. A dark spot stained the chest, and her finger found a hole.

"Is this your husband's coat?" Edward asked.

Jem nodded, choking back tears.

"Where did you find it?" Edward demanded.

"On the battlefield," Theo defended.

The conductor told them to sit. The train was building steam and leaving the station.

Jem sat next to Theo. Clyde and Edward sat in front of them.

"I didn't do nothin' wrong," Theo said. "Soldiers call it spoils of war to take things off the battlefield."

"You're not in trouble, Theo," Jem said. "I want to know about the coat. You said you found it?"

"After we chased the Yankees back to Centreville we gathered prisoners. I saw a man lyin' on the bank of Cub Run."

Jem pointed to Ben in her photograph. "This man?"

Theo stared. "What is that, ma'am?"

"It's a photograph. Haven't you ever seen one?"

"No, ma'am. They all look so real like I could touch them." He pointed at the image of Herman. "This one. He was soaked and bleeding from his head. He moaned, and they hauled him off to join the prisoners."

He moved his finger to Ben. "I found him nearby. His uniform was wet like he'd been in the water. He was face down, and when I turned him over, he was dead." He poked his finger through the hole in the jacket. "Shot in the chest."

"The men were scavengin' the battlefield. Taking guns, haversacks, anything they could find," Theo said. "He was dead, ma'am, and I figured he wouldn't need his coat no more. I didn't have one. Only a cotton shirt. I didn't kill him, ma'am, honest."

Theo had greasy hair and dirty fingernails. His hands hadn't seen soap in weeks. His pants were too short, and his shoes didn't match. But his eyes were steady when he spoke.

"I believe you," Jem said.

I remember the scar on his forehead." He touched the stain on the coat. "He was hit in the front, ma'am. He wasn't running away."

She nodded.

Theo stared at the photograph. "What happened to the other fellas?"

"This one is in prison in Richmond, and this one returned home to Ohio."

"You from Ohio, ma'am."

Jem nodded as she stroked the velvet cuff.

"I'm from Gopher Springs, Virginia." He stared at her hand. "Did you make this coat, ma'am?"

"I made it for my husband as a wedding present. The velvet is from a dress I wore when we first began courting."

Theo removed the coat and offered it. Jem stroked the wool fabric, her hands tracing the dried stain. Her husband's blood. The hole was near his heart. She opened the coat. The stain was larger on the inside. He had bled to death. She found her name embroidered above the inside pocket. Her hands caressed the silk lining, and she discovered a thickness beneath. Her fingers slipped inside the fold she had made and withdrew a packet of letters.

"I found those, but I can't read so I put 'em back, ma'am," Theo said.

Jem recognized her writing on the envelopes. He had saved the letters she had written him the last few months. They were tied in a bundle with one of her hair ribbons. He was always taking something of hers—a hair ribbon, a comb, or little memento. He said he was taking a part of her. Her hand trembled. One letter was apart from the others. The handwriting wasn't hers. Ben had written a letter before the battle but never mailed it. She burst into tears.

"You can keep the jacket, ma'am. I couldn't wear it now knowing who it belonged to."

"But you said the coat is spoils of war," Buck argued.

"Shut up!" Edward ordered.

Jem dried her tears. "I'll see that you have another coat. I'll make you one."

"You don't have to do that, ma'am."

"I want to. I want you to know how much this means to me." She studied him. "Do you prefer a long coat or a shorter one? Some of the men say it's easier to maneuver in the shorter coats."

"What's maneuver?"

"Move."

"I think I'd like a short one. I do a lot of maneuvers."

Jem bit her bottom lip to suppress a smile. "What color should I make it?"

"Most of the fellows are wanting gray like the officers wear."

"With some gold piping?"

"Nothing too fancy, ma'am. I'm a private."

Jem clutched the coat. "I'll send it to Mr. Vandal's home in Richmond. I have the address." Jem studied Edward. "Can you make sure Theo receives it?"

Edward turned to Theo. "Are you stationed at Manassas?"

"Yes, sir."

"I'm not an officer. I'm a politician."

"Ain't they important?"

Jem searched the other pockets. She withdrew a bag of tobacco.

"That's mine, ma'am."

Jem handed him the tobacco and a corncob pipe she found. "My friends call me Miss Jenny."

"Are we friends?"

"I hope so. I wouldn't make a coat for a stranger."

"Why don't we go to the front of the car and share a smoke," Edward suggested. "Would you excuse us, Mrs. Collins?"

He was giving her privacy to grieve. "Thank you."

"I'm real sorry about your husband, Miss Jenny."

"God bless you, Theo."

Jem sat near the window and read Ben's letter. *"Dearest Miss Jenny,"*

The familiar greeting was reassuring.

"Herman, John, and I are waiting to march out of Arlington Heights. A man named Matthew Brady took a photograph of us. John stored the claim check in his Bible where he stores all his valuables. I figure I'll buy a print when we return to Washington City to remember my time in the army. Three months has been a lifetime. I've read your letters so many times, I've memorized every word. When I read your letters to the other men, I realize how lucky I am to call you my wife. I know I don't say the romantic words a man should say to the woman he loves, but I hope you forgive my shortcomings. The column is moving now. We're heading for Richmond and victory."

The writing was shakier on the second page and dated July 20.

"It's evening now, and we're resting before the battle. The coat you made me is covered with dust from the days of marching, but I think of you when I wear it. The other soldiers are envious I have such a talented wife. Tomorrow we meet the enemy, and the war will come to an end. Herman is excited about fighting, but John worries killing will darken his soul. I want to do my duty, but wonder if war is the answer to reuniting the Union. I wrote last time about re-enlisting, but there will be no need once we beat the Rebels and become one nation. I'm coming home as soon as they discharge me. You're never far from my thoughts, Miss Jenny. I believed being part of the victory would make me a great man, but all I want is to love you.

Your devoted husband,
Benjamin."

The tears had begun with the first line, but now she let them flow freely, letting her grief find release. He hadn't read her last letter, didn't know her love had faltered, and had decided to return home without her ultimatum. Ben loved her. She clutched the letter along with the others as the train headed northwest to Manassas Junction.

Ben was dead. She had her answer although it wasn't the one she had hoped for. He had died on the battlefield. He may have saved Herman's life by dragging his unconscious body from the water. The location of the hole in his coat and the amount of blood meant he had died quickly if not instantly. That was small solace. Ben had turned twenty-one last fall. Now he was in an unmarked grave in Virginia.

She was nineteen and a widow. What did that mean? She hadn't entertained the idea Ben could be dead, thinking it would make it real. But hoping he had survived was no longer an option. He had been killed. He was dead. John was wounded, and Herman in prison.

She twisted her handkerchief. All because politicians couldn't do their job. They should have abolished slavery in 1808 when they abolished the international slave trade. Instead they argued over a balance of free and slave states that ultimately tore the country apart.

The war would be long and costly. She had already seen the price paid by Thornton and other men maimed from the weaponry. And how many young men like Ben would die? Their dreams would never come true.

By the time they arrived at Manassas, Jem had cried out her sorrows and subdued her anger. She wiped her face and put the letters back into the inside pocket of Ben's coat. She ate some fruit Esther had packed, but it was tasteless. Edward, Buck, and Theo had left her alone on the train ride to Manassas but joined her on the depot platform.

Jem used the privy and found a pump to wash her face and hands.

Edward checked the schedule. "This train heads west, but a train to Alexandria departs in two hours."

Jem looked around. Camp Pickens had been established to guard the railroad crossing. "How far are we from the battlefield?"

Theo pointed. "North of here."

"Can you show me Ben's grave?"

"We buried the Union soldiers in mass graves."

"Can the caskets be exhumed?" Edward asked.

"We didn't have time to make caskets. Yankees

were in such a hurry to leave, they didn't bother gatherin' their dead. The sun was hot, and the bodies were attracting animals."

Edward put his kerchief to his mouth. "Shut up."

"It was better than letting the bodies rot in the open."

"I said…"

Jem laid her hand on Theo's arm. "Thank you for being honest." She looked toward the road. "What about the bridge? Where is the Cub Run Bridge?"

"I can show you."

Jem hadn't thought to leave her bag or basket at the station. She draped Ben's coat over the top of the basket through the handles.

"Would you like me to carry something?" Theo offered his hand.

She gave him the medical bag, which was heavier. "Thank you."

"Buck, you carry her basket."

Jem pulled away when Buck reached for it. "It's not heavy."

"Suit yourself." He looked around the hilly landscape. "Can't wait to see the battlefield."

Theo led them north along Sudley Road. A rocky bluff was to the left and a clump of trees to the right opened on a ridge facing Warrenton Turnpike. The cornfields to the left were flattened or shredded as if a great storm had passed through the countryside. On a hill to the right a one-story framed house suffered broken windows and missing boards. The fields around it had not been planted, and the exposed dirt was scarred with ruts.

"What is this place?"

"The Henry house." Theo crossed the war-torn property. "Widow Henry was killed during the battle."

Theo paused in front of the house where a mound of dirt marked a grave. "She's buried here."

"How close was the battle?"

The Confederate line was spread across this hill." He pointed at the Warrenton Turnpike below. "That's where the fighting was fierce. Evans, Bee, and Bartow commanded their men in this area."

The names of the Southern generals were unfamiliar. "Did any of these regiments fight at Stone Bridge?"

"Evans was located at the bridge early in the day, but when the Union troops flanked our left side, he moved to engage them."

John said they had seen troops moving away from their position and heard fighting in the distance.

"Stonewall Jackson took position next to them."

"Who?"

"His real name is Thomas Jackson, but he earned the name Stonewall because he wouldn't budge from Henry Hill." Theo said their names with reverence. War made heroes of ordinary men. Was that the reason they risked life and limb in a battle that had claimed so many lives on both sides?

Theo helped Jem descend the steep hillside to Warrenton Turnpike. A two-story brick house marked the intersection. "Both sides used Stone House for a hospital. Lot of shoes and clothing left behind."

A broken shoe lay on the ground, its sole torn from the leather. Caught on a thistle, a piece of blue cloth flapped in the breeze. Jem stepped on a hard object, a fragment of a cannonball shell embedded in the dirt.

The signs of battle littered the tortured landscape. Theo grabbed a discarded bag and shook it. "Empty." He tossed it on the ground. "That's the Robinson House." Theo pointed to a small white house along the road. Ahead was the Stone Bridge.

Jem crossed the bridge and stood near the stream. Ben had fought on this ground. Trampled grass, footprints along the bank, and discarded debris testified of heavy traffic. Men had picked through the abandoned Union property, leaving the worthless items to rust or disintegrate with time.

She closed her eyes and imagined what Ben had seen, heard, and experienced on that Sunday more than a week ago. She was standing next to Theo, the enemy, and yet he seemed no different from Ben, Herman, or John. How did they shoot at each other, knowing death was the result? Some had been friends, some brothers, and now they were enemies. How did it make sense?

Chapter Twenty-Seven

She returned to the road. The bridge crossing Cub Run had been nearly destroyed in the panicked retreat. Mismatched boards had been nailed across the cross supports to fill the gaps. A wagon wheel was stuck in the bank with a few broken boards. Other useless items were scattered along the bank. Panic had made this spot a struggle for escape.

Theo pointed downstream from the bridge. "That's where I found your husband, Miss Jenny."

Jem made her way along the grassy bank to the spot Theo identified and whispered a prayer for Ben.

Theo handed her a clump of wildflowers. The bouquet was an unexpected gesture of kindness. She smiled and thanked him before placing them on the ground.

"We'll leave you alone." Edward and the others stepped away. She could hear them talking about the battle. Why would they want to relive something so awful? Water rushed along the discarded armaments in the stream, a breeze shook the broken branches lining the banks downstream, and she thought of her husband. She gathered more flowers and placed them with the others. She sang a hymn, "Nearer My God to Thee," written by Sarah Francis Adams two years ago. She had sung it in church with her sisters. It had been Ben's favorite.

Jem finished the hymn and bowed her head. A bird echoed her song, and peace filled her heart. Ironic that Ben had died in such a quiet pastoral setting amid a violent battle. She removed the photograph from her pocket. Ben would forever be the young, smiling man captured in an image by Matthew Brady.

Voices drew her attention to the bridge. Three men in gray uniforms were approaching at a fast pace. One was an officer. She joined them.

"This is Colonel Chauncy LaDonte." Theo saluted the officer.

The colonel had a mustache and short beard. He removed his wide-brimmed hat. His hair was dark and matted. His two companions were privates. One was eerily familiar. Buck's brother, Clyde Cassell sported a black eye. She looked at Buck. "Why didn't you join with Clyde?"

"Mr. Vandal pays better."

Clyde studied her. "How do you know me?"

Buck and Clyde were stout, hairy men. Tyler had told her the Cassell brothers had spent their youth working in the coal mines before becoming chasers for Edward's father. When Tess ran away, Edward hired them to hunt her down. They had nearly killed Noah and had threatened to rape Tess. They terrified her, but showing fear was not an option. "We were never formally introduced. I'm Jennifer Collins." She nodded toward the stream. "You could probably find leeches in the water. They would help with your swollen eye."

Edward shuddered. "I hate leeches."

The colonel studied her. "Are you called Jem?"

No one called her Jem but family and one man. "Family does."

"Her husband was killed at the bridge." Theo pointed to her basket. "That's his coat."

The colonel stared at Theo, his face hard and unfriendly. "Did you obtain the supplies?"

He snapped to attention. "Yes, sir. They're at the depot, ready for transport."

"Take them to the quartermaster." He jerked his head at the unknown private. "Go with him."

Theo handed Jem her bag, made a sharp left turn with his mismatched boots, and hurried back to the depot.

Edward extended his hand. "Colonel LaDonte, I'm Representative Edward Vandal. What do you want with Mrs. Collins?"

"Nothing, yet," he said. "How do you know her?"

"She's a midwife." He pointed to the bag in her hand. "She took care of my wife after the birth of my son. We were waiting for the train, and she wanted to see where her husband had died."

Chauncy studied the blue coat draped over the basket. "What regiment was your husband's?"

"He was a volunteer in the 1st Ohio."

"I didn't think the Ohio boys fought in the battle."

"They were in reserve until the retreat. Then they guarded the rear."

"You seem to know a lot about the battle."

"His friends told me what they remembered."

"Friends in Washington?"

The colonel was fishing for information. "Some of them have returned to Ohio. Others are in prison in Richmond."

"Come with me," he ordered, "please."

What did he want with her?

They headed for a military camp on a farm along Warrenton Turnpike outside Centreville. Rows of tents surrounded a log house and several outbuildings. Men stared as she walked past. They were digging ditches, building mounds, and adding logs for fortifications. Did they expect another attack? She stared straight ahead, keeping pace with the colonel.

"Mr. Vandal, I'd like you as a government official to witness a hanging," Chauncy said. "We've caught a spy."

Edward brushed dirt from the lapel of his coat. "I'd be happy to serve in my official capacity."

The colonel stopped walking and turned to Jem. "The spy heard you singing and started shouting, 'Jem.'" He removed something from his coat pocket. "He said you were this woman." He showed her the photograph Davy had taken of her in Brady's studio. Only one man possessed a copy.

Jem's legs trembled too much for her to continue walking. Logan wouldn't have been foolish enough to follow her. He was aware of the dangers. What had Chauncy said? They were going to hang the spy. "What's his name?"

"Logan Pierce."

Everything went dark.

****

When she opened her eyes, Jem was inside a room. The cabin had exposed beams across the ceiling and mud between the cracks in the walls of hewn logs. She sat and a damp cloth fell from her forehead. "What happened?"

"You fainted," Edward said.

She put her feet on the ground but didn't trust

herself to stand. Her collar was open, and the odor of tobacco clung to her dress. Who had carried her into the cabin? She saw Buck grinning. She shuddered. "Logan!" Did they hang him? Was she too late? "What have you done with him?"

The colonel was seated at a desk. Her belongings were in front of him. Chauncy was searching them. "How do you know him?"

Jem crossed the dirt floor on unsteady legs and placed her hand on the desk for support. "Logan is here to help me, Colonel LaDonte," she pleaded. "He's not a spy. I swear it."

Buck spat a stream of tobacco juice on the floor.

"These are my quarters," Chauncy said. "If you have to spit, do it outdoors."

"Inside or out, it's still dirt."

Chauncy turned to Edward. "You should teach your man better manners."

"I hire him for odd jobs," Edward said. "Jobs that don't require manners."

"Then your ill-mannered servant can wait outside."

Buck didn't budge until Edward spoke. "Out."

Chauncy watched Buck exit and turned his attention to Jem. "What do you know about Logan Pierce?"

"He's a civilian, not a soldier." If anything happened to Logan because of her, she wouldn't forgive herself.

"Most spies are civilians."

She collapsed in a wooden chair next to the desk.

"Maybe you should eat something." Items had been removed from her basket. She took a sandwich Esther had made with shredded dried beef and cheese and bit into it. Chauncy had found her collection of photographs inside her medical bag and had spread them on his desk. He showed her the group photo and asked her to identify the three men. "Where are they now?"

"My husband is dead, Herman is a prisoner in Richmond, and John returned to Ohio."

He showed her Logan's photograph. "How do you know this man?"

"He was helping me find my husband."

He lifted Ben's coat. "This was your husband's coat?"

She reached for it. "I made it for him."

She stroked the fabric and rubbed the velvet against her cheek. She hadn't been able to save Ben, but she wasn't going to allow Logan to die. "He's here because of me and because of you." She looked at Edward.

"Me? What did I do?"

"You delayed my return to Washington. Logan worried and crossed lines to find me." She repacked the food in the basket and gathered the photographs. "Please, let me speak with him."

"He fought with my men," Chauncy said. "He's in bad shape."

"If Logan needs medical care, I'm asking you to allow me to see to his needs."

"Aren't you a midwife?"

"My father is a doctor. I've been trained as a nurse."

Chauncy stood. "Bring your bag."

She took the basket with Ben's coat draped over it as well.

Chauncy led them to a smokehouse behind the log cabin. An S was painted below the angled roof. Clyde was guarding the door and banged on the side of the wall. "No trouble, or I'll give you more Southern hospitality."

Nothing prepared Jem for the sight of Logan. His coat was gone, his white linen shirt was stained with blood, his left eye was swollen closed, and his lip was split. He was covered in dust as if he had rolled on the ground, and his blonde hair was matted where he had bled from a cut near the crown of his head. "Logan!"

"Jem!" His outcry was silenced by a punch to the gut from Clyde with the butt of his rifle. Logan collapsed on the ground.

"Stop!" Jem dropped her belongings and blocked Clyde from smashing his gun on Logan's prostrate form. He grabbed her around the waist and lifted her with one arm, pressing her tight against his chest. She struggled to separate her body from his. His foul breath nauseated her as he spoke through tobacco stained teeth. "Been a long time since I had a woman."

Logan struggled to stand. "Leave her alone."

Clyde laughed, yanking Jem closer.

"Put her down, Private Cassell," Chauncy ordered.

Clyde hesitated.

"If you don't obey my order, I'll have you locked in the smokehouse instead," Chauncy warned.

Clyde shoved her.

She stumbled, but Logan caught her. His hands were manacled with a short length of chain connecting them. He stood in front of her to protect her. His shirt was shredded, revealing a swirl of bruises on his body and open cuts from a whip crisscrossing his back. She tugged on a loose strip of his shirt, but it stuck to the fresh wounds. She turned to Clyde. "You beat him? He's not an animal." She looked at the colonel. "Did you order this?"

"Clyde said he was dangerous. Said the prisoner hit him."

"Logan would never attack without provocation." She turned to Clyde. "Clyde Cassell needs no reason to beat, kidnap, or rape."

"He's a Yankee spy," Clyde said. "We're going to hang him from the tree near the railroad so passengers can see his rotting corpse."

"You're wrong!" She examined Logan and stroked his blood-streaked hair back from his face. She had denied her feelings because of Ben, but he had died July 21st on the battlefield. Even though she had discovered she was a widow only a few hours ago, she wanted Logan to be a part of her future. She couldn't lose him. Careful of his wounds, she put her arm around his waist to support his weight and prevent him from collapsing.

Logan squinted his good eye, and his dimples deepened as he attempted a smile. "Hey, I know you."

He was battered and bruised, and the sight of him made her heart quicken until she realized what he had done. She put her hand on her hip. "What are you doing here?"

"What are *you* mad about?" He frowned. "You lied to me. You said you were going home."

She stroked his bruised face. "I didn't want you to follow me. For this reason."

"Did you find Ben?"

"Yes."

His hands dropped, the chain clanging with the weight. "I'm glad."

She looked toward the basket, and his gaze followed.

"Why do you have his coat?"

Jem handed it to him. "He's dead." She waved her hand toward the distance. "He died near the creek below."

Logan examined Ben's coat. "I'm sorry."

Ben was gone. "I said goodbye."

"Is that why you were singing?"

"It was Ben's favorite hymn, 'Nearer My God to Thee.' "

He returned Ben's coat. "Will you sing it at my hanging?"

He accepted his impending death, but like Ben, she hoped for a different outcome and refused to acknowledge his request.

She fisted her hands. "Don't joke about death."

Logan shook the manacles as he waved at the soldiers around them. "These men are serious."

She touched his swollen eye. "I wish you hadn't come."

He rested in the palm of her hand. "I wanted to rescue you."

She stepped away, putting her hands on her hips. "Do I look like a damsel in distress? They think you're a spy. Why do you think I didn't tell you about my trip?"

"I didn't care about the risks. I couldn't live with myself until you were safe. Did Sydney Carton stay out of Paris?"

Jem recognized his reference to *A Tale of Two*

Cities. Sydney had helped Charles Darnay escape from the Bastille by taking his place on the guillotine, the one noble and daring act of his self-indulgent life. "You're noble like Sydney Carton, and I'm going to rescue you."

"Save yourself," he groaned.

Jem turned to Edward. "I'm not leaving without my friend."

"You can take him back in a box," Clyde said.

Jem gasped. "He isn't a spy. He's a hard working secretary in the department of the treasury."

Logan groaned. "Jem, darling, you told them more in one sentence than I've uttered all day under torture and threat of death."

"It's not like you work for the secretary of defense." She turned to Chauncy. "He isn't here to uncover military secrets. He's here to rescue me." She turned to Edward. "You promised Reggie you'd keep me safe. That includes Logan."

"I'm not responsible for anyone, not even you."

"But you gave your word."

"The train to Alexandria leaves in an hour. Whether you board it or not, I plan to return to Richmond."

"But I can't leave Logan." She led him to a wooden bench under a tree.

"That's your choice, but I fulfilled my obligation," Edward said. "I don't like leaving Regina alone at night. Don't you remember? She's afraid of the dark."

Reggie had good reason to be afraid with Buck in his employ. "Can't you use your influence to free Logan before you leave?"

Edward looked at Chauncy. "Where's your

commanding officer?"

"General Early is in Richmond reporting on the progress of the barricades around Centreville and Manassas."

"Does he know about your prisoner?"

Chauncy hesitated, measuring his words. "Not yet. I'm in charge until he returns."

"Then you don't want to make a mistake." He nodded toward Jem. "Let her tend his wounds."

"It's a waste of time."

"It's her time."

Chauncy slapped his hat against his thigh. "He hangs at dawn."

"Then let him spend his last hours with the woman he loves."

Jem looked at Logan. He loved her. What other explanation was there for his foolhardy rescue. And unfortunately she loved him, a man condemned to die.

Chauncy carried her belongings to a shade tree. "Do you need anything?"

Where to start? "Leeches for his eye." She removed an empty jar from her bag.

"Fetch some leeches from the creek," Edward ordered Buck.

Clyde snickered.

"I wouldn't want to deprive him of the experience," Buck said. "Maybe you should put some on Clyde."

He sneered at Jem. "I'd like to see you try."

Chapter Twenty-Eight

After his brother left, Clyde moved to the shadows of the smokehouse where he leaned his rifle against a wall. He removed his Bowie knife from his boot and whittled on a stick, watching Logan from a distance.

Jem removed a towel and alcohol from her bag. "This is going to burn." His shirt was stuck to the wounds. "I can't remove his shirt with these chains on him."

Chauncy turned to Clyde. "Remove the manacles."

"He'll escape."

"He's not going anywhere as long as she's here," Edward said. "And if he is stupid enough to run, treat him like one of my slaves and shoot to wound. We don't want him to miss his hanging."

Chauncy stared at Edward. "How many slaves do you own?"

"Had a dozen at one time. A couple escaped." He looked at Jem. "Abolitionists helped them get away from Buck and Clyde."

She had witnessed Edward's fragile love for Reggie, but his hate for Tyler and her family hadn't waned. He didn't care what happened to her once he left. His hands were clean of any responsibility.

Clyde swaggered toward them, the key ring in one hand and his knife in the other. He threw his knife at Logan. The blade struck the tree inches above his head.

He wrestled it free as he leaned in close, but Jem heard his words. "I'll keep your pretty widow friend company after you're dangling from a rope." He turned and grinned. "We're old acquaintances."

He unlocked the manacles, and Logan rubbed his wrist. He cocked his head as he looked at Jem. "How do you know my friend, Clyde?"

"We met last summer along with his brother, Buck."

"You reunited the Cassell brothers?" Logan squinted. "You didn't think one of them was challenge enough for me? You had to invite his brother for a visit?"

A lesser man would have been defeated by the challenge, but Logan's deep dimples meant his spirits were revived. "I wouldn't want to deprive you of their charming company."

Logan looked toward Edward. "Who's the fellow in the fancy suit?"

"Edward Vandal."

Logan's jaw dropped. "Did you invite everyone to the party?"

Jem shook her head. "You were not invited."

"But I'm the guest of honor."

"Maybe that's why they insisted upon meeting you." She looked around. "I'll need some clean water to wash his wounds. Do you have a pump or spring nearby?"

The colonel waved toward the cabin. "In the yard."

Edward pointed at a wooden bucket. "Fetch some water for Mrs. Collins."

"I don't work for you anymore," Clyde said.

"You work for me, though," Chauncy said. "Fetch

it."

Clyde grumbled.

"In this army, a private says yes sir when he's given an order," Chauncy said.

Clyde saluted the colonel, but the exaggerated gesture bordered on insolence.

"I hope you can control him," Logan said to Chauncy.

"We had to take away his bayonet."

Logan grimaced. "This is the man you leave in charge of prisoners?"

"Brutes get results."

"We murdered the natives for their land, we enslaved the blacks for labor, and we torture the enemy for naught. What's happened to our moral compass?"

"You're the moral compass like your brother before you." Jem carefully removed his arms from his tattered sleeves.

When Clyde returned, she took the bucket from him and examined it.

"I didn't spit in it," he said. "Wish I had."

She carried the bucket to Logan, who splashed water on his face and drank from his cupped hands. He touched the wound on his head.

"I'll take care of it after your back." Jem used the water to ease the fabric of his torn shirt off the stripes of opened flesh. "Is this your handiwork, Clyde?"

He grinned for a response. "I used a riding crop. If I had a proper whip, he wouldn't have any flesh left on his back."

"You always did enjoy your work." Edward turned from Clyde to the colonel. "Did he talk?"

"No," Chauncy said. "But the motive wasn't for

information. It was for inflicting punishment. Battlefields aren't tourists' attractions."

"And men claim they're civilized." Jem focused on easing Logan's pain. She cleaned the whip marks and trimmed the flayed flesh. Each snip produced a shudder, but Logan remained statuesque, biting back any outcry as she worked to mend the damage to his back. Finally, she applied salve over each stripe, tracing each one with her finger. She counted six strokes cutting open the skin. Others had left ugly welts.

Buck returned with the jar. Floating inside muddy water were several leeches. "Ugly creatures."

Jem hooked a leech with a bent fork. "Close your eyes and tilt your head back." She placed it on his cheek near his eye where the swelling was worst. "Don't move."

The colonel groaned and turned away.

"What did you put on my face?" Logan raised his fingers.

Jem grabbed his hand. "Don't touch."

"It feels like something is crawling on my skin."

The leech swelled, its body pulsing as it withdrew blood. "It won't hurt."

He stiffened. "What won't hurt?"

Full, the leech fell off. Jem scooped it into the jar and chose a smaller leech to continue the draining of excess blood from the bruise.

"I think I can open my eye," Logan said.

"Keep it closed."

"Hey, something is on my face."

Jem rubbed salt on the leech to release it before Logan could smash the blood-filled parasite. Logan opened both eyes. He stared at the jar. "What's in there?"

"Leeches."

He pointed at the colonel and Edward. "Are you on their side?"

She examined his eye. "It reduced the swelling." She opened the picnic basket. "Are you hungry?"

Clyde slammed the lid. "You're not going to feed him."

"Even a condemned man has a right to a last meal," Logan reminded him.

"Eat, drink, and enjoy your final night together," Chauncy said. "Tomorrow at dawn, he hangs."

Jem unwrapped a sandwich and handed it to Logan. Her hand shook.

He clasped her fingers. "I won't eat unless you join me."

She bowed her head so he wouldn't see the tears beading on her lower lids. "I can't."

"Take a bite, for me." He tempted her with a peach.

Her teeth nipped his fingertips. She laughed when he examined his fingers.

His dimples showed. "It's good to see you smiling."

She sat next to him on the bench. "What good can come of this?"

He handed her a muffin. "I understand now why Derek risked his reputation and his life to be with Hannah. His life meant nothing without her."

"What meaning will my life have without you?" She turned away. The colonel was watching them. She offered the muffin.

He took it. "Thank you."

A train whistle echoed nearby. The train to

Alexandria. She'd missed her ride.

Chauncy took a bite. "Are you staying the night?"

She put her arm in Logan's. "I won't leave."

Logan leaned toward her. "You need to escape."

"I'm not the one they want to hang."

"I'm not afraid of dying." He nodded toward Clyde. "It's the sadist who wants to prolong my suffering I fear. I can't protect you after tomorrow."

"I'll be on the morning train."

Theo had returned and was making coffee. Jem joined him by the fire and offered a slice of pie.

"Thank you, ma'am."

"Where's mine?" Clyde stepped forward. He and Buck had been lurking in the shadows.

"Theo gave me news of my husband. I'm showing my appreciation."

Clyde spat on the ground. "How fortunate he's dead."

"What an awful thing to say." She turned away.

Clyde overtook her. "Would you want him to know of your adultery?"

Jem turned, jabbing her finger in his face. "Mr. Pierce is my friend. Unlike you, he knows how to behave like a gentleman."

"And like a gentleman, he'll only dream of you tonight." He jabbed Buck with his elbow. "We're men of action."

Buck stripped her with his eyes, the way he had undressed Reggie. It made her flesh crawl. The Cassell brothers respected no woman, slave or free. She hurried to Logan's side. She didn't want him to know how upset they had made her and carefully cleaned and packed the dishes and towel in the basket. She folded

Ben's coat and placed it on the lid.

Logan touched the velvet sleeve. "How did you find Ben's coat?"

"I was outside the prison after visiting with Herman."

"Herman?" Logan interrupted. "How was he?"

"Better than expected. I made him write his mother."

"You were outside," he prompted.

"Edward was looking for a midwife for Reggie. I saved her life, but his gratitude is limited. He ordered Buck to show Ben's photograph around at the other prison, and someone recognized the coat. We traveled to Manassas on the train with Theo, who showed me the place near the creek where he found Ben."

"I heard you singing."

"You recognized my voice?"

"You have the most beautiful voice I've ever heard," he said. "I wondered if I had gone crazy. I started screaming your name."

"When the colonel asked me if my name was Jem, I had an awful feeling you had followed me." She twisted her handkerchief. "How can I lose you and Ben? It isn't fair."

Theo offered her a cup of coffee. She sipped the bitter brew.

"Mrs. Collins told me how you found her husband's coat," Logan said.

"He was near the Cub Run Bridge on the battlefield," Theo said. "I didn't shoot him, but he was dead and didn't need his coat no more so I took it."

Logan nodded. "It was kind of you to return the coat."

"Miss Jenny promised to make me a new coat."

"Miss Jenny." Logan shook his head, and his dimples deepened. "Does every man who meets you, adore you?"

She tilted her chin. "Unlike you, I know how to make friends."

"Don't you know? Children love me."

Jem gasped. "What are you going to do about Deidre?"

****

Logan had forgotten his promise. Who would take care of a little girl? He'd made a solemn pledge to Hannah and in a way, to Derek. After his hanging, Deidre would be the last family member left in the world. He met Jem's gaze. "I couldn't ask you to take on such a huge responsibility."

"I have Ben's coat and letters to remember him. I would be honored to have your niece to raise as my child to remember you."

Logan caressed her cheek. "I should have stayed in Washington and waited for your return, but any logic was lost by my madness your absence inflicted upon me." He glanced at the soldiers surrounding them. "Thank you for taking care of Deidre." His lips brushed her cheek and sought her lips.

She shared his passion, refusing to retreat and returned for one more taste of his lips. When they parted, the deal was sealed for eternity. Deidre was their child.

"Good man," he called to Theo. "Do you have pen and paper? I need to make a will."

"I know the colonel has some." Theo waited as Logan struggled to stand.

Jem was staring at his bare chest. "I'm much better."

She blushed. Was she thinking about something other than his health?

He placed her arm around his waist. "But I could use your help."

Clyde and Buck approached. "Where are you going?"

He didn't trust the two men. As long as he was alive, he would protect Jem from them, but who would protect her after his hanging? "Colonel's cabin. Do you want to join us?"

Theo led the way to the cabin. After knocking, they entered. Clyde and Buck loitered outside.

Chauncy and Edward were having a lively discussion while they puffed on cigars. Chauncy stood.

"I would like to make a will." Logan held a chair for Jem.

Chauncy stared at Logan's back and turned to Theo. "Weren't there shirts in the supplies from Richmond?"

"Yes, sir." Theo saluted.

"Fetch one for Mr. Pierce." He turned to Logan. "Sit."

Every muscle ached as Logan lowered his bruised body onto the chair.

Chauncy searched his desk for paper. "You need a will? Are you a man of wealth?"

"No. I recently agreed to be guardian of my niece. My brother is dead, and the child's mother is dying. She'll have no one to care for her after you hang me."

Jem gripped his arm.

"I want to name Mrs. Collins as her guardian in my

will. It needs to stand any challenge in court. I'll need it witnessed."

"Nobody knows us," Chauncy said.

He looked at Edward. "Your signature is known by Tyler Montgomery. He'll vouch for it."

The colonel turned to Edward. "Who's Tyler Mongtomery?"

"A lawyer and Mrs. Collins brother-in-law. Tyler lived in Vandalia, the town my grandfather founded. He's arrogant and sneaky, but he'll make sure the will is executed."

Logan didn't agree with his assessment of Tyler but was grateful. "Thank you."

"My wife reminded me that Tyler was kind to her when she was a frightened child. I don't want to be indebted."

Chauncy gave Logan paper, a quill, and an ink well. Logan carefully wrote his will.

"You have beautiful penmanship for a Northerner," Chauncy said.

He looked at Jem. "You know I'm a secretary. My penmanship is required to be legible."

"Does Mr. Chase know you're here?"

"He believes I have a short-term illness, which will make it difficult to explain my death."

"You lied to him?"

"It doesn't matter. He'll find another secretary to take my place."

Chauncy signed his name to Logan's will. Edward did the same. Logan folded the signed document and presented it to Jem.

Edward checked his watch. "It's time for the train to Richmond."

Chapter Twenty-Nine

After knocking, Theo entered. "I found a shirt."

Logan stood, and Jem helped him dress. He groaned as he slipped his arms into the sleeves.

"You're lucky," Edward said. "Clyde usually doesn't leave much flesh on a man's back."

"How can you employ animals like the Cassell brothers?"

"They do the ugly tasks civilized men don't dirty their hands with," Edward said. "Your back will heal."

Logan raised his bruised wrists. "If I wasn't sympathetic to freeing the slaves before, I am now. Lincoln said every man who supports slavery should wear manacles. He should feel the sting of a whip, too. If that doesn't convince him, nothing will."

"Slavery serves a purpose."

"It's outdated and overdue for abolishment."

Edward put on his hat. "The Confederacy thinks otherwise."

"If you don't believe in the Union, why form another? Shouldn't Virginia stand alone and defend its state's rights? And is this the way to treat a visitor to your country?"

"Are you only a visitor?"

"I made no plans to remain." He exposed the lining of his pockets. "No money."

Jem helped Logan hitch his suspenders over his

shoulders and back. "Didn't you wear a coat?"

"Clyde took it with my hat."

They crossed an open area to the tree where Jem placed the will in her bag next to the photographs.

The Cassell brothers were sharing a bottle of whiskey. Edward signaled Buck to approach. "We're leaving."

"I ain't goin'," Buck said. "Me and Clyde decided to fight the Yankees together."

Edward showed no signs of regret. "I don't own you. Goodbye and good luck."

"I didn't like working for him anyway," Buck said as soon as Edward had disappeared from sight. "But I sure did *like* his wife."

Jem met his gaze. He grinned. She knew what he meant and understood why Reggie had been afraid of him.

The colonel pointed at Buck. "Are you enlisting?"

Buck stepped forward and saluted in an exaggerated manner like his brother's earlier disrespectful example. "Yes, sir."

"Follow me." Buck went into the cabin, and both exited a few minutes later. "Clyde, do you have Mr. Pierce's hat and coat?"

Clyde smiled, his teeth black from tobacco juice. "He need them for the hangin'?"

"I like to be well dressed for public appearances." Logan smiled at Clyde's angry reaction.

"I want to examine his clothing," Chauncy said.

Clyde stooped to enter a tent near the smokehouse and returned with the garments. The wool coat was ripped and dirty. The wide-brimmed hat was dust covered but in one piece. The colonel searched the coat pockets and found them empty. He examined the hat but gave them back to Clyde.

"Those are mine," Logan protested.

"They're spoils of war," Clyde said.

"Then that fancy coat belongs to Theo." Buck reached for the coat on the basket.

Jem snatched it. "I promised to make Theo another coat."

Clyde spat at her feet. "How will you know what size to make it?"

"Put on the coat, Theo." Jem held the coat by the shoulders.

He backed away. "I gave it to ya."

"I want to measure you." Theo turned and slipped his arms into the sleeves.

"Show Private Cassell to the quartermaster to obtain his supplies," Chauncy ordered Clyde.

Buck hesitated, and Clyde tugged on his sleeve. "Orders."

"I'm going to have trouble with those two," Chauncy muttered as he poured a cup of coffee.

Jem removed a cloth tape from her medical bag used for measuring babies. She placed it against the sleeve and wrote how many inches to subtract in her notebook. She measured the length from his shoulder to his waist and recorded the number. "You can take it off."

The letters in the inside pocket fell out as Theo turned the coat over his arm.

Logan retrieved them. "What are these?"

"Letters I wrote Ben." She took them and headed for their spot beneath the shade tree.

****

Logan joined her. "Sid said Ben read these to the other men in the 1st Ohio."

She nodded. "They found them amusing."

"Would you mind reading them to me?"

Her blue eyes widened. "Why?"

"We don't have much time left together, and I would like to spend the last hours learning as much as I can about you." It was the truth. He also wanted to take her mind off his impending death.

Hot tears cascaded on her cheeks.

He put his arm around her. "Don't cry." He brushed a few strands of hair back from her face. "Your hair is like fire when sunlight touches it."

"I forgot to put my scarf on this morning, and it's a mess." She searched for her brush in her bag. After removing several tortoiseshell combs, the chignon at the base of her neck tumbled free. She removed the rubber bands holding her braids and ran her fingers through the woven strands to separate them and remove the ribbons.

Logan couldn't resist touching the wave of fiery curls and wrapped a section around his hand. "Your hair is soft like I imagined."

She brushed, starting at the bottom and working upward. "I need to braid it."

He stroked a length along her back. "I like it this way."

"It will be a tangled mess in the morning if I leave it free flowing." She braided her hair in a single loose braid, leaving several inches free below the rubber band. She tied a ribbon around the band.

Logan chuckled. "You're such a girl."

"Because I like ribbons in my hair?"

"Ribbons, braids, pretty dresses, and musical laughter. I could spend a lifetime enjoying your feminine ways." His lifetime was tonight.

Jem turned away, sorting through the letters. Tears splashed on the top envelope. He pulled her against his chest. "I'm an insensitive clod."

She leaned against his chest.

Even if their behavior was scandalous, the closeness of her resting in his arms was too precious to worry about rules of society. He rested his cheek against hers and played with the curls at the end of her braid.

She opened the first letter and cleared her throat.

Theo squatted nearby. "Do you mind if I listen?"

"If you become bored, I won't be offended if you leave." She smiled at Theo before reading the words she had penned. "Dear Ben."

By the time she had read through the first letter, other soldiers had gathered, some conspicuously close. Chauncy sat in a canvas chair under the neighboring tree. Buck and Clyde had returned, lingering in the shadows of the smokehouse. They posed no threat but didn't join in as the soldiers laughed when Jem described the antics of her sisters.

"Colleen and Jessica nearly caused a riot in Akron yesterday. A man was in town bragging about what an expert marksman he was and challenged any shooter to compete for a five dollar gold piece. Naturally, Jessica wanted to compete. You know how she loves to win. She paid ten cents for the competition and waited her turn. The man was good. He beat everyone until Jessica shot. She hit all the marks, and he missed one. He said a man had sneezed and wasn't going to pay the prize money to

325

a little girl. Colleen said he better pay, or they would tie him to the back of the Irish Rose and drag him to Cleveland."

"What's the Irish Rose?" Theo interrupted.

"It's a canal boat my grandfather owns. My sisters work on it."

"Do you have any brothers?" Theo asked.

"My father prefers girls."

Theo made a whooping noise. "Is he crazy?"

"No, he's a doctor. Dr. Sterling—"

Logan squeezed her arm to prevent her from revealing the Beecher name. She met his gaze. She had almost stumbled again. Her ties to the abolitionist's family could turn this crowd against her.

"Thank you," she whispered.

"Let's hear more from your letter," Logan urged. "Your sisters are amusing."

"Do you know them?" Theo asked.

"Only two of them," Logan said.

They forgot they were surrounded by Confederate soldiers as Jem read the next letter. Her voice was animated and elicited laughter at the antics she described. She was winning the enemy with words describing home and family. These men were no different from the soldiers in the Union. Yet, they had killed each other on the nearby battlefield, and in the morning, they would hang him. He wasn't afraid of dying. As a mortal, he couldn't fight God's plans. He trusted God's outcome was for the best. Yet he prayed Jem would be safe and think of him a little after he was gone.

Dusk made it difficult to see the print on the page, but Jem finished the last letter a little after the lanterns were lit. She folded it and returned it to the envelope. She gathered the letters, tied them with a ribbon, and placed them in her medical bag. She yawned.

"A bed is inside." Chauncey nodded toward the cabin. "I can sleep under a tent."

"I want to stay here," Jem confided to Logan. "I'll feel safer with you."

Logan agreed. "We could use a couple of blankets."

Theo left to fetch them. The other soldiers departed to their tents. Clyde saluted, and Buck joined him in his tent near the smokehouse.

Logan couldn't see the two men hidden behind canvas, but the odor of tobacco, an expensive brand Edward smoked, drifted from the tent. They were watching and waiting. "How well do you know Buck and Clyde?"

"They planned to rape Tess when she was a captive," Jem said. "My cousin Jake and his friends rescued her."

"Rape?" They were more dangerous than he had thought.

"Once I'm on the train, I'll be safe."

"When does the train leave?"

"Around sunrise." She grabbed his hand. "I wish you were going with me."

"Jem, darling, so do I."

Theo delivered blankets for them and made his bed nearby. He was chaperone and guardian.

Logan arranged the blanket over Jem's shoulder as she snuggled against him. Death was worth these precious moments with her close by his side. She relaxed in his arms, and he listened to her steady breathing. He remained awake on guard. Tomorrow he would begin his eternal rest.

The colonel wandered to the fire. Theo stood, ready to do the colonel's bidding. "At ease." Chauncy poured a cup of coffee.

"Hang me after she's on the train," Logan said. "Don't let her witness my death."

"Why do her feelings mean so much to you?" Chauncy asked. "She's not your wife. She's only recently discovered she was a widow."

"I don't want to subject her to any more grief than she's already suffered."

"She must care a great deal for you or you wouldn't be concerned about her reaction to your death."

"I don't know how deep her feelings are toward me. But I wish to spare her the horror of my gruesome death. Certainly, you can understand my concern."

"We would all like to spare Mrs. Collins further pain." He studied her sleeping form. "Are you in love with her?"

"Did I tell you how we met? She attempted to run me over in the street with her buggy?"

"That doesn't answer my question."

"She constantly tumbles out of any carriage. She's a disaster waiting to happen."

"But you risked your life to secure her safety."

"She makes lists. She organizes work crews. She had me emptying chamber pots. Why would I want to spend the rest of my life with a woman who thinks I'm a chambermaid?"

A smile crept across the colonel's mouth. "Because you're in love with her."

He loved her, but it would be cruel to declare it. "That's my misfortune and my secret."

"You understand I have to do my duty," Chauncy said.

"You're in charge. You make the rules."

"That I do." He headed for the cabin.

****

Jem nestled closer to Logan's hard chest. Was it morning? She opened her eyes. The embers of the fire were barely discernable in the darkness. What had awakened her?

Logan had fallen asleep. His steady breathing rose and fell beneath her. How long had he been sleeping? A twig snapped, and from the shadows, the thick figures of Clyde and Buck emerged. She screamed.

Logan bolted, but Clyde jumped on him, pinning him to the ground.

Buck grabbed Jem, his hairy hand clamped over her mouth to silence her.

Theo stirred from his blanket. "What's going on?"

"Now that I'm a soldier, I'm collecting the spoils of war," Buck said. His bitter breath was inches from her face. His hand caressed her breast.

It was small comfort he touched more corset than flesh. His intentions were clear. Jem struggled to retrieve the knife in her skirt pocket.

"Let her go!" Theo was alerting the camp. He attacked Buck, pulling on his arm to free Jem. Buck threw an elbow into his midsection and knocked him to the ground like a sack of grain, the air swooshing out of his lungs from the impact. But Theo had created enough of a distraction for Jem to retrieve her blade. Buck had kept one hand over her mouth, squeezing her cheeks in

329

a dirty vise. She slashed the back of his hand, cutting deep enough to sever an artery. Blood squirted from the wound.

He howled, releasing her, but as soon as she screamed, he backhanded her with his other hand.

Her head reeled from the impact, and she stumbled. Buck shoved her and, dazed, she fell. He stuck his boot on her butt, pinning her to the ground.

"Let her go! Miss Jenny is a lady." Theo tugged on Buck, who was three times his size.

He hurled Theo through the air and knelt, shoving his knee into the small of Jem's back. Buck leaned close to her face. "Miss Regina is a lady. Once Edward filled her belly, he wouldn't touch her. Seemed like a waste not to use a woman for the purpose she was made for. She screamed at first, begging me not to hurt her baby, but then she'd lay there, shaking and whimpering. I liked it better when she fought back."

Poor Reggie. "Edward allowed you to violate his wife?"

He exposed rotting, black teeth. "He don't know, and ladies never tell."

From her low vantage point, she saw Logan and Clyde rolling on the ground, unable to determine who had the advantage. Theo was pounding on the cabin door, calling the colonel's name. Jem tightened her fingers on the knife in her hand, but it was useless in her position.

Buck yanked her head back by her braid and showed her his Bowie knife. His hand was wrapped in a dirty kerchief soaked with blood. "You think you can win a knife fight with me?" His weight was gone. She turned her head. He had switched the knife to his uninjured hand and was straddling her.

"A little help here!" Clyde called as Logan pinned him to the ground. He had Clyde's knife.

Buck was distracted. She slashed her knife between Buck's legs above her, guessing where she could do the most damage. He howled, falling to his knees beside her.

She rolled away and dashed for the colonel's cabin. He was answering Theo's pounding and caught her as she collided against him.

"What the hell is going on here?" Chauncy strode to the fire. Logan released Clyde and handed the knife to the colonel, handle first. Buck was curled in a fetal position, his hands between his thighs.

"They attacked Miss Jenny," Theo said.

"We was the ones attacked." Clyde went to Buck's side. "What's wrong, brother?"

Logan put his arm around Jem's shaking shoulders. "Are you all right?"

She melted against him. "Buck assaulted Reggie."

"Edward's wife?"

Jem nodded, a shudder convulsing her body.

Chauncy touched her shoulder where the sleeve was torn. "Mr. Vandal know about it?"

"I don't think so." He couldn't be *that* evil. "Edward is too proud to allow an insult to his wife, and therefore, to him."

Clyde turned to Jem. "What did you do to my brother?"

She raised the bloody knife in her hand. "I cut him. Maybe I can stitch the cut, or maybe it's gangrenous. I might have to cut more."

"She's crazy!" Buck reached for Clyde. "Don't let

her near me."

"I thought she was insane when I first met her," Logan said, his dimples deep. "Better have a doctor repair the damage."

"Take him to the surgeon," Chauncy ordered.

"What about him?" Clyde pointed at Logan. "He attacked me."

"With your knife." Chauncy threw the Bowie knife at Clyde, embedding it in the ground at his feet. "Since you like rising before dawn, you can dig the grave for Mr. Pierce."

Clyde smiled at Logan. "My pleasure." He helped Buck to his feet. He was bent over, his hands remaining on his crotch. "Your bandage is dripping blood. We better find that doctor."

Through narrowed slits, Buck looked at Jem. "Bitch."

She had hit her mark. Reggie wouldn't have to be afraid of the dark anymore."

Chapter Thirty

Theo served breakfast of scrambled eggs and slightly burnt biscuits as the sun rose. Jem didn't have much appetite so Logan finished hers.

The colonel joined them. "Let's finish this unfortunate business. The train to Alexandria will be at the Union Mill junction soon. We want to give them something to stare at besides the scenery."

Jem sobbed. "How can you be so heartless?"

Logan put his arm around her and squeezed. "Hush. He's doing his job."

"But you're not a spy."

"In spite of the risk, I had to find you." Logan displayed his dimples. *"It is a far, far better thing that I do, than I have ever done; it is a far, far better rest that I go to than I have ever known."*

Jem pounded on his chest. "Don't you dare quote Dickens!"

The colonel frowned. "You've read *A Tale of Two Cities*?"

Logan gathered Jem's medical bag. "She didn't like it."

"At least the husband lived." Jem faced the colonel. "I have nothing because of you."

His expression softened. "You remind me of my wife."

"Would she be proud of you for hanging an

333

innocent man?"

"I don't know. She died a month ago." Chauncy appeared older, beaten. "She was alone."

"I'm sorry." Jem reached for him but didn't touch him. "I had my family after Ben left for war. It's awful to be alone."

"I agree." He signaled for Theo to drive the wagon toward them. In the back along one side was a plain wooden casket. Chauncy placed Jem's basket with Ben's coat in the back of the wagon. Logan added the medical bag and helped her climb aboard. On the bed was a length of rope. "I hope it's a new rope."

Jem burst into tears.

Chauncy joined Theo on the driver's bench. "You need to work on your comforting skills, young man."

"You promised to sing my favorite hymn. I'd like to hear it." Logan sat on the casket.

She waved her arms. "Get up!"

He patted the lid. "It's empty."

She hesitated but joined him. She placed her cape and bonnet beside her. He held her in his arms, and she began the song "Nearer My God to Thee," choking on the chorus. She had reached the second verse when they arrived at the hanging tree.

Theo halted the wagon under an outstretched limb, and they stood. The depot was visible nearby. Passengers would have a clear view of Logan's body swinging in the morning sun. The colonel ordered Theo to tie a hangman's noose. He tossed it over the branch and secured the other end to the tree trunk.

The noose swung back and forth in front of Logan's face. Jem stood beside him, clutching his hand, staring at the circle of death.

Chauncy turned to Logan. "Are you going to tell me the truth, or do I hang you in front of Mrs. Collins?"

"If you're a decent man, you'll take her away from here." He turned to Theo. "Take her to the depot." A train whistle sounded in the distance.

"I'm not leaving you." She threw her arms around his neck, locking their bodies together as one.

They hadn't tied Logan's hands yet, and he caressed her bruised cheek. "If you only knew how much I love you. How much I could have loved you given the time. Remember me fondly."

She kissed him. This was the last memory she would have of him. His lips upon hers, his arms around her in a final gesture of love. She loved him. She didn't measure the quality or quantity against her love for Ben. She loved them both and would have to bear double the grief.

It was an eternity before his arms released her. Jem's bruised lips trembled as Logan gazed into her eyes, his hand gently swiping a tear from her cheek. "What am I to do without you?"

His hands rested on her shoulders. "Promise me you'll live a full life. Live it for Ben. Live it for me. Don't you dare wear widow's garb for long. I'll haunt you if you do."

"But I love you."

"I love you, but fate has other plans for us." The noose swung above them, and Logan kissed her for the last time. He pushed her away. "Now join Theo. It'll be easier on me if you leave with him."

She wrapped her arms around his waist. "Then suffer like I'm suffering. I won't go."

"Get them out of here," Chauncy ordered.

Theo smacked the reins on the horses, and the wagon rolled forward. Jem and Logan clutched the sides of the wagon to keep from falling. "What's going on?"

"We took your husband in battle," Chauncy said. "I won't kill the man you love. He's no spy, but don't come back to Virginia. I may not be in as forgiving a mood."

"What about a body?" Logan stomped on the lid of the coffin. "Won't Clyde know it's empty?"

"Take a look."

Logan lifted the lid, inhaled, and dropped it. He turned to Chauncy and pointed at the casket. "There's a dead man inside."

"Died yesterday of battle injuries."

"What if Clyde peeks?"

"Grab that hammer and bag under the seat." Chauncy pointed below him. "After digging a hole, he'll be too tired to pull nails from a coffin."

Theo stopped the wagon at the station and helped Jem down. He carried her bags to the depot. Logan finished nailing the coffin tight and joined them.

Jem hugged Chauncy. "Thank you, sir." She hugged Theo. "I'll send your coat care of the colonel. I don't trust Edward's promise to deliver it."

Chauncy handed Logan two tickets and passes to cross the picket line.

Logan extended his hand to Chauncy. "Thank you for not hanging me."

"War doesn't mean we abandon all acts of decency. Take care of her."

****

Logan and Jem rode the train in silence to

Alexandria, huddled in the back seat to escape any scrutiny by other passengers. They were a pitiful pair. Clyde had inflicted fresh bruises on Logan's face, and his new shirt was dirty and torn at the sleeve. She had worn the same dress for four days, and it was torn and smeared with bloodstains, none of her own. Her corset was uncomfortable, and Buck had bent the wires in her crinoline when he had stomped on her butt. She was bruised, tired, and hungry. Logan had eaten everything Esther had packed. She wished she had eaten more breakfast.

"We're almost in Alexandria." Logan clutched her hand. He didn't let go until the train released its last puff of steam and the conductors placed wooden blocks for the passengers to disembark at the depot. He retrieved the medical bag, basket, and Ben's coat from the floor where Jem had hid them with her skirt.

Union soldiers barely noticed the weary couple. Jem used the outhouse and washed her hands and face. They looked at the long road to Washington City. "I don't think I can make it."

Logan searched his pockets, but as before, they were empty.

Reaching beneath her corset cover, Jem removed a dollar. "Let's ride."

He helped her into the carriage and slowly climbed in after. "Is there an illness causing bruises?"

"Why?"

"I wrote Mr. Chase I had become ill after interviewing soldiers to explain my absence. I may be unemployed when he sees me."

"I'll tell him how you charmed Colonel LaDonte out of a hangman's noose, and he won't dare reprimand

337

you."

"I wish he would fire me."

Jem gripped his chin. He needed a shave. "Why?"

"As long as I work for Mr. Chase, I have to stay here. Washington City is a long way from Ohio."

Since he would remain alive, Jem had to be practical. "We can't see each other. I'm a widow."

"How long will you be in mourning?" His words were flat and emotionless.

"I'm not sure. I think a year or two is expected."

"It's a lifetime." He took her hand. "We could correspond. I'd like to hear about you and your family."

"I'm not sure. Mr. Wheeler isn't a gossip, but Darrow Falls is a small town. Someone will see your letters addressed to me or mine to you and share the news."

"Like Mrs. Stone?"

"I don't care what they say about me, but I wouldn't want my family to be embarrassed by my actions."

Logan leaned back into the padded seat of the carriage. "What if I write to Tyler Montgomery and enclose a letter to you through him?"

Jem considered his proposal. "It might work."

"You could send your letters to me the same way, and I'll visit."

"On what reason?"

"Mr. Chase will have assignments for me to travel to Ohio. I'll want to visit Tyler to talk about the state of Kanawha. If you happen to be visiting, we could talk."

Jem considered his words. "And Tyler and Cory would invite you to meet the Beecher family. We would be seen together, and people would begin to accept us as a couple."

"You may develop a fondness for me," Logan said. "I don't expect you to love me as much as you loved Ben, but I'm willing to settle for less."

Jem crossed her arms. "I'm not. What makes you think I can't love you as much as Ben. I certainly hope I love you longer."

"How about forever." Logan kissed her.

"Is that a marriage proposal?"

Logan cringed. "Is it wrong to talk of marriage so soon?"

"I almost lost you. I can see the hangman's noose swaying over your head." She calmed her voice. "I'll go home, and we'll correspond in the next few months, but when Hannah can no longer take care of Deidre, you'll need a wife. I think that's a good reason to marry, even if it is rushed after Ben's death."

"We'll keep our plans secret," Logan suggested. "I'll court you and win your heart. You may have to try a little harder to win mine." His dimples contradicted the seriousness of his voice.

Jem frowned. "I could change my mind in five months."

"I won't let you." He kissed her. When he released her, his eyes strayed to the basket on the floor. "Would it be ungallant of me to ask if there is anything left in your basket?"

"I wish there was. I didn't eat breakfast like a condemned man."

"It was my last meal." He handed Jem the jacket and lifted the lid. "It's full."

"Theo must have packed it." Jem grabbed a hard biscuit. "I'm never getting rid of this basket. Every time

I empty it, someone fills it."

****

The carriage stopped at the Southern Belle. Sid was walking back and forth in front of the building.

"Am I glad to see you!" Sid helped Jem as she stepped without incident from the carriage. "I finished that book you loaned me. Do you know the man switches places with her husband and goes to the guillotine?"

"They don't have guillotines in Virginia," Logan reassured him.

"But they have hangman's ropes," Jem added.

"I was worried this book may have given you some crazy ideas." He pointed to his head. "See these gray hairs, Miss Jenny. I'm too young for gray hair. What were you thinking of going into enemy territory?"

"I had to find out about Ben."

Sid stared at the coat draped over her arm. "Dead?"

She nodded. "But Herman is alive. He's a prisoner at the Alms House in Richmond."

"I'm sorry about Ben."

"I have my answer," Jem said. "I know what happened."

"When are you going home?"

"Tomorrow." She hugged Sid. "I'll write and send you some homemade treats."

"Don't forget you promised to send supplies to Miss Barton."

"I haven't forgotten. I plan to enlist the help of my sisters and other women in Darrow Falls. The wounded will have plenty of supplies."

Sid shook Logan's hand. "I'll see you around."

Logan nodded toward the building. "Mrs. Sharpton

didn't mind you marching in front of her place?"

"I think she left. They put Mrs. Greenhow under house arrest for spying. Scared some of the other female spies out of town. Was Mrs. Sharpton a spy?"

"Probably," Logan said.

Sid waved and headed to camp. She rang the bell and entered the boarding house when no one answered the door. "Do you think Annabelle will return?"

"I hope not. I didn't like the woman."

"I never would have guessed." His laughter was the only sound in the building. "Miss Annabelle!" Jem searched the bedrooms. Her belongings were where she had left them. She placed her father's book and medical bag on the bed. She opened the door to the bedroom belonging to Annabelle and found it empty of personal belongings. She joined Logan downstairs. "She's left."

Logan was nearly asleep on a sofa. "Probably in Richmond telling them all our secrets."

"I paid my rent. I'm going to take a bath and sleep."

"I'm tempted to join you."

"Logan! I allowed your kisses because I thought you were dying. It doesn't give you license to tumble in bed with me."

"Jem, darling, I'm too tired to make my intentions dishonorable." He looked around. "But I don't like you staying here alone. Maybe I should sleep on the sofa."

She leaned close to his ear. "You should find out if you have a job."

He headed for the door. "I'll be back later to make sure you're safe."

Logan's words made her uneasy, and Jem searched the house again. Once she was satisfied no one was hiding in any of the rooms, she hauled water from the pump for a bath. She heated a large pot of water on the stove and mixed it with the cold water in a tub in a room off the kitchen. On a shelf were soaps and lotions next to a Godey Ladies Book of recipes. She chose one that smelled like peaches and added it to the water.

Jem soaked the dirt and grime from the past week from her bone-aching body. She washed her hair, wrapped it in a towel, and relaxed in the warm water. Widow Collins. She was a widow. She hadn't had time to think about what it meant. She had no body to bury. Only a coat with a hole and a few memories of her life with Ben. But she had closure. She wasn't sure why the colonel had changed his mind and released Logan, but she was grateful. Logan was her hope for a future with a husband and family.

A board creaked, and she jerked forward, the water splashing onto the floor. She grabbed the knife she had taken from her skirt pocket and placed on the stool next to the soap and extra towel.

She stood, wrapped the towel around her body, and was stepping out of the tub when the door opened.

"Here you are." Logan stood in the doorway and stared.

"I was taking a bath."

"I see."

She waved her knife. "Get out."

"Put that blade away if you desire my children."

"I have the desire, but I can wait. Can you?"

"Is the water hot?" He stuck his hand in the tub. "Tepid. How long have you been soaking?"

"I was relaxing."

"Do you mind if I relax?"

"What?"

He shook his dusty clothes. "I need a bath. It might help my back."

Jem had forgotten about his beating. "I'll heat more water."

"You're going outside to the pump in that itty bitty towel?"

Jem tugged on the bottom, which barely reached mid-thigh. "I have a nightgown and robe." She looked around.

Logan found them. He examined the nightgown. "Pretty."

She snatched it from his hand. "Go fetch the water so I can dress."

****

Logan was pouring the water into a pan on the stove when Jem joined him in the kitchen. Her hair tumbled freely, and her lightweight robe and gown molded to her figure. He ached to touch her. He wanted to make love, but patience was required when courting a woman with the intention of marriage. She determined the timeline, and Jem had been generous with hugs, kisses, and a declaration of love. He would wait until their wedding night to satisfy his passion. Until then, they would share their lives through letters and visits.

"I'm still employed," he said. "I told Mr. Chase about the fortifications around Centreville and the prisoners in Richmond. He said the government wasn't officially planning any prisoner exchange, but some wealthy men are working on a private one."

"For Herman?"

"It's for Congressman Ely, but one freed prisoner

might lead to others."

"But Herman isn't important."

He wanted to reassure her. "That makes it easier to throw him in with the group."

"How can I repay you?"

"Put salve on my back."

"I'll fetch my medical bag."

"I'll be the naked man in the tub."

Epilogue

A wet snow blanketed the outdoors and filled the corners of the glass pane of the window Jem stared through. Behind her, an evergreen was decorated with red velvet bows and small lit candles clipped to the boughs. Presents were stacked beneath the tree. The fire crackled in the background as Cass played a Christmas hymn on the piano and Jules, Cole, and Jess sang. "Come join us, Jem," Cole urged.

"I think someone is coming." Sleigh bells grew louder outside. Jem turned to announce the visitors. "It's Cory and Tyler."

Her mother joined her by the window. "You sound disappointed."

"I was hoping it was Logan."

Maureen put her arm around Jem's waist and squeezed. "The bridegroom won't be late on his wedding day."

Jem smoothed the lace on her pale blue gown. A white gown didn't seem appropriate for a second wedding. "I hope not." She looked at the Reverend Lawrence Davis and his wife, Mary. They were eating slices of cheese from the wedge Thornton and Ellen had sent. Jem and her sisters had packed food and supplies for the 7th Ohio camped a hundred miles west of Washington City. Sid had written he wanted to join another Ohio regiment after the 1st was mustered out.

Her cousin, Jake Donovan, was also in the 7th. Ed and Art Herbruck had joined the 29th Ohio and were waiting for orders to travel to Camp Chase in Columbus.

Jem didn't have to believe in war to support the men who fought. She had shared the letter from Colonel Chauncy LaDonte with her family. Theo had received the coat she made and was grateful. The Cassell brothers had deserted, and where they had gone was anyone's guess.

Blake Ellsworth, who had business dealings in the South, had delivered the letter after smuggling the coat to Theo. She would thank him personally once she returned to Washington City. Logan had bought the Southern Belle at a bargain price and renamed it Pierce House, their future home.

Sid had sent a photograph of himself in his uniform. She had placed it on the piano next to the photograph of Ben, Herman, and John. The photograph of Logan was placed with hers on the table between two candles and a Bible to be used for the wedding ceremony. A ceremony waiting on the bridegroom.

Cory entered the parlor carrying a bundle wrapped in blankets. As soon as she was safely inside, she knocked off the snow covering her wool cape.

"I want to see my nephew," Jules squealed.

Cory unwrapped the blankets to reveal Sterling Beecher Montgomery. He was three months old with a hint of dark hair and huge blue eyes like his father. He seemed surprised by his surroundings but smiled as his mother reassured him he was safe.

Maureen helped remove the layers of clothing on her grandson. "Where's Tyler?"

"Putting the horse and sleigh in the barn."

"Does he have presents?"

"Jules!" Maureen reprimanded her youngest daughter.

"He has presents for everyone." Cory lost Sterling to Cole, who took first turn holding him. Jess, Cass, and Jules crowded around him for their turn.

Tyler carried in a stack of packages. "Look who I found on the doorstep."

Jem had expected Logan, but John Herbruck and Herman Stratman entered instead. "John, Herman!" She hugged them.

"We wanted to show our support for you marrying Logan," John said. "I think Ben would have approved."

"I wanted to thank Logan for helping free me from prison," Herman said.

"He won't take credit. It was Randall who paid the money for a private release." Logan had confided in his last letter that a large prisoner exchange was being talked about after the first of the year.

"I'm working for Randall at the bank," Herman said. "I promised I'd pay him back."

"Your mother must enjoy having you home," Maureen said.

"She's constantly feeding me. She thinks I'm too thin."

"You are too thin," Maureen said. "We're having a ham and turkey for dinner, so you'll have plenty to eat."

The Reverend turned. "When is dinner served?"

"After the wedding ceremony," Maureen said.

He looked around the parlor. "Are we ready to start?"

"I don't know where Logan is," Jem said.

"Behind you." Logan stood in the hall doorway. Deidre stood beside him. She was bundled in a fur-lined hood and blue wool cloak.

Jem rushed to greet them. "Hello, Deidre."

"Hello, Aunt Jenny." She looked at Logan. "You said I should call her Aunt Jenny, right?"

"I want you to meet the rest of your family." Jem unbundled Deidre and introduced her. She took an interest in the presents and bonded with Jules, who pointed out at least one gift for the little girl.

"I made a doll for Deidre and sent one to Inga," Jem confessed in a whisper.

"Like the doll in the box in the story you told her on the train?"

"Yes. I want to share the story with Deidre before she opens her gift."

Logan removed his cloak and hat. "You said not to take any rooms at the Darrow Falls Inn. What are the sleeping arrangements?"

"Deidre can sleep with my sisters. We furnished the room above Papa's office for us. It's small but private." She took his and Deidre's belongings and hung them on the pegs in the hallway behind the staircase. Logan pinned her against the wall. "Logan."

"Mistletoe hanging in the entranceway. I think you owe me a kiss." He nuzzled her neck.

His lips were cold but warming rapidly. "My family is in the next room."

"I have a ring in my pocket and a license to marry you if they have any objections."

"I think we should start the ceremony. We've waited long enough."

"You sound anxious to become Mrs. Logan

Pierce."

Jem fought to clear her head. "I have a long list for tonight's activities. After all, it's Christmas Eve. After the wedding, we'll eat, and then Papa will read the ending to *A Christmas Carol*."

"Do you open your presents in the evening?"

"Oh no, we wait until morning to open them after Papa reads the second chapter in Luke."

His hand examined the lace on her gown. "I was hoping to unwrap one present tonight."

"But you can't." Jem pouted. "I hope you're not disappointed with the gift I'm giving you."

"Jem, darling, I'm not talking about any gift under the tree." He kissed her cheek below her earlobe and mapped a trail to her lips. Jem's body trembled with anticipation. They had waited out of respect to Ben, her family, and society's rules, but tonight, they would share a bed as husband and wife.

"We better start the ceremony," Cole called out to the others from the hallway. "Before they start the honeymoon."

A word about the author...

Laura Freeman has been a reporter for the past ten years covering the historic town of Hudson, Ohio. She has won the Press Club of Cleveland's Ohio Excellence in Journalism award twice and the Ohio Newspaper Association award several times.

Her novel *Impending Love and Death* is the sequel to *Impending Love and War* and takes place in the fictional town of Darrow Falls and Washington City after the Battle of Bull Run in July of 1861.

She lives in Ohio, where she is working on her next book, *Impending Love and Lies*.

Visit her on Facebook.com/laurafreeman.5648 and Twitter@LauraFreeman_RP She can also be found on her blog: Authorfreeman.wordpress.com

CPSIA information can be obtained
at www.ICGtesting.com
Printed in the USA
BVHW050201180523
664410BV00011B/257